GUNS OF THUNDER

OTHER FIVE STAR WESTERN TITLES BY LAURAN PAINE:

Tears of the Heart (1995)
Lockwood (1996)
The White Bird (1997)
The Grand Ones of San Ildefonso (1997)
Cache Cañon (1998)
The Killer Gun (1998)
The Mustangers (1999)
The Running Iron (2000)
The Dark Trail (2001)
Guns in the Desert (2002)
Gathering Storm (2003)
Night of the Comancheros (2003)
Rain Valley (2004)
Guns in Oregon (2004)
Holding the Ace Card (2005)
Feud on the Mesa (2005)
Gunman (2006)
The Plains of Laramie (2006)
Halfmoon Ranch (2007)
Man from Durango (2007)
The Quiet Gun (2008)
Patterson (2008)
Hurd's Crossing (2008)
Rangers of El Paso (2009)
Sheriff of Hangtown (2009)
Gunman's Moon (2009)
Promise of Revenge (2010)
Kansas Kid (2010)

GUNS OF THUNDER

A WESTERN DUO

LAURAN PAINE

FIVE STAR
A part of Gale, Cengage Learning

GALE
CENGAGE Learning

Detroit • New York • San Francisco • New Haven, Conn • Waterville, Maine • London

GALE
CENGAGE Learning

Set in 11 pt. Plantin.

LIBRARY OF CONGRESS CATALOGING-IN-PUBLICATION DATA

Paine, Lauran.
    Guns of thunder : a western duo / by Lauran Paine. — 1st ed.
    p. cm.
    ISBN-13: 978-1-59414-908-5
    ISBN-10: 1-59414-908-9
    1. Large type books. I. Paine, Lauran. Phantom trail. II. Title.
PS3566.A34G876 2010
813'.54—dc22
                                      2010028395

First Edition. First Printing: November 2010.
Published in 2010 in conjunction with Golden West Literary Agency.

Printed in the United States of America
1 2 3 4 5 6 7 14 13 12 11 10

TABLE OF CONTENTS

PHANTOM TRAIL 7

GUNS OF THUNDER 119

5

★ ★ ★ ★ ★

PHANTOM TRAIL

★ ★ ★ ★ ★

I

The wagon had a soiled canvas top stretched across ash bows, and in the fierce midday heat with the canvas slack the rig looked like a tortured gaunt old soiled beast with its ribs showing making its clumsy way along the edge of the Casadora Wash—called an arroyo by the Mexicans—somewhere between the town of Montoya and the more recent *Yanqui* settlement called Fort Triumph.

There was no fort down there and if the "Triumph" signified a variety of victory, no one seemed to know what it was. Once, there *had* been a fortnightly bivouac by pony soldiers at the large spring northeast of where the settlement came to be, and palpably the name of the town derived from that fact—soldiers had stopped there—while the name Triumph undoubtedly came from the Mexican name of that cold-water spring—Triunfo.

The world between Montoya and Fort Triumph was hot this early summertime of year, heat-hazed in its long distances, blue-blurred in the fragrant dusks, and bell-clear, fragrant, and beautiful just before sunrise, although few people were abroad that early in the day.

It was a flat, seemingly endless flow of gritty soil and upthrusts of bone-bleached rocks, catclaws, paloverdes, and tiny little delicate wildflowers of pink and violet hiding at the coarse base of flourishing thornpin bushes. It smelled of creosote during the height of the heat each day, and it smelled of ancient dust and those shy little flowers every evening. Once, it had all belonged to Indians. They had effectively pushed Mexican civilization back hundreds of miles and kept it there. When the whites arrived, war came, too, and this time the Indians lost. Had lost in fact five years before they were finally forced to give up entirely.

Since then cattlemen had arrived, along with freighters and stagers, storekeepers, blacksmiths, even doctors, although at Fort Triumph there was none of the last, unless one included Father Eusebio Halorhan, who ministered equally to ailing humans, horses, cattle, dogs, and cats.

In a flat countryside visibility should normally be great, but on the lower desert flourishing great stands of underbush could and very often did limit visibility to less than a hundred yards. Sometimes less than a hundred feet. It had been this natural condition that had enabled the Indians to hold their heartland for so long. They had perfected tactics and strategy created exclusively around blending with the undergrowth.

Now, out where the old wagon was slowly moving, someone had fired the undergrowth for miles in all directions. The obvious purpose had been to minimize those everlasting, and very lethal, Apache ambushes. No one had considered the natural after-effect; no one had cared a damn about that.

And Mother Nature, or someone anyway, had come right back with a surprise and a blessing—grass! It now grew over miles of thin-soiled lower desert countryside nourishing herds of cattle.

After the Indians had been corralled and hauled away, the burning had gone on. Grass had come everywhere the meager rain helped. Behind the grass and the cattle, came trees, ranches, even settlements like Fort Triumph, roads, and public conveyances such as the red-bodied stages of the Montoya-Fort Triumph line.

Civilization returned to the lower desert, and right along with it had come something else—outlaws—commonly on the run from up north somewhere, and bound over the border into the security of Mexico where neither U.S. lawmen nor soldiers were permitted to pursue. But there was another variety of scourge too, *bandoleros, guerrilleros, pistoleros, bandidos, renegados,* whatever one chose to call the cruel, crafty infiltrators from up out of Méjico. It was more because of these deadly Mexican renegades that travelers on the lower desert rarely went very far without forming into a company. The *gringo* outlaws never murdered and plundered just because they did not like the color of someone's eyes. They actually were scarcely a threat at all; they did not want to draw attention; they wanted to get over the line like wraiths. It was the border jumpers, the Mexican killers and torturers, horse thieves and ambushers, which made it necessary for the old wagon moving along the eastern rim of Casadora Wash to have a pair of coursing scouts out ahead cutting back and forth looking into every dry wash, clump of thick thornpin, around behind each sharp-etched, mottled old rock upthrust.

The man on the seat of the wagon herded his jennies along with the sure hand on slack lines of a lifelong mule man. He was grizzled, lined, slit-eyed, and chewed rhythmically, occasionally spewing amber tobacco juice, never overlooking movement close by or miles distant. His name was Pete Redd. The Mexicans called him either Viejo—old one—or Viejo Rojo. What Pete Redd called most Mexicans was not the same at all. He had been on the desert most of his adult life. He had served the Army, the freighters, the lawmen, and now he hired out his wagon and little mules for long individual hauls. He and his two tame Apaches, who coursed ahead like greyhounds.

He watched until they could turn clear of the wash and aim toward the stage road, then he spat over the side, hauled a soiled sleeve across chapped lips, leaned, and spoke to someone back under the canvas.

"Got Triumph in sight, if you'd care to look."

She was gray-eyed and leggy, with close-cut curly hair the color of taffy, with darker streaks. She could have been in her mid-twenties, or older. The way her head sat on a classical neck, the way her eyes assessed, the way she held her heavy mouth, and the way she leaned out to come down gently upon the splintery old wagon seat beside Redd, added up to perfect co-ordination, health, and strong resolve. Pete had sized her up back at Montoya where he had met her southbound stage. He had liked several things about her, but Pete Redd had never married, had never considered women as much, and still did not consider them as much, so, along with his grudging approval, there just naturally had to be something he didn't like. It was simply that she was female. The south desert was not a place for females. Even squaws and *mestizas* wore out fast down there.

He jutted his jaw toward the dull clutch of yonder buildings, mostly of adobe, mostly with three- or four-feet thick mud walls—not for defense but to keep the searing summertime heat out—and shifted the cud before he could say: "Ugly place before they commenced setting out them trees. Now. . . ." Pete chewed, squinted toward the settlement, spat, then finally continued: "Now . . . it's ugly in the shade."

She turned a quick, warm smile. He laughed and reddened a little. "Well . . . Montoya's closer to the north mountains, so they got some board buildings up there. At Triumph all they ever had was mud bricks. Hard to make things pretty when all you got is wet mud to do it with." He continued to study the distant settlement. "Last time I come down from Montoya they'd just hanged some Mexicans. They'd dry-gulched some cowboys, and made the mistake of not scoutin' in back. There was more cowboys behind 'em. They killed four and took the other two on into Triumph and folks hanged 'em from a wagon tongue."

She was watching Pete's face, probably trying to decide something about him, but his expression rarely changed. He never looked mean or angry, or very amused or very compassionate. He always looked watchful and inquisitive.

He met her questing look with a slight shrug. "It ain't like back East, missy. It never was and I don't see how it ever can be." His eyes twinkled at her. "For one thing we eat beans and meat three times a day out here. They don't do that back East . . . do they?"

She smiled. She liked Pete Redd. "Ham and chicken on Sundays, Mister Redd, and very seldom beans any other time." She continued to study him. "And if you think it is necessary to prepare me for Fort Triumph"—her smile widened—"it's kind of you but unnecessary. I've seen frontier towns before."

"Back East?" he asked, a trifle skeptically.

"No. In Texas and out on the Kansas plains."

He awaited an explanation but none was forthcoming so he herded his mules along, watched his tame Apaches reach the roadway and swing off to squat upon the edge, talking and smoking while they waited, and after a while he sighed, surreptitiously eyed her handsome and strong profile, and with immense difficulty decided she was tough. That was the greatest compliment Pete Redd paid anything, two-legged or four-legged. She was also extremely easy to look at. Pretty as a spotted fawn, in fact, or a speckled pony, or one of those ladies they put on the horseshoe calendars.

It did not occur to Pete at this time, but it would occur to him later, that she was both beautiful and brainy, a combination he had been swearing up and down for forty years existed only in story-book tales.

"Why do they call it Fort Triumph?" she asked, giving him a

fresh opportunity to demonstrate superior masculine knowledge. But after he had explained, she ran off a rapid sentence in flawless Spanish, bringing out the foreign word for triumph among other things, leaving Pete, whose Spanish was not rightly Spanish at all—it was border Mex—hanging in a sort of uncomfortable vacuum.

She leaned back. He was conscious of her full, round blouse and her classical side-view features. He was young enough, still, to be interested while at the same time being old enough to be concerned. He said: "You never told me who you was going down here to see, Miss Hamblin."

"Father Halorhan, Mister Redd. He's my father."

Pete almost lost the lines, groped for a fresh hold on them, and recovered in a moment. "Your . . . father?"

She smiled at him. "His name in those days was Eustace Halorhan. He was a printer. He did not become a priest until the years after my mother died." She returned her dead-level gaze to the upcoming village. "I haven't seen him since I was eleven years old . . . Mister Redd?"

"Yes'm? Say, does he know you're coming?"

"Well no, Mister Redd. We've corresponded for many years, and we just always assumed that someday I'd come out to visit him."

Pete leaned with gentlemanly concern to expectorate, then straightened up with a little worry line directly between his eyes. "Lady, you hadn't ought to never do something like that. It's not decent."

She blinked. "You mean . . . just come out to visit?"

"Yes'm. That's exactly what I mean. It's not a decent thing to do to folks. For all you know. . . ." He chewed, considered, then changed the sentence. "Well, folks out here don't live in big houses with lots of extra rooms, and sometimes they got big families, or maybe aren't even around."

14

"Mister Redd, he has lots of extra rooms. He's written me at least a dozen times about the size of the old mission. And he wouldn't have a big family, would he?"

Pete reddened a little. He had known a lot of priests on the lower desert who had families. Not Eusebio Halorhan, but plenty of others. Pete avoided a direct answer by saying: "Well, there's no turning back."

She waited, then began gently to scowl. "Are you trying to prepare me for something . . . warn me about my father, perhaps?"

Redd shook his head. "As fine a man as you'd ever want to know. Nothing to warn you about . . . except that this ain't back East by a long shot. That's all I'd try to prepare you for." He got off this uncertain ground, too, by pointing. "See that scrawny little wooden cross leaning northward atop that big old tiled red roof yonder? Well, sir, that's the old mission. Been here a couple hundred years, so they say, but I'd guess it's been here a lot longer'n that. Anyway, a long time ago the mission had big herds, lots of Indian *vaqueros,* acres and acres of crops and grapes, and *jacales* all them mission Indians lived in. Then along come Mex politics and the missions was all disen- . . . disfran- . . . well, they was all told to disband their herds and cut loose their redskins, and get rid of their priests." Pete leaned over to let fly again. "Then us *gringos* come along, taken the Southwest from the Mexicans, and we let the *padres* take over the missions again. But not like before. They'd never again be like that."

He sighed. Pete Redd, who certainly did not look like anything other than what he seemed to be, struck Marie Hamblin as an incurable romantic. She liked that in Pete, and smiled her encouragement to him.

He cleared his jaws of chewing tobacco, settled the old sweat-stained hat more squarely atop his unshorn graying head, even sat up a little straighter as they reached the roadway, finally, and began to rumble, jolt their way straight on down to the northernmost outskirts of Fort Triumph.

II

Pete Redd drove her directly over the northeasterly side of the dusty settlement, over where Mex town was, and, after turning her over to the Mexican woman—dressed all in black with a face to match for gloom and gravity—who did the washing and cooking for Father Eusebio, Pete leaned upon a mighty adobe wall beneath a very old *ramada* and wondered about leaving her alone.

Father Eusebio had been called away, according to the dolorous woman in black. She had rolled up her eyes. He had been called to give Last Rites to an old Mexican shepherd—very old and very devout, the shepherd was.

"They die," murmured the woman in sepulchral tones. "There has always been a time."

Pete cleared his throat, looked disapprovingly at the woman, then smiled toward the beautiful girl. "He'll be along directly. It don't take long once they are really fixing to die. I'll sort of wait around for a spell." He was reaching into his pocket for the plug of Kentucky twist when she said: "You'll do no such thing, Mister Redd. Those mules are thirsty. Besides, what harm could come in this place?"

He looked at the mules. For a fact they would be thirsty. He saw the sidelong look of distaste the Mexican woman was bending in his direction, and pocketed the plug without gnawing off any.

She crossed to lay fingers lightly upon his arm. Her smile dazzled him completely. "You have been wonderfully kind, Mister Redd."

He left, after that, waved once, saw the Mexican woman standing primly, arms folded, watching his departure with an aloof glance, and waited until they could no longer see him, then said to his mules: "Why in hell couldn't she have come along forty years ago? Well, maybe forty-five then. . . . Josephine, darn your long-eared hide, get up into that collar and quit letting Esmeralda do it all." He followed up the admonition with a light tap on Josephine's rump. If Josephine was intimidated, she gave no evidence of it; she was still hanging slackly when they turned back onto the main thoroughfare and headed down in the direction of the public corrals.

The heat had been building over the past couple of hours. It did not bother Redd's pair of ragheads; they were already off-saddled and hunkering in tree shade by the time Pete got down there with the rig. Generally Fort Triumph turned inward at this time of day, borrowing from the Mexican residents of the lower desert the delightful characteristic of taking a pleasant *siesta* when it was too hot to do much of anything else.

Inside, the mud buildings were cool. Often as much as fifteen degrees cooler than the roadway. That old mission, for all its dilapidation, its overgrown cemetery out back enclosed within a crumbling adobe wall on three sides, and its clear look of great, sad age, was probably the coolest place in Fort Triumph. Not only did it have extraordinary mud walls—six feet thick all around—but it had the typically high, forked ceiling of old Spanish missions, and far below was the cool red tile floor. On the hottest days people came to pray dressed heavily, wearing scarves—the women—as well as high necks and long sleeves. The heat could not reach to the ancient altar.

Out back, where Marie Hamblin went, guided there by the Mexican woman, was the longest covered porch Marie had ever seen. It ran the full length of the old building. Someone at the north end could, of course, be seen by someone at the south end, but they were too distant to be recognized by their features.

There was more of that glazed, Spanish tile, and along the

rotting eave ends swallows had made mud nests. Beyond, was the very old and very overgrown cemetery.

The Mexican woman left Marie out there. She had said scarcely a word since Pete Redd had unloaded the valises and had set Marie down out front. Beyond asking for Father Eusebio, his daughter had said nothing, which was probably just as well.

The Mexican woman's name was Olivia. That much Redd knew and had told Marie. He did not know her last name, and, during the course of this short exchange, something about the way Pete Redd spoke and looked left Father Eusebio's daughter thinking Pete Redd did not like Mexicans. She was correct but it would be a while before Pete Redd confirmed this to her satisfaction.

It was drowsily serene and fragrant out upon that vast and empty *ramada*. Marie was lulled almost to sleep several times during her lengthy wait. The last time she roused herself was when the housekeeper brought her a glass of lemonade. Marie's surprise pleased the older woman. In careful English she said: "These are lemons from Sonora, the Mexican province below the border from here some distance. We do not have lemon trees at Fort Triumph."

The lemonade was delicious. Marie smiled. "Do they bring the lemons up here to your town to sell them?" she asked. That was how it was done in the border country of Texas.

Olivia nodded gently, eyeing Marie with fresh interest. She clearly had not thought Marie would know such things. Few unmarried, handsome women had to know about the origin of lemons along the lower desert. Of course, once they were married that changed; they were required to know not only when the peddlers would come through with their laden burro trains, but also how to haggle and squeeze out the last lemon for their coins. Olivia had been married at thirteen. She was forty-five now and could not really recall what her life had been like when she had not been married.

But she had an uncomfortable presentiment about this handsome, lean, tall woman in front of her, who looked so uncommonly like Father Eusebio. It bothered Olivia more than she ever would have admitted. Olivia Gomez was a very moral person. Something like this upset her terribly, and yet, there it clearly was—the eyes, the gentler cast to the same strong jaw, the shape of the head, and the very direct and uncompromising gaze, with its little quizzical lurking smile.

Well, of course it happened. The great patriot priest of Mexico had offspring. So also did the historical political priest, Juan Almonte, who was himself an illegitimate son of. . . . It did not matter. Juan Almonte had been dead many decades. What did matter was this beautiful woman who clearly, despite her different name, could—to be charitable—be Father Eusebio's niece, but who Olivia Gomez knew in her hurting heart was Father Eusebio's daughter.

God had been outraged. Still, who did you blame? Not this handsome woman certainly. Not some warm and wanting woman who had, as had Olivia Gomez, found Father Eusebio Halorhan both handsome and charming. Then who? Father Eusebio—whose great honor and whose good works reached all the way down to Sonora and Chihuahua?

Marie said: "Is Father Eusebio the only priest hereabouts?"

Olivia had to pull herself back as though from a great distance before answering. "*Sí*. This is a poor parish, but it is very large. Father Eusebio travels far." Olivia's magnificent dark eyes in the gloomy, very pale setting, looked gentle now. "He takes the Sacrament to an old shepherd this morning. This afternoon he will baptize triplets born day before yesterday to *Señora* Gutierrez of Mex town." Olivia turned. "No other man could possibly do it."

For a moment Marie was captivated by something she saw in the older woman's face. Then she slowly turned back to regarding the ancient, weathered headstone out where birds were constantly fighting among low tree limbs and high stands of durable weeds.

A tall, bronzed horseman appeared around front, tied his mount, and climbed the wide, low steps to the front of the church, spurs ringing. Olivia cocked her head, waited, then excused herself, and disappeared through a little door. It did not occur to her guest, but women raised in territories where men went constantly booted and spurred learned early to know the different sounds of different spurs.

A very old *mestizo* came shuffling from the far end of the *ramada* muttering to himself and looking indignant, until he saw Marie, then with a hasty hand tugging off the old sombrero the old man widely smiled. His dark eyes were lively with frank admiration. Evidently the desert air, or perhaps the desert water, something anyway, permitted even the very old to retain their basic instincts right on up into ancient age.

The old man spoke softly in Spanish, but hesitantly because clearly he did not expect the statuesque *gringa* to understand.

"It has been a beautiful day, miss, and now it has also been a memorable one."

She almost laughed. He did not look like a man whose command of flowery Spanish would be that good. On the other hand, perhaps he had heard the smooth-speaking younger men say that and had memorized it. In her twinkling look was also a woman's appreciation when she answered him in Spanish: "I am honored that you noticed me, horseman. It has indeed been a beautiful day."

The old man's eyes popped wide, then he momentarily lost command, bowed, clutched his old hat, and hurried away in clear retreat. Now, she did laugh, but not aloud.

Olivia returned, graceful hands tucked modestly inside a dark *rebozo*, and, while she and Marie were discussing the woeful condition of the old cemetery, with Olivia deploring how it was nowadays when everyone expected pay even for doing their duty, Father Eusebio returned.

Olivia disappeared again through that little oaken door and Marie watched her father striding across from the tumble-down horse shed. He was grayer, naturally, but otherwise he did not look very different from the pictures she had of him.

He was a large man, six feet tall or perhaps even a little taller, and thick, with a columnar neck and mighty shoulders. She was so absorbed in watching that she simply sat. When he finally discerned someone over on the porch sitting upon one of the ancient benches in overhang shade, he started dutifully to veer in that direction.

Then he halted, dead still.

She smiled through a forming mist and arose with a pain in her throat and chest.

He moved up more slowly now, stepped into the shade, and opened his arms to her. For a full minute she lay against him thankful for her hidden face while she fought down the spiraling, tearful emotion of this overdue reunion, and, when he finally held her at arm's length and said—"What a beautiful woman you have become, Marie. Uncommonly like your mother."—she smiled at the blur of his handsome, strong face without trusting herself to speak.

At her age, half a lifetime had been spent thinking of him. Wondering what he was like now? How he did the Lord's work? Why he did it in such a place as the low desert?—and now his powerful hands were holding her upper arms while he looked at her.

Suddenly he cleared his throat, dropped his hands, and took

her back to the ancient bench where they could sit quietly for a while.

"I should have warned you," she said, conscious of Pete Redd's particular disapproval. She groped for a silly, tiny lace handkerchief and dried her eyes a little.

He was understanding. "And deprive me of this wonderful surprise?" His wide mouth curled. "Of course, for a moment I almost had a heart seizure."

They laughed, which made it easier for her right away. He straightened up and widely gestured with both big arms. "This is my world. An old dilapidated mission, an overgrown cemetery full of people who have been out there at least two hundred years . . . so long no one even remembers their families let alone their names. . . ." His arms dropped as he settled thick shoulders against the smooth adobe bricks at his back. "And hundreds of miles of rattlesnakes, thornpin bushes, gila monsters, fever ticks, outlaws and renegades of every possible kind . . . and this village."

She was watching his profile and detected a hint of tiredness. "Acolytes . . . ?"

"Yes, I have a couple of reliable ones, and they're a great help." He shook off the weariness to look at her with another smile, gentle as before, but this time wistful. "Twenty-five now, Marie?"

She blushed in spite of herself. "You have an old maid daughter."

"That's impossible. You are beautiful. Really, Marie, you are a very handsome woman."

"But unmarried."

He used his hands often to gesture, for strong emphasis. He did it now. "I don't know that it's written where a woman can't be fully mature before she marries." He allowed that to hang a moment between them, then slapped his legs as though to arise and said: "You need a room. Where are your things? I have a housekeeper, Olivia Gomez, she will help you get settled."

Marie was uneasy. "Here, Father?"

He looked surprised "Yes, of course here. Marie, these old Spanish missions are not like the churches back East. Once, they were complete settlements unto themselves. I have here the shop of a sandal maker, a tanner, a baker, even a small sick apartment as well as a nursery. And rooms for everyone who, generations ago, ran this place as a church, a local presidio, a governing unit for five thousand square miles of sand and heat." He arose, smiling down into her lifted face. "Were you thinking of the good name of the parish priest?"

She nodded. "Something like that, Father."

"Not here, Daughter. Here, people don't just go to church on Sunday. Here, this old mission is as much a part of their daily lives as the sun and the sand. You'll notice the difference in time. Now come along. Where did you say your things were?"

III

The settlement itself looked Mexican without having more than a handful of Mexicans employed over in *gringo* town. The stores were all shady and very cool inside, ugly and functional and massively squat outside. Except for the trees, here and there a flower garden or a flourishing bean or corn patch, the place probably would have been hotter than it was, and full summer had not arrived yet as Marie Hamblin went exploring.

No one in *gringo* town had the faintest idea who she was. In Mex town, lying to the east, with its back to *gringo* town, although the buildings were back-to-back, everyone knew at once who she was.

Father Eusebio had ridden away immediately after breakfast with three tight-lipped, heavily armed range men, leaving his daughter to help Olivia for a while, then to wander down through the village.

Before Marie had gone strolling, Olivia's strong disapproval had translated itself into denunciation. "They will work him to death," she said to Marie, "and this time for what . . . those cowboys are ingrates, drinkers, and worse. Why don't they look after their own?"

It was at this juncture Marie discovered that her father was a self-taught physician and, in extreme emergencies, a self-taught surgeon. Those *vaqueros* rode for a man named Dennison who ranged thousands of head of cattle over the low desert five or six miles to the north and west of Fort Triumph. One of Dennison's men had been accidentally shot, which was why Dennison had sent for the priest.

Marie had watched her father's departure in that band of rough men, feeling something special about him, and afterward went strolling through the village, and was nearly bitten by a nervous little fierce mongrel dog when she stepped past a narrow, smelly passageway between two buildings. The dog had been lurking just inside. When she started past, it snarled and lunged. There was no contact, and she had been more surprised than startled, but a nearby range rider saw what had happened and with a quick curse took two long strides over the plank walk, right hand dropping to his holstered Colt. The little dog looked up at him and also showed teeth, crouching as though to spring. The cowboy's face showed cruel anger as he started his draw.

Marie, having recovered from one surprise, now had to face this fresh surprise, but this time she was ready. Without delay she moved up, pushed the cowboy roughly so that he was off balance as the gun slid forth, then she took a position directly in front of the little dog.

She said—"There was no harm done."—and the cowboy

looked long at her, gun hanging loosely at his side, before he answered.

"She was going to bite you, lady, and if you let her get away with it, next time it could be a little kid. Just step aside."

"Do you know why she was willing to fight?" asked Marie. The cowboy kept studying her face without answering. "She has a baby puppy in there in front of her. It's instinct for them to protect their young."

The cowboy did not care to verify what he had just been told. He was suddenly irritated and disgusted, so he swung on his heel and walked back over to the tie rack, yanked loose the shank to a saddle animal, turned the beast, and mounted it without another glance in Marie's direction, and rode northward.

A second man, leaning in the gun shop doorway close by, drying stained hands upon an oily cloth, said: "Miss, the darned little dog is mine. She and I appreciate you stickin' up for her."

This man came forth, shoving the oily rag into a hip pocket. He was no more than average in height but he was thick and powerfully hung together, like her father. He had a shock of light brown curly hair and deep-set gray-blue eyes. He sank to one knee and reached. The little bitch snarled, glared, bared her teeth, and did absolutely nothing as the gunsmith picked up the tiny puppy from between her front legs. But as soon as the man stood up, the little dog came forth and got just as close to him as she could, whining softly and looking up.

The man smiled at Marie. "Her name is Lady and this darned pup . . . how do you like Santa Anna?"

She wanted to laugh. "It's a large name for so small a dog, isn't it? Who was Santa Anna?"

"Big Mex hero," he answered, looking at the snuffling little unsteady puff of warm hair in his hands. "Yeah, I expect you're right. Well"—he raised his eyes to her again—"what do you think of . . . General Grant?"

Now she did laugh. "How about . . . is it a male dog . . . then, how about just plain Bob?"

The gunsmith considered. "This is the only pup she had. It's her first litter, too, so I figured it had ought to have a kind of special name." He leaned to look at the bitch. "Lady . . . how about Bob?"

The bitch whined and raised a forepaw to brush the man's lower leg.

"By golly, she likes it." The burly gunsmith smiled at Marie. "All right, we'll name him Bob." He motioned for Marie to precede him into the shop. "I had no idea he could climb out of that box. His eyes aren't even open yet."

Marie watched the man gently replace the pup and watched as the bitch sprang into the box very possessively, thumping her honey tail and smiling widely at the man—completely ignoring Marie.

The gunsmith shook his head. "The sides of that crate look high enough, don't they?"

Marie thought they did indeed seem too high. It then crossed her mind that perhaps the bitch had lifted her baby out, for some reason known only to herself. "She might want to take him somewhere else. Perhaps where there won't be people around. Aren't they particularly protective at this time?"

The gunsmith was a good-looking gentleman. "All I know is that one morning about a year ago I opened the back door and there was this little brown dog, sick as she could be, with some other bigger dogs trying to chew her to pieces. I brought her in, fed her, got her feeling good. . . ." He turned a slow grin toward Marie. "And wouldn't you know it . . . she came home the other day and climbed into her box and presented me with . . . Bob." He shook his head downward and the bitch thumped her box with that bony tail again. "She's the first dog I ever owned.

I don't know much about them."

He stopped talking, looked steadily at Marie, then suddenly seemed to remember something. "I owe you my thanks for keeping that gun-happy cowboy off the dog for me. Would you care for a cup of coffee?" He pulled out the oily rag and commenced drying his hands again. "Aren't you new in town?"

She did not want the coffee, especially served by hands covered with gun oil, so, after declining that, she moved quickly to the other topic. "I arrived yesterday." Now, in order to make her explanation of who she was palatable, she selected words in advance, and sounded them out on this first person she had met in Fort Triumph. "Years ago my father was a printer back East. After my mother died he went into the church and became a priest."

The gunsmith stared. "Eusebio Halorhan?" She nodded, and the gunsmith tossed aside his oily rag as he took a moment to make the adjustment to all this. Then he said: "Wonderful man, miss. They never made 'em any better than your paw." He abruptly smiled at her. "Maybe he's the first priest I ever knew who. . . . Well, it don't matter. By the way my name is Will Emerson."

She gripped his hand and immediately let go with an oily feeling to her fingers. He stepped to a bench and picked up a shotgun. "Care to see something beautiful?" he asked, and handed her the gun. "Ever see one silver and gold engraved before?"

She hadn't, but then she had not seen very many shotguns of any kind before. The gun was heavy, but it was indeed inlaid with some of the most exquisite scroll and floral designs she had ever seen. As she handed the weapon back, she asked if he had done that work. He laughed.

"Someone with a lot more talent than I'll ever have did this. The gun came from Mexico. Cowman named Dennison brought it back from there last month. I'm just honing the fire mechanism a little for him. It didn't respond very well. I figure the man who made this gun was really more nearly a jeweler than he was a gunsmith. Inside, it's not the best gun I've ever seen, but outside. . . ." He accepted the gun back and shook his head as he raised it to admire the intricate, exquisite inlay work.

The little puppy was out of the box again. Marie pointed, and, when the gunsmith looked around, Marie laughed at his expression. "You'll either have to find a crate with higher sides or nail some boards on that crate," she told Will Emerson.

He had what he thought might be a better suggestion. "You take him." At her look of blankness he said: "Really . . . you take him as soon as his eyes are open and he can navigate. Everyone should have a dog, miss."

"But I'm just visiting down here and I don't have a place to keep. . . ."

"Are you staying up at the old mission?"

"Yes, but. . . ."

"There's enough room up there to keep a herd of horses. Father Eusebio is very good with dogs. He likes animals. In fact, he's the one sewed up Lady here, after I got her away from those dogs in the alley last year. He's the best man for doctoring animals . . . people, too . . . anywhere around."

Marie had recovered by this time and had her resolve up when she firmly said: "It's very kind of you to make the offer, Mister Emerson, and I do appreciate it, but no thank you."

She edged toward the door with Will Emerson coming along. "Well, maybe your father would like Bob. When you talk to him this evening, you could mention I'll save the pup for him."

She walked southward to the lower end of town where a huge old tree shaded a wide, dusty expanse of ground where old men sat whittling, or arguing, or just quietly chewing and smoking. Every old eye turned solemnly as she went past, and a moment later, when she had to walk back, every old eye followed her again. When she was no longer in view a lively discussion started up.

But not only at the whittlers' benches. The paunchy individual who owned and operated the general store sauntered out front to stand and watch Marie walk northward. Next door the café man stepped forth and also watched, then he said—"Who is that?"—but all the paunchy storekeeper could do was wistfully smile and wag his head because he had no idea who she was.

It did not take long to explore Fort Triumph. Marie completed the entire expedition in less than an hour. On her way back through the litter and decaying débris over at the upper end of Mex town, she had one more encounter, when a bright-eyed Mexican lad and his lolling-tongued mongrel dog met her just south of the old mission, and returned her smile, even the old dog. The boy said in soft Spanish that his dog's name was Alejandro and that his own name was Roberto, and that her name was *Señorita Padre* Eusebio.

She laughed and the handsome child laughed with her, not because he understood but because, at this stage of his life, he could laugh easily.

He told her it had been his grandfather who had died the morning before; the old shepherd for whom Father Eusebio had brought his stole and beads. The child grew momentarily solemn; it had been his first encounter with death. Marie could see how deep and terrifying the impression had been, so she paused long enough to say, in gentle Spanish, that it was truly a blessing for old, and people in pain, to depart. When the child dutifully nodded because he had been told this at least ten times in the past twenty-four hours, she also said: "Roberto, you must be tranquil and never fear because where you will go someday . . . well . . . your dog will be waiting, and your grandfather, and of course all the sheep."

She was not too sure the church believed this way, but Roberto was a little boy. Right now, a little boy did not need lofty abstractions, he needed to know something closer and more friendly, for the sake of his sore heart. She leaned to scratch the smiling old dog's head and he looked straight up at her with trusting and adoring eyes.

"My aunt said that my grandfather must first do penance. He had lived a very long while, miss, and had done many bad things, of course, therefore he must suffer before reaching heaven."

Marie went right on scratching the old dog while she waited for her annoyance to diminish to the point where it would not interfere when she answered. Then she smiled at the child. "It may be, Roberto, it may be. And yet I think your grandfather's God is a very understanding individual." She kept smiling. "Your grandfather did not have to be afraid. Neither do you."

She left them, and went the balance of the distance to the mission, found Olivia out back picking beans in the shady early afternoon, sank down, and told about her encounter with the handsome little boy named Roberto.

Olivia was interested so Marie told her all of it; how she had felt angry because of the aunt who had added to the child's terror.

Olivia straightened up and brought her bucket of picked beans into the *ramada*'s coolness to be snapped and washed. While seating herself and avoiding Marie's gaze, Olivia said: "He had an old tan dog with him named Alejandro, this child?"

Marie nodded.

Olivia leaned to do her work with nimble hands. "He is my nephew. I am the aunt who talked to him."

Marie sat in a long silence. The only sound between them was made by Olivia's long fingers snapping the beans.

★　★　★　★　★

Elsewhere, some horsemen came walking their animals into town, and across from *gringo* town into the ancient dust and lassitude of Mex town. Father Eusebio was with them, riding a fine dappled gelding a Mexican family had given him for saving the life of their only son.

It was one of the most handsome horses in the entire Fort Triumph countryside. Father Eusebio had had many opportunities to sell it, but there was the matter of ethics; a man never under any circumstances sold a gift. Never.

IV

The moon was full and huge and golden, with a rusty look to it as the hours passed, as it steadily soared, ultimately giving it the look of something older than the world, older than time, as old perhaps as God, and equally aloof.

They sat out back watching in the wonderfully benign magnificence of a low-desert night, listening to the faraway sounds of coursing coyotes, little, swift foxes, and a slow breeze that brought southward, from a very considerable distance, the faint fragrance of greenery.

She told him of her *faux pas* and how afterward she had sat there like a dullard, unable to think of a single thing to say to Olivia.

He smiled. "Wait, Marie. Wait until you get to know her. Olivia has two sides . . . the extremely devout side, and the . . . ah . . . womanly side. Be patient, as the Mexicans say. As for Olivia being offended, or deciding that now she doesn't like you. . . ." He gently wagged his head. "It's not her way." He turned with an expression of tolerant understanding. "Give yourself a chance to get to know her."

His defense of the woman with the white skin and the

magnificent liquid large eyes drove Marie into a slightly prolonged silence, and during it he spoke of that ancient moon, of the equally as ancient land where they were sitting, of how something as normally hostile as the low desert grew on people, and finally he said: "I buried a young cowboy today. He was a couple of years younger than you. I tried to keep him here but he just slipped away from me. I will tell you something . . . there are times when it shouldn't happen. Not too much blood loss, not a really fatal injury, a healthy body full of youth and strength." His big shoulders gently rose and fell. "You can feel him slipping away right under your hands. No reason, Daughter. No physical reason, and yet . . . they slip quietly away."

She understood, or thought she did anyway. "His time, Father?"

Eusebio Halorhan smiled at her, grateful for her understanding. If he'd had to explain what he'd meant, it would not have been the same at all.

"Yes, that has to be it, Marie. His time. Well, if a person did not especially believe . . . and I think many people fit that category . . . but they saw how this happened, they would have to believe."

She knew about faith. She had not only seen it in the East, she had also seen it in frontier Texas. But the low desert was different in all other ways, therefore it was undoubtedly also different in this way.

"They don't much believe down here, is that what you're suggesting, Father?"

He raised a powerful paw to scratch lightly the tip of his nose. "About calling me . . . Father. . . ."

They laughed together before she said: "I suppose I could call you Eusebio . . . without the 'Father'."

He considered the alternatives. "Dad?"

It did not fit him, but she yielded. "Dad . . . Dad . . . they don't believe very strongly down here?"

"Every Mexican family and perhaps a third of the *gringos*," he told her, then enlarged upon that. "The community is not entirely composed of storekeepers and people like that, Marie. There have been outlaws here by the dozen. There are always renegades passing through. Commonly, of course, they try to make it in the early springtime. The best time to cross the desert. But they can't always do that, you see. Well, we who have lived down here for any length of time . . . we know a general secret. Most of the range riders, some of the prominent cattlemen even, along with merchants and whatnot, all established in the Fort Triumph countryside . . . have been wanted men somewhere. May still be wanted somewhere if their crimes were bad enough. . . . They don't come to church Sundays, you understand?"

"I would imagine people whose pasts have clearly been forgiven if the law hasn't caught up with them, Dad, should be the exact people who would come to church."

He grinned. "It's a nice way to think, Daughter."

"But they don't do it?"

"Something like that," her father acknowledged. "Marie," he said in a crisper tone, "you haven't mentioned your mother's sister and brother-in-law, the Hamblins." He turned again to watch her handsome features in the warm night.

"They died," she replied simply. "There was an epidemic of typhoid fever."

"Both of them?" He was shocked. "I owed them so much. They wanted to take you in and raise you as their own child. Marie, they did a wonderful job. You are a perfect lady . . . and so handsome." He turned away, considered the old moon for a while, and, when she got over her own emotions, she told him how she had loved her aunt and uncle, how she had striven hard to be the daughter they hadn't had. Later, she also said:

"They sent you a letter, written just as the epidemic struck. I have it in my room. I'll get it."

He said: "No . . . tomorrow will be fine." A moment later he spoke again, softly. "If you'd care to stay, I'd be very happy to have you here . . . but, you can see, it's not a lovely countryside, the people are different from anything you are accustomed to, there isn't much to hold a beautiful woman down here . . . no, well, good music, for example, or stimulating companionship, not even very many other young women, at least of the kind you'd want to be close to."

From a vast distance a lowing bull sent forth his combination challenge and mating call. It was on a two-toned level, one high, piercing bawl, a short pause, then a lower, deeper bellow. No cows answered. They would not have done so anyway. The sound lost even its echo after a time, which allowed the depthless desert silence to resettle.

"I've only been here one day," she told her father. Then she laughed. "There is a gunsmith in the village who is saving a little puppy for you."

Father Eusebio considered this adroit switching of topics, wryly smiling to himself. She was a clever, quick, and capable woman, no question of that. Her mother had also been that way—so wonderfully gifted at turning awkward or painful things aside, so gifted at maintaining an even kind of blended humor and gentleness in their married life. He swallowed hard.

"A puppy? Why a puppy?"

She explained. Told him the entire story from beginning to end, and, when she was finished, he looked gravely at her. "Marie, don't ever do anything like that again. Pushing an armed range man when he is drawing his pistol." His intentness increased. "This just isn't like any country you have ever been in. I know . . . you spent a summer in Texas . . . but that was not border Texas the way this is the low-desert border country of. . . ." He let it trail off and continued to sit facing her.

She understood his exasperation and was contrite in the face of it, and, of course, if she'd had a little time to think, perhaps she would not have bumped that cowboy to prevent him from killing the little female dog. . . . Yes she would have! What gave him or anyone else the right to kill the little dog just because he wore a gun?

Her father said: "Either Olivia or I will go around with you for the next few days. . . ."

She was twenty-five, dammit, not ten! But that wasn't fair, either; he had only one thing at heart—her welfare. She smiled at him, even though it was an effort, and did what she—and her mother—could do so well.

"It's a very little puppy, and the gunsmith seemed to think you needed a dog . . . Dad."

He sighed, willing to be turned aside with his anxiety for her in this raw place. "Look out front any day, Marie, and you'll see dogs by the dozen rummaging around the mission. I think if there is one thing I don't need, it is a dog. Not even a puppy dog." He changed that. "Particularly not a puppy dog."

The moon was high, the night was advancing, she knew he had been tired at supper, and she also knew that Olivia would not approve of her keeping him up this late. Olivia . . . ?

"Dad, will she resent me being here?"

He blinked. "Who? We were talking about dogs, weren't we?"

"Olivia."

"Why should she resent it, Marie? You are my daughter."

Marie nodded about that; she was his daughter, and she also happened to be a woman. "Dad, are Mexicans very different from us?"

"In what ways, Daughter? Generally, no, I don't think so, but they certainly have a different background and heritage."

"The women . . . are very jealous?"

He considered a moment, then said: "That's what's bothering you. Marie, Olivia is the housekeeper here. That's all. There has always been someone . . . altar boys, acolytes, maintenance men, a housekeeper . . . that's how we run these big old missions. No one priest, or even two or three priests, could do it alone. . . . Sometimes I've wished I had a smaller place, just a simple little church." He made a little fluttery gesture with both hands. "Instead, I have this. Well, Daughter, I'm not as young as I once was, so, after watching that magnificent moon rise. . . ." He arose and stood thickly powerful and solid, looking tenderly at her. "Marie, having you with me is an answer to a constant prayer. Good night, dear."

After he had departed she continued to sit for a time in the cooling, softly fragrant late night. Her mother had died when she had been quite small. Since then he had been fully occupied with his faith, his work, his separate world

Marie arose and went slowly to the very edge of the tiled old patio and gazed up at that more distant, less golden, high old moon.

Maybe he thought Olivia was just a housekeeper, the way all missions had them for their busy priests, but Olivia was a woman. What did she think?

Marie turned slowly to go down through the hushed and ancient corridors to her little room, which—so Olivia had told her—had once housed a sacred nun named Theresa who had, of all miracles, possessed the stigmata. Sister Theresa was buried out beyond the rear *ramada.* Olivia had volunteered to show Marie the little grave.

There was a high, recessed window where moonlight filtered in while Marie got ready for bed. The room itself was like a vault. Its furnishings were very old: two rawhide-bottomed chairs, a bench, a smoothly worn old table with two uneven legs, the cot made into the north wall, and that deep-set very narrow long window.

As she got into bed, she told herself almost defiantly that tomorrow she would find a vase, cut some flowers, and bring some light and life and beauty into her room—her darned cell, then.

One distinct advantage about such a place, and such a room in such a place—people slept well. There was never a sound, and, if someone had fired a cannon out front, the racket would not have penetrated all those six-foot walls back to the rear of the place where her room was.

She slept as though she had been drugged, awakened only when the sun, replacing moonlight, sent its golden brilliance down through her recessed high window and across her bed and face.

The silence was serenely everlasting, morning or night. She had to leave her room to wash but the dark corridor beyond, worn down the centuries with the passage of many feet, was now as empty and likely to echo her footfalls as a tomb.

She returned, eventually, to dress fully, and now she stood below the little window, looking out. All she could see was the sky, which of course had been no accident of the builders. Everyone, it appeared, had been anxious to scourge themselves every way they could, had been stubbornly dedicated to eschewing the sordid earth in favor of heavenly loftiness, even, she told herself a trifle tartly, when they had to do it on an empty stomach.

Olivia never changed. She was a vision in lengthy black, great soft eyes solemn, wealth of handsome dark hair sternly unswept and piled, her full mouth compressed with inherent asceticism. She did not return Marie's smile, but she nodded and said: "Good morning."

The breakfast was simple and nourishing, and always the same because, Olivia explained, Father Eusebio never really seemed to care what he ate as long as it kept his body strong.

Marie considered this idea and held back all comment. She wanted to like Olivia. She was going to like Olivia if it killed them both, but no man alive was beyond caring what his food tasted like. Or looked like, for that matter.

"He left early," the older woman announced, and gave her customary expression of pained resignation over this. "It is that Dennison outfit again. This time *Señor* Dennison came himself in the top buggy."

Marie frowned. "How early?"

"Five o'clock. I was just boiling his food when the buggy arrived out front." Olivia pointed accusingly. "He ate half, then took the little bag and hurried away." She allowed the hand to sink to her side. "Sickness. Yesterday he buried one out there. Today it's a sickness." Clearly Olivia had no use for the Dennison cow outfit. She may not have had any use for the man who owned and operated the cow outfit, either. She certainly gave no hint of approval about anything having to do with the Dennison outfit, and at least for the time being Marie was inclined to agree with one aspect of all this. The Dennison Ranch indeed did demand an awful lot of her father's time, and they seemed to do it with small regard for her father's own personal well-being.

After breakfast, partly in order to be busy and partly in order to make amends for what she had done yesterday, she went out to the garden patch with Olivia and picked beans until her back ached, her fingers were sore, and she did not care whether she ever saw another bean, on a bush or on a dinner plate.

She also marveled at Olivia's physical endurance. Even after the heat came in late midmorning, Olivia remained out there, stooped and busy.

They conversed very little. Thus far they had always talked to one another in English, and this may have inhibited the older woman a little, for while Olivia was almost fluent in English, it was not native to her and she did not think in English, therefore conversing in it was not as easy for her as speaking Spanish.

Also—and Marie had already discovered this—Olivia only spoke when she had something to say.

V

Her father fell asleep eating his meager supper that night, and this time Marie's indignation matched the anger of Olivia Gomez. There was no excuse for people to take such advantage of a man, priest or no priest. She roused him, got him off to his room, another of those little meager cells, then she returned to the kitchen to help Olivia clean up, and let go with her pent-up annoyance.

She spoke in swift Spanish and Olivia turned to stare, having until this moment no idea Marie knew the language. Then Olivia turned back to her work and remained impassively silent for a while. Marie's final remark was to the effect that someone ought to manage her father's time for him, ought to make some laws governing how people could, and should not, impose on him.

Olivia shrugged, keeping her face averted.

Marie looked at her. "Do you want to help him, or just feed him gruel for breakfast?"

Olivia stiffened, continued to wash dishes for a time, then finally straightened up and reached to dry her hands. In Spanish she said: "My place is here, to cook and clean and help when I can. *Señorita,* I am a woman. That is my place." Olivia hung fire a moment before saying: "*Señorita,* you are also a woman."

Marie sensed a meaning that eluded her. "Meaning what?" she asked.

"Meaning, *señorita,* you have a place exactly as I have my place. Father Eusebio is a man."

Finally Marie understood. She reddened a little but she understood, and, thinking back to her conversation last night out under that magnificent full moon, she felt like snorting. Perhaps if her father had been there in the kitchen she would have snorted. Basically he had gravely said that no, the Mexicans are not different. Well, her answer to that had to be that he had been buried down here on the low desert where nothing ever seemed to change from century to century, but elsewhere in the country there had been a lot of change within the past twenty years.

But instinct told her not to make any pronouncements in front of Olivia. Certainly not on her second day here and certainly not after making that awkward *faux pas* only yesterday. All the same it was hard, so, as she turned aside to pile dishes on a nearby shelf, she said with great restraint: "But hadn't someone ought to help him, Olivia?"

The older woman did not take her gaze off Marie's back for a long while. Eventually though she turned back to the sink as she said: "Yes. It is true, *es verdad, señorita?* I have been troubled by this for several years. He does not budget either his strength nor his time. But . . . well. . . ."

Marie turned. "Yes, I understand," she said in Spanish. "You are only a woman."

"You, too, *señorita.*"

Marie smiled coldly.

The dishes were finished and Olivia impassively donned her shawl, her head and shoulder covering, to depart for the day. As they stood gazing at one another, separated not just by age and background, Olivia said: "Good night . . . I hope you will be good for him."

Later, as Marie went outside to share the night again with that rusty old moon, she was fairly certain she understood Olivia's concern for Father Eusebio, whether Olivia understood it herself, or would ever have acknowledged it.

What Marie wanted to do was form an alliance with Olivia, if it were at all possible, so that between them they could prevent this condition of people taking advantage of her father from continuing. It had hurt her to see how drawn and gray and stooped he had been this evening.

Later, as she was lying in bed watching that high old moon get into the correct position to send shafts of ghostly paleness through into her room, she thought back to her life since early childhood in the East, and that made her more than ever disagree with her father's notion that there was not much difference between those two parts of the same country that, in her eyes, could have been entirely different worlds.

She did not remember sleeping. When next she opened her eyes, the sun was coming, and that made her realize that one difference certainly existed. In her mission room she heard no horse cars clanging their bells in the street, no hawkers with their pushcarts crying out what wares they had to sell, and she heard no men shouting or dogs barking or young boys with piping voices, hurrying past her house front.

Olivia greeted her with the same unsmiling gravity. If there was any residual antagonism from last night, Olivia did not allow it to show, but Marie, basing her feelings upon what her father had said about the older woman, did not believe she was hostile, even remotely so.

Her father was out in the horse shed, Olivia said, looking after the dappled gelding. He would be along soon because he and Olivia had to make poles and string twine for the beans to climb upon.

"We would be glad if you would help, *señorita.*"

Marie smiled at the older woman, and on impulse blurted out a feeling she had. "Olivia, I do want us to be friends. If I say something I shouldn't, if I offend you, it's not from the heart."

She had spoken in Spanish and Olivia's beautiful soft eyes seemed to brighten slightly although otherwise her expression remained the same. Then she answered. "We will always be friends, *señorita*. We have the same interest at heart." Then Olivia swiftly turned to reach for a little wicker basket. "If we can just get those beans strung high before it gets too hot. . . ." She kept her back to Marie all the way out to the garden.

Early morning was wonderful on the low desert even during midsummer. Father Eusebio was already out there, perspiring from having sledged long wooden stakes into the flinty earth at the end of each bean row. His face shone with perspiration when he smiled at them, and Marie, who happened to be looking, saw Olivia's classically perfect, pale features almost smile back.

It took patience more than time, actually, to string the twine once the stakes had been driven into the hardpan. Olivia said several times—in English, which Marie had always heard her use around Father Eusebio—that they should have done this a month ago, and Marie, detecting an undercurrent, looked at her father. He kept busy, face slightly averted. He was being nagged. She was so surprised, she almost laughed out loud.

The heat gradually built up. Off to the north where low, thick mountains stood against an azure horizon, a solitary soiled cloud was hanging, high and motionless, otherwise in all directions there was nothing but a very pale, bleached sky reflecting sunlight.

Two elderly Mexicans came around back, hats in hand. There was this dispute, one of them explained, would the good father come with them into a private place and give a judgment?

Olivia looked exasperated but kept right on stringing beans as Father Eusebio, with a sidelong wink at Marie, took the old men over into the shade near a thick, fairly large old oak door heavily studded and reinforced with iron.

Olivia spoke without turning. "Do you see that door behind where they are standing now, *señorita?* Well, down below is a very cool room that smells powerfully of the wine priests made down there a hundred years ago. Now . . , does not your father take the old ones down there beyond that door?"

Marie looked. The door was ajar and there was no one in sight. She said: "Is there still wine down there, *señora?*"

"Still? There is wine down there . . . a few gallons. We make it every summer." Olivia reached for another long strand of twine. "Those old men had no argument. They do this once a month. Oftener if they did not believe Father Eusebio would comprehend. Now he is listening to their trumped-up argument. Two minutes from now he will draw off three glasses of wine. Then two more. . . ." Olivia held out a hand. "That length of twine, *por favor, señorita.*" Marie handed over the string, and wanted to laugh but Olivia's face was totally unsmiling.

"There are others besides those old men. There is the *Señora* Esteven, always with a sore stomach, and *Señorita* Soto . . . something in her eyes. *Hah!* And *Señor* Dennison, or the storekeeper, or the saloon man." Olivia had to stand on tiptoe to tie the twine. She was surprisingly lithe and slender and handsomely willowy, Marie decided. A definite contrast to most of the Mexican women Marie had seen lately. But there was a basic difference Marie would not understand for some months yet. Olivia Gomez was not, strictly speaking, Mexican, although she spoke the language of Mexico and had relatives in Mexico. She was a descendant of the *gachupins*—wearers of spurs—the Spaniards who had conquered and ruled Mexico for so long. Otherwise, she never would have had that alabaster skin.

Father Eusebio emerged from the dark old cellar, heaved his weight upon the oak door to close it, waved at the pair of happy old men who were shuffling briskly away, and turned to catch his daughter's eye. He winked again at her, locked the door, pocketed the immense brass key, then began to whistle as he light-footedly strode over to take up where he had left off with the bean-stringing. Olivia looked over her shoulder at him. He stopped whistling.

They finished with the sun nearly directly above and the flat, pale lemon-glare over the entire low desert. Olivia had lemonade for them, but, when the priest and his daughter wandered out to the *ramada* to enjoy it, Olivia did not join them, and afterward, when she and Marie met in the huge pantry and Marie said they had missed her, the older woman handed Marie several jars to carry back to the kitchen, loaded her own arms, and said: "I know how long it has been since he has seen you. There will be days of talking, no?"

Marie reached and lightly touched the older woman's arm. "Olivia . . . you are delightful."

For just a moment Olivia Gomez looked as though she might yield, at least a little. Someone out front, striking one of the ten-foot massive chapel doors with the great wrought-iron ring, interrupted, and Olivia's face closed down as she turned and briskly walked to the kitchen to put down the armload of jars.

"*Norteamericano,*" she said, avoiding the word *gringo* deliberately. "Who else would come to a church and feel he had to knock on the door? Excuse me."

But Marie went along, like a gray shadow in the wake of the black dress. Olivia had been correct. He was not just an American, he was a ruggedly handsome one with gray at the temples and dazzling blue eyes set on each side of a gently predatory hooked nose and a big, smiling mouth. Clearly he was someone of substance. Aside from an ivory butt on his holstered Colt, his magnificent black horse at the distant rack wore silver.

Olivia said—"*Señor* Dennison."—in a voice so softly flat it sounded venomous.

The handsome man looked past at Marie, and blinked. Olivia's mood swiftly changed. "What is it you want . . . this time?"

John Dennison was a strong, capable man, intuitive and wise. He was also wealthy and independent and able. He returned his gaze to the older woman, and now it showed a trace of iron. He was reacting to Olivia's very obvious dislike. But he did it tactfully. He even smiled at her, when he said: "I would like to see Father Eusebio."

"He is at prayers."

Dennison stood a moment bracing into the cold look of Olivia, then reached inside his light jacket, brought out a doeskin pouch, and, while looking Olivia directly in the eye, he said: "A token, *señora*. I can never fully repay him for all he's done."

Olivia made no move to accept the pouch. She had both hands clasped over her stomach when she replied: "You might try doing a few things for yourself, Mister Dennison. Father Eusebio is only flesh and blood and you are not the only person he tries to help. Last night he came back worn out and so tired he fell asleep halfway through his supper."

The handsome cowman still held out the pouch, but now there was high color beneath his heavy tan. He clearly would have liked to say something, but he just as clearly would not allow himself to do it. He leaned, pressed the pouch into Olivia's hand, turned with a slight, bleak bow, and went back out to the beautiful horse.

Marie lingered at the partially ajar door watching John Dennison turn to ride over into *gringo* town. Behind her in the perpetual gloom of the high-vaulted chapel Olivia said: "Sainted Mother . . . look."

The little pouch was full to the choker with gold coins. Marie was impressed. She thought there had to be at least $50 there. But it was $100! More than most of the men around Fort

Triumph earned all year. Olivia put a hand to her mouth in remorse. "What did I say to him?"

Marie side-stepped an answer. "Hadn't we better take it to Father Eusebio?"

"He is still at prayers," murmured the older woman, and led the way back to the kitchen where she sank disconsolately down upon a wall bench. "May I be forgiven." She looked up. "Father Eusebio will be angry."

Marie used the older woman's given name for the first time. "Olivia, I don't believe Father Eusebio could ever be angry with you."

From the doorway in the back wall, beyond which there was a very long, narrow corridor, the priest said—"Why should I be angry?"—and strode into the room.

Olivia switched instantly to English and blurted out her story. Father Eusebio picked up the little pouch, hefted it, began to frown as he hefted it again, then turned and up-ended the pouch upon a table.

He was silent for so long that Marie said: "Dad . . . it's one hundred dollars."

He blew out a rattling long breath and turned toward Olivia. She met his gaze with a wet look, so he stepped across and leaned slightly to brush upward on her cheek with a finger. In gentle Spanish he said: "I told you five years ago . . . you bring good fortune to the mission . . . and to me." He smiled, then stepped back and became brisk again. "Well, now we can prevent the whole mission from turning into a mud slide when it rains again and washing us all way. We can fix the roof. And after that . . . Olivia, a decent floor in your kitchen to replace this ancient one that has been worn into trails?"

"No, Father . . . a new stole, some new robes for you in the Sunday services." Olivia had regained her composure. Marie saw her actually smile at Father Eusebio. She was beautiful.

VI

Sonora lemons had a distinctive tartness. Marie's father told her one evening—through a mighty yawn—it was rumored that otherwise only in the Holy Land could they grow such flavorful lemons. It was pure hearsay. A paunchy priest named Father Domingo, who had stopped at the mission for a week on his way to Texas from San Xavier in Alta California, pinched and squeezed a Sonora lemon and pronounced it wholly inferior to California lemons.

The day after Father Domingo and his mud-complexioned *mestizo* companion and horse holder departed, a handsome, lithe *vaquero* with wickedly bold black eyes and a beautiful mouthful of teeth came to the mission, found Marie on the *ramada,* removed his hat with a flourish, and said in flawless English he was looking for the *Señora* Gomez.

Marie was flattered by the obvious surprise and the ensuing near rapture of the handsome *vaquero* as he stood studying her. She was also suddenly very much on guard, so, when she replied in Spanish saying that the *Señora* Gomez had gone over to the general store, she put it almost coldly.

The handsome youth sighed and, without allowing his eyes to leave her features for even a moment, said: "It is her husband, *señorita* . . . if you please, it is *señorita,* is it not?"

Marie considered. Since everyone else seemed to know by this time she was Father Eusebio's daughter, this handsome Mexican cowboy must not be from Mex town. She said: "*Sí,* it is *señorita,* and what of *Señora* Gomez's husband?"

"He is dead," stated the *vaquero,* saying it as though he were making a statement of fact concerning the weather.

Marie did not move on the bench but her eyes steadily widened. In Spanish she said: "How can this be, man?"

"Brigands, *señorita.*" The *vaquero* pitched his shoulders up and down in a callous small shrug. "The desert is full of them, but mostly they don't attack Mexicans. Only *gringos*. But this time. . . ."—another of those small shrugs—"this time it was different. He was riding a very good horse. One of *el jefe* Dennison's fine cattle-working horses. I was with him, but we were hunting cattle about a mile apart. I heard the gunshot and raced over. We traded a few shots. There were four of them. One was taking the horse when I was close enough finally to fire . . . but they all raced southward . . . *señorita?*"

Marie looked white to the eyes. "I'm all right, *hombre.*"

"You don't look it."

Marie struggled for composure and arose to step past the lithe range rider. They were of an equal height, but, while she had been sitting, he had seemed taller. Probably because he was lithe and lean-hipped.

At the edge of the *ramada* facing those weed-grown plinths of native stone, some askew over ancient graves, she told him she would tell *Señora* Gomez. She then thanked the *vaquero* for bringing the message and kept her back to him until she heard his huge-roweled Chihuahua spurs fade around the corner of the mission's south wall, then she turned to stroll aimlessly northward.

Her father was in the little windowless cell that he used as a study. The door was open, so she leaned there watching him at the magnificent, very old carved oak desk that surely must have arrived long after disenfranchisement, because, had it been at the mission during those times, someone would have hauled it away as they had hauled away everything else they could lift, or which they would wrench and prise loose from the walls and floors. It had someone's proud coat of arms beautifully carved in the front panel amid a magnificent floral, oak and chestnut, frieze.

He raised his head, sensing rather than seeing her presence, and slowly put aside the pen he had been writing with to straighten up a trifle more. "Marie," he said gently, "what is it?"

She told him.

He put his head in his hands for a moment, rallied almost immediately, and asked where Olivia was. Marie's answer was curt. "At the general store over in *gringo* town." It came out so naturally she had no idea she had said it with that faintly underlying tinge of prejudice that went with any such pronouncement by the people of Mex town.

Father Eusebio arose. "Marie, I need you very much."

She understood. "Anything I can do, anything at all. Do you want me to walk over and find her . . . take her walking for a while, and tell her?"

"No. I'll do that. If you would mind the chapel and the mission?"

She nodded. There was nothing, really, to mind. The chapel had its sandaled—and occasionally a booted as well—visitor at different hours of the day, but they entered without announcement, prayed, and departed in the same privacy. Unless someone in the rear of the immense old building left a corridor door open, the normal residents of the place had no idea who might be in private prayer in the chapel. It was one of the discreet, age-old unwritten laws neither to spy upon nor intrude upon prayers, even though, and this had often happened the good Lord knew, it was suspected that outlaws or brigands might be in there praying.

She moved to allow her father to squeeze past on his way out. The look of intense concern on his face was perhaps no more than she might have expected on the face of any man—or woman—who had the ability to feel very deeply. She made no attempt to analyze his expression. She loved him, which meant she also implicitly trusted him.

Shortly after his departure when she wandered through the

faintly echoing, lofty-ceilinged old rooms that were so blessedly cool, she wondered about Olivia and her husband/wife relationship. What brought that on was the fact that Olivia had not once in the ten days Marie had been at Fort Triumph mentioned being married, mentioned her husband, nor her family—if she had one.

Someone arriving out front, spurs ringing as he marched up the wide, long steps to the chapel, caught her attention as she passed one of those deep-set narrow high windows. She hardly heeded the sound. Someone, instinct—erroneously—told her, had arrived at the chapel to pray. She wandered back to the upper end of the *ramada* beyond which was that rather large bean patch where they had tied string to stakes some days earlier—and he was standing there in deep shade, hat in hand, white shirt open at the neck, high black boots and silvered spurs dusted over as though he had ridden a fair distance. He did not smile when he said—"Miss Hamblin."—and gave one of those little courtly bows the *gringo* men had learned from the better-class Mexicans of the Southwest.

She wondered how he had learned her name, but decided that, after the length of time she had been in the area, even cowmen six miles away had probably heard of the daughter of Father Eusebio.

She said: "Good morning, Mister Dennison. Can I help you with something?"

"*Señora* Gomez," he murmured, moving a little closer in the deep, fragrant shade.

"She is not here, and if it's about her husband, a cowboy came by an hour or so ago."

"She knows, then?"

"No, she was over in *gringo* town. But my father is looking for her now, to tell her. Mister Dennison . . . maybe if we left it to my father . . . ?"

50

He conceded at once, destroying some myth of hers that he was an arrogant, forceful man. "No one could tell her better, Miss Hamblin, I sent that *vaquero* on ahead, but the reason I came along, too, was to give her the details as best we know them right now. And also to tell her . . . she will not be in want because her husband no longer draws wages."

It was a generous gesture and Marie was impressed by it. She was certain very few ranchers ever went to this extreme when one of their riders was killed, particularly when the rider had met his death through no fault of the outfit he was riding for.

She invited him to be seated on one of the smooth old wooden benches, and she moved to seat herself nearby as she said: "The cowboy said it was brigands, Mister Dennison."

For the first time harshness crept into his voice. "Horse thieves, Miss Hamblin. They had just raided my north range where all the ranch loose stock is kept. One of them had an accident. His horse broke a leg in a dog hole out there. They left the horse . . . didn't even shoot him . . . and came down with that particular renegade riding double until they saw the *señora*'s husband. They didn't have to kill him. All they had to do was ride on up, throw down on him, and take his horse."

"Throw down on him?"

"Point their pistols at him, Miss Hamblin. There were four of them. No man in his right mind would argue with four pistols. It wasn't necessary to shoot him down like they did. . . . They'll pay. I promise you they'll never do it again." He paused and watched her profile briefly, then turned his attention to the faraway misty hills. "I would also like to know whether to fetch the body to town or to bury it at the ranch." He swung back toward her. "They hadn't lived together, you know, for all those years."

She hadn't known any such thing and it stunned her. How many years hadn't they lived together? Since Olivia had come to look after her father? She was afraid to ask so she gave an indeterminate response to his question.

"Really, I doubt that Olivia will be in any condition to make decisions like that right away, Mister Dennison." It was a long ride for him to make for the answer to his query, but on the other hand he had to have a reply quite soon, so she said: "Could I help to the extent of riding out to your ranch when Olivia decides?"

He smiled very suddenly. "That would be wonderful." He arose and stood gazing at her, still smiling. "Do you know . . . has Father Eusebio told you . . . how we mark trails out here? The way out to my camp is marked by stones about this size, painted bright green." The gesture he made with both hands indicated stones slightly larger than melons.

She hadn't heard that this was how trails were marked on the low desert and right at the moment it struck her as unique. Why didn't they use painted wooden signs like everyone else?

He must have read her thoughts because he explained: "Any wood you use down here, even posts and the boards nailed to them, disappear within a couple of weeks. That kind of wood is the most valuable thing around. Everyone has a shack or store or corral needing wood." He stood watching her a moment longer, then bowed again and departed.

She went to the edge of the porch to watch him ride over to *gringo* town. He had not said anything about there being a posse, or any kind of pursuit being in progress, nor had he mentioned the possibility that those horse thieves were marauders from below the line, or outlaws from north of the low desert, although she had picked up some inference, perhaps without real justification, that those horse thieves were from below the border. Mexican *bandidos*.

He rode as though he were part of his mount, and he had the posture of the Southwest, which was part pride and part nonchalance. She did not understand what this was. All she knew was that he was handsome on a horse, too.

One of the elderly men who did odd jobs around the mission came in search of her. A very large bird was in the chapel, the result without question, the old man said, of someone, no doubt a *gringo*, leaving one of the huge old oak doors ajar, which was the primary reason why all doors at the mission were kept closed. The priests had never minded birds nesting elsewhere, on the outside of the church for example, even making their wretched mud nests in the eaves, but clearly this matter of a bird in the chapel was something requiring prompt attention. The old man did not go into detail. Nor did he have to. Marie went with him through the cool corridors until they emerged through a back doorway into the handsome old chapel with its inherent scent of incense, and the bird was indeed large. It was also black, like all crows, and, while without question the old man knew exactly what kind of bird it was, when it landed upon a wooden pew facing the altar—shiny black, tawny eyes, bill partly open—the old man crossed himself twice and murmured a swift prayer of which Marie heard only two distinct words: "*Señor* Satan."

She went down the longest aisle, opened both huge oak doors so that sunlight immediately flooded into the chapel, then she picked up a faggot broom left discreetly near the doors in case someone entering during the rainy season had to sweep mud off their sandals or boots, and went after the lively crow, whether he was the devil in disguise as the old man clearly thought, or not. The bird took a close look at the determination of the handsome long-legged woman with the broom in both hands, and flung upward to make a high circuit of the ceiling in his search for a way out.

He came lower only when he was tiring, and she was right there, broom upraised. He tried to get past. She swung with surprising power and the rush of air sent him more swiftly on his way. He squawked once in consternation, finally saw the source of all the sunlight, dropped down, and went with unerring accuracy to the wide exit. Without a single slackening of wing beat, he shot straight back out into the brilliant hot morning.

Marie went over to replace the faggot broom, to pull with all her strength to get the huge oak doors closed, and, when the old man came over, beaming a somewhat admiring smile that nonetheless harbored some hint of misgivings, she said: "Do these hinges have to work this hard?"

In contrite Spanish he assured her that he would go at once, find some tallow, and grease each spindle. He also told her because he powerfully admired her bravery, that he hoped with all his heart and soul the crow had been nothing but a simple crow. Then he bustled away leaving her to wonder why, if that had indeed been the devil, he had decided to visit a place as dull and uninspiring as Fort Triumph.

She lingered a while in the cool and gently gloomy chapel, went up to the foremost railing, knelt, and, for the first time since arriving here, bowed her head in a simple little prayer—for Olivia, and for Father Eusebio, and also for the departed soul of the man she had never known, would never see, and had not heard a single word about—Olivia's husband.

VII

For Marie the absence of her father's housekeeper meant assuming the domestic duties, and, while they were far more varied than she had anticipated, and required what she thought had to amount to about ten miles of walking from one end to the other of the huge old building every day, she was willing.

All her father had told her of the murdered *vaquero* was that he and Olivia had been married while in their early teens, one of those "arranged marriages" in which their people sometimes indulged, and that her husband had never really wanted to stay married, that he had been cowboying from his twenties, and had never chosen to relinquish that life for one of a family man.

Otherwise, Father Eusebio said nothing about Olivia's husband, but there was something else, and Marie deduced that it probably had to do with dislike, or at the very least disapproval, because a priest came down from Montoya on the morning stage to perform the interment ceremony and Father Eusebio rode out on the dappled gelding to care for an ailing woman named Esteven, who had stomach trouble. Marie was confident that normally her father would have performed the burial service, especially for someone as close to him as his own housekeeper. But she asked no questions, watched her father ride out, and thirty minutes later when a lanky, taciturn man named Jim Young came over looking for her father and she saw the badge on his shirt front, she asked him pointblank if Olivia's husband had been a worthwhile individual, something she would never have done under other circumstances, and shrank from doing now even as she did it. It helped, too, that Constable Jim Young was a complete stranger to her. It was easier to make such a request of someone she did not know.

He considered her for a moment before saying: "Well, Miss Hamblin, if you mean was he the kind of feller folks like and all. . . ." Jim Young shrugged wide shoulders. "He was tolerably well liked, I'd say. But if you mean did I like him or your paw, or some other folks around town . . . well, then I'd have to say he was one of those men who never took no responsibility. At forty-five he was still hootin' and hollerin' and drinkin' and gamblin' like he was a twenty-year-old range rider." Evidently this variety of individual was no novelty to Constable Young because he also said: "Every cow outfit's got 'em by the dozen . . . grown men still thinkin' and actin' like they was eighteen years old."

She had about as much of an answer as she needed, so she took a message for her father to the effect that Dennison's hard-riding range crew had got between the horse thieves and the Mex border, that Constable Young was now going south with a town posse to get in behind the outlaws, and, if Father Eusebio had the time and the inclination, he could fetch along his medicine satchel and ride down there, too, just in case someone got hurt.

Of course someone would get hurt. Marie watched the unsmiling, long-faced constable striding back in the direction of *gringo* town. He was her idea of what a Western range man was—lanky, close-mouthed, grave, and unsmiling, always armed and booted, tough and courageous. And now she added something else—thick as oak.

Her father did not return until early evening. Olivia appeared soundlessly in her black attire upon the rear *ramada* where Marie was snapping beans she had picked from the garden. She had found a little free time and she had seen Olivia fill out her hours this way, so she had done it, too. When she glanced up and saw the very dark eyes in the white face, she did not know whether to smile a greeting or not. She gravely inclined her head, pulled her skirt closer so there would be room for the older woman on the bench, and, after Olivia had seated herself, Marie remained discreetly silent and busy snapping beans.

The older woman's classical profile was in the direction of the old graveyard when she said: "I knew you could do it all even without my guidance." Then she turned a gentle little smile on the younger woman. "Father Eusebio?"

Suddenly Marie remembered. Olivia, in her moment of biting scorn a few days earlier, had mentioned a *Señora* Esteven as pretending to have stomach trouble in order to be visited by the parish priest. Marie especially did not want to add a burden to those Olivia was already carrying on the day she had buried her husband—whether she loved her husband or not—so all she said was: "He rode out about an hour after breakfast."

"With his medicine satchel?"

"Yes," answered Marie, and shifted the subject. She relayed the lawman's message in case Olivia encountered Father Eusebio before his daughter met him.

Olivia settled her shoulders against the ancient wall, let both strong hands lie idle in her lap, and said, in inflectionless but soft Spanish: "Certainly now everyone rushes forth with his loaded gun, no? One man has died, so the most natural thing in the world is to make certain three or four also die. Miss, does not that make logical sense, then? What must people always do if not kill one another?"

Marie did not know how to answer the quiet bitterness. Primarily because she believed those murderers deserved to be punished. It was fine to be religious, commendable to believe in the sacredness of human life, but still. . . . She snapped beans and stepped carefully through the thickets of her private thoughts. She and Olivia were different. That was the only summary she arrived at right then. Olivia was more nearly like Marie's father in her asceticism, at least Marie came to this conclusion while they sat there. Then Olivia turned and slowly studied the lowered head and thoughtful, sober eyes of the younger woman, and smiled, and said something that undermined Marie's conclusions.

"But there must be an orderly world, must there not? There must be protection for those who wish to make better the lot of humanity."

Marie looked up, and, when their eyes met, Olivia reached and gently lifted away a tumbled lock of the younger woman's hair. "They will catch the *guerrilleros,* or whatever they are, and men will die." The strong shoulders gently rose and fell. "It is wrong, is it not? But to take lives to make life safer. . . . How do we decide about those things?"

Marie smiled back, softly. "We don't. Olivia . . . we are only women."

This time though that was no answer at all for Olivia Gomez, the widow. "I once saw a priest shoot and kill an outlaw."

Marie was not entirely shocked but clearly Olivia had thought she would be—or at least thought Marie should have been badly upset, because Olivia gravely inclined her head for emphasis before giving the details.

"It was nine years ago when I was thirty-six . . . even then I was older than you are now. This outlaw stole the money from the mission's offering boxes, and, when one of the acolytes came up, the outlaw killed him with one shot. The priest . . . his name was Gregorio O'Brien . . . he stepped into the chapel, and, as the outlaw aimed again, Father Gregorio shot him, then dragged him out onto the steps in front, flung down the gun, and went into seclusion with prayers for seven days. And fasted." Olivia waited for Marie's reaction. "Well, we are flesh and blood, it is true, but our way is clearly marked, *señorita.*"

"Olivia, are you telling me you don't think . . . are you saying he should have let the outlaw kill him, too?" demanded Marie.

"What I am saying, child, is that I don't know. I do know the correct road, I just don't see how under some circumstances we can travel it, try though we must."

Marie felt a quick depth of pity and warmth for the older woman. If Olivia's seeming outward intransigence had resulted in her being unable to excuse the priest, or alibi him, it would have made things much more difficult for Marie. She softly said: "Olivia . . . I love you."

The older woman leaned. They touched cheeks, then Olivia straightened away and, by averting her face, kept her expression secret until, moments later, they saw Father Eusebio cross diagonally in the direction of the horse shed, then Marie decided to finish snapping beans in the kitchen. "It's getting too hot out here," she said in English, took her pans, and departed. Olivia looked after her for as long as Marie was in sight, then arose, smoothed her somber black dress, and went as far as the southernmost edge of the *ramada,* there to stand in shade until Father Eusebio emerged from the shed and saw her.

He came at once.

She met his gaze and held it until, arms wide, he was up into the shade. She fell against him, buried her face against his powerful chest, and shuddered from head to toe.

For Marie, the transmittable mood of Olivia Gomez lasted until she was cleaning up from the beans and a pair of shuffling old men came to the rear kitchen door, hats in hand, lined and almost entirely toothless, with very bright, very wise black eyes. They regarded her with sly interest, and, when she came to the door, one of them asked in almost incomprehensible English if he and his companion might have a word with the *padre,* because they had this unresolvable dispute between them, and in order not to allow such ungodly passions to overwhelm them that they might attack one another with knives or pistols, and thus fall from God's sweet grace. . . .

Marie eyed them calmly. In Spanish she crisply said: "At the present time, *hombres,* Father Eusebio cannot be disturbed." She held the door open and motioned for them to enter. Then, when they were standing there smiling with obvious uncertainty and clutching their hats, she pointed to a pair of benches. "Sit," she commanded.

Both old men went over and seated themselves. Now, they were scarcely smiling. It was not just unseemly for a woman no more than a girl to order older people around like this woman was doing, it was also inexcusably shameful and also, of course, disrespectful.

She went to a low cupboard, rummaged, brought forth a

crockery jug, blew dust from it as she had seen Olivia do, swung its solid weight to the unsteady table, got two thick cups, and set them beside the jug. In border Spanish she then said: "Guzzle, old ones, and let this be between us. So . . . drink!"

They filled both cups, drank, refilled them, and under her steady regard, arms crossed where she leaned watching, they downed the second cup loads. Then one of them, the taller of the raffish old pair, pulled himself to his full majestic height, adjusted sagging shapeless baggy old trousers with a flourish, and, speaking with the deliberation and the precise enunciation of someone who chooses not for others to realize how quickly he had become half drunk, he said: "Thank you, *señorita*, for this favor. I am heading for distraction because of your beauty and my heart weeps that I cannot more splendidly reward you for your charity, for your graciousness and understanding. . . . One more half cup then?"

She stoppered the jug and swung it back to its lower cupboard, and, when she faced around, they were both merrily smiling at her. She reached for the sturdy faggot broom and leaned upon it as she said: "I blush for the compliments, horsemen, and now I have work to do." She pulled the sturdy broom closer with both hands.

The slighter of the pair of old men shuffled expertly toward the door, moving sideways. From over there he smiled straight at her. "*Señorita*, I tell you honestly . . . our parish has needed someone like you for a long while. Good day."

After she saw them hastening southward more erect than ever, with more spring to their strides, she turned and regarded the empty cups, and laughed. Then she got to work, preparing supper, for while it was still early, at least the sun was still up there, she had never taken over the whole responsibility before and chose not to be rushed now that she was going to do it alone.

Neither Olivia nor her father appeared until daylight was ending, until the first soft fall of a little evening breeze swept the length of the tiled old shadowy *ramada* when she stepped out to look for them.

The meal was prepared. It was different; she had never cooked a tortilla in her life nor concocted an entire supper around *carne con chili,* so she had misgivings. Still, she consoled herself with the knowledge that someone besides Olivia was going to have to do these things for the next few days, and, since she seemed to be the only available alternative, she would prepare what she knew how to cook, and if there were complaints—well—they could take them to the priest.

Finally she saw them, sitting relaxed and holding hands around the north end of the *ramada* up where the bean patch was, talking now and then, very quietly, obviously unaware of another soul on earth right at this time.

Her father seemed very grave while Olivia, with her head back, her beautiful classical neck and throat fully exposed, seemed at peace. If he had accomplished that for her on the day she had buried her husband, regardless of how she and her husband had got on, why then he had accomplished a wonder.

Marie returned around the corner, stood there a time gazing around into the softly settling dusk and wondering whether even to mention supper. Right at this time it seemed to be almost a blasphemy to call someone to come and eat.

There was no moon, and, although the sky was steadily darkening, going through an entire spectrum of pastels from soft rusty-gray to warm purple, there were only a few visible stars and over where the northward low hills stood immutably stark and insensitive, each coarse outline was visible right up until Marie decided not to intrude, and slowly turned to go back down by the kitchen, removing the apron as she walked.

Well, it wasn't much of a meal anyway, actually. Not to people who were accustomed to an altogether different kind of cooking.

But ten minutes later they arrived, Olivia preceding Father Eusebio, her beautiful liquid dark eyes sweeping from the waiting table with its lighted candles to the face of the younger woman. She smiled.

Someone opened and closed a chapel door out front. Marie sighed. The maintenance man had sworn he would grease those hinges. Another thing for her to do tomorrow, apparently.

Father Eusebio came close, kissed his daughter's cheek, then went to his place at the table to raise both hands and simultaneously to drop his head.

VIII

He departed right after supper, but Marie did not realize he had gone until Olivia returned for her shawl. She had gone as far as the horse shed with him.

"I tried to keep him here," she sighed in Spanish.

Marie turned. "Where did he . . . ? Not down where those outlaws are bottled up . . . in the dark?"

"*Sí.*"

"Olivia!"

The older woman adjusted her shawl to cover both her hair and shoulders. She had up until this night never called Marie by her given name, and perhaps under different circumstances she would not have done it this night because by nature and heritage she belonged to a very formal class of people.

"He will not be in direct danger, Marie, but even if this were not so . . . could you or I stop him? Would we? He is both a man of God and a doctor." Olivia shrugged gently. "Well, as a matter of fact I did try to talk him out of it. Useless of course, and I knew it would be. He is a man who serves. In time you will adjust to it. . . . I did, and it took me a long while." She went to the door and Marie went over there with her to walk down the dark *ramada* and see her on her way.

Nothing more was said until, nearing the edge of the long tiled walkway Olivia hesitated and faced the younger woman. "He is grateful for you, Marie, and so am I." She walked on.

It did not occur to Marie until Olivia was dim in the darkness that the older woman was going home to a dark night of poignancy. She started impulsively to go after her, then halted and turned back, slowly. Olivia would want to be alone this particular night, pain not withstanding.

Marie understood this even though she was not at all certain it was wise for Olivia, nor was she certain she could have done it. Still, if it had been between Olivia and her dead husband as it now seemed it must have been. . . . A mongrel dog sprang away in astonishment and Marie's heart nearly stopped. She had not been the least bit aware of her fear of being alone, but there it was. The dog was probably one of those foraging mongrels that did their most productive work after nightfall. Fort Triumph, like most cow towns, had its share of dogs like that.

In the morning Marie went out to the horse shed first. It was empty. She had thought it might be, for even though she had not expected to be roused by the return of her father in the night, she had felt fairly certain the mission would still be her sole charge come daylight, and it was, so she made breakfast for herself, very light, and prepared coffee for Olivia, should she show up. She did, but it was almost 10:00 A.M. and the heat was rising again, coming up from the earth, rolling down from the mountains, spreading from the sun's overhead heights in wave after wave until it met with those other sources, then a haze emerged. Olivia was as always dressed in black. Otherwise, she seemed the same in her expression, in her quietness, in her calm efficiency.

They were changing the position of a rock in the little *acequia* that supplied water to the melon and tomato patch, when a horseman rode around to the rear of the mission without dismounting, and finally swung to the ground when he spied them.

Marie recognized the lanky, taciturn town constable except that this morning he looked dusty, soiled, tired, and dehydrated. He had beard shadow to make his normally somewhat elongated face look more horse-like than ever.

He waited until he was certain of their attention, stood hip-shot, trailing braided rawhide reins from his left fingers, and, when Olivia finally left the patch and approached, still holding her skirt out of the dust, he said: "Came back to town a little while ago, *señora,* to dispatch a wagon with hay in it down where we come onto those border jumpers."

She said: "Father Eusebio . . . ?" Marie saw a hand rise slowly to her throat.

Jim Young's sole indication that he was not as calm and nerve-less as he appeared to be was a little flip of the hand holding the rawhide reins. "It was a bad fight," he told Olivia, and let his eyes stray past to where Marie was standing erect, listening. "They're going to fetch back two posse men who got shot and two shot-up greasers, plus a dead greaser. One got away. Some of the Dennison crew went after him. Me, I couldn't authorize no one to go down over the line into Mexico. It's not allowed."

Olivia's hand was still at her throat while she stood patiently waiting for all that drawled information to be passed along, then she reiterated her earlier question. "Father Eusebio, Constable?"

Marie suddenly caught the shock of a bad premonition. It turned her to stone where she was standing in the fierce sunlight. It stopped her breath for a moment.

"He rode into a bushwhack," stated Constable Young. "We

never had no idea there might be one behind us after Denni-son's crew pushed 'em back toward my crew, but there was . . . a Mex sneakin' around behind to stampede our horses, set us afoot so them outlaws could still make it down across the line. Father Eusebio rode right into. . . ."

Olivia's sharp voice cut across the endless drawl with three words. "Is he dead?"

Constable Young shook his head. "Nope. He sure got cleaned out of his saddle, though. I was lookin' back and seen it hit him. Took him out of leather like someone in back had grabbed the collar of his shirt and yanked hard."

Marie walked over. "How badly is he hurt, Constable?"

Constable Young faced them both. "Shot through the lights," he reported, and Olivia had to interpret that.

"The lungs," she told Marie in a quick murmur.

"The Mexican that shot him is one of the wounded men they'll be bringing back. Olivia, I figured you'd have to know so you can get some rooms ready." Constable Young eyed their ashen faces. "Ladies, he never lost consciousness . . . was joking with John Dennison when I rode back, and, except for spittin' blood now and then. . . . Ladies, I've seen 'em recover from a lot worse shots than he's got."

Olivia's gaze at Constable Young hardened with either dislike or distaste just before she turned away, speaking over her shoulder. "We will have the rooms ready."

Constable Young turned, and, instead of mounting his head-hanging horse, he started to walk heavily away, leading the animal. There were heat waves beginning to dance like gelatin by the time he got over to the edge of *gringo* town; they broke and re-formed when he passed through them.

Marie saw Olivia watching her, so she walked part way toward the older woman before saying: "I could borrow a horse and take some lemonade or something down to him."

Olivia did not argue, she simply said: "Marie, you are not accustomed to the kind of heat you'd be riding through. On cooler
days than this I've seen my own people . . . after two hundred
years here . . . drop unconscious as red as beets in the face. . . .
Marie, stay with me, we'll have enough to do."

"Olivia . . . !"

The older woman nodded understanding, reached for one of
Marie's hands, and held it in a cool, firm grip for a moment,
then released it. "Come along."

They prepared four of the little priests' cells for the pair of
injured posse men and for the two injured Mexicans. They spent
most of the time preparing Father Eusebio's room.

The also made quantities of fresh lemonade, put some pep-
permint beside each cot, and Olivia finally took Marie to the
chapel and they prayed. It was about 1:00 P.M. before they were
able to go to the kitchen. Olivia drank black coffee and urged
Marie to eat something. The best Marie could do was drink
some lemonade. Her stomach was in no mood for food, not
even for coffee.

Constable Young reappeared, freshly bathed, shaved, and attired. He announced that the posse men were just now entering
town and that they had reported to the liveryman his straw-
filled hospital wagon was only about an hour behind.

Marie eyed the bitter lemon-yellow sun and had to clench
both fists to keep herself in hand. Constable Young, who had
impressed her rather favorably the day before, now struck her as
stolid, unfeeling, and needlessly dense.

Olivia seemed to understand, and, when the wagon finally
appeared, being escorted by John Dennison and that handsome
young *vaquero* who had clearly been swept off his feet by Marie
only a short while back, Olivia took Marie's hand and they both
hurried over to walk the last few hundred feet beside the old
wagon.

The teams were wringing wet with sweat, the driver, the gun guard, the escort of riders, and the men lying out in the straw under that unrelenting sunshine were all wringing wet.

Dennison did not say a word except to growl at his *vaquero* the moment the rig halted. They began carrying in the injured men, Father Eusebio first, and, although he smiled at Olivia and winked roguishly at Marie, they could both see the bled-out pallor beneath the sweaty sunburn of his strong face.

Afterward came the pair of injured range riders and neither of them smiled at all. One had a leg broken above the knee. That long haul under the blazing sun in an ancient wagon that had no springs had caused him to faint several times from pain. The other posse man had been hit a glancing blow up the back, which opened a furrow from hips to shoulders. He had been bandaged quickly enough to stop much of the bleeding but he looked sick and feeble after they got him to his cot inside the blessedly cool old mission.

The dead Mexican had been off-loaded over in *gringo* town. The two wounded Mexicans were greasy with dark sweat. One had a body wound that seemed not to be bothering him very much, while the other Mexican had a broken arm and a gash in the side where the same bullet had smashed into two ribs, breaking them both.

It took a full hour to get the wounded men settled and afterward Marie was kept busy bathing dirty, overheated bodies to bring temperatures down as much as possible, while Olivia demonstrated that she had served Father Eusebio often as a nurse.

When the wagon turned back and Dennison's *vaquero* accompanied it as far as the saloon in *gringo* town where all the victorious posse men and range men were loosening in more mud-walled shade, Marie assumed everyone had gone. She did not observe Constable Young briefly in conversation with John

Dennison out back on the tiled *ramada*. Nor did she see Constable Young finally turn away, too, leaving Dennison to drink deeply from a hanging *olla*, roll and light a cigarette after sinking wearily upon a bench against the mission wall.

He was still out there an hour later when the sun, and at least a little of its heat, had shifted around until the full massive bulk of the ancient mission was between it and where Dennison was still sitting, when Marie strolled forth to catch a breath of afternoon breeze, drying her hands and lower arms upon a towel. She did not see him, but stepped tiredly to the edge of the tiles to stand under the eaves looking far beyond the patiently leaning old headstones.

He waited a long while, studied her with frank interest, and finally softly said: "How is he, Miss Hamblin?"

She whirled, taken totally unawares. For a moment she regarded the fresh layer of red-bronze over his deep tan, the slump of powerful shoulders, and the looseness of his strong body, then she stepped a few paces closer, where the shade was deeper but where the breeze had not reached yet, and replied quietly to him: "He's asleep, Mister Dennison."

It was as though her father was the only injured survivor. Neither of them mentioned a name, and they both spoke as though there could be no question of their concern for any individual other than Father Eusebio.

"Jim Young told you how it happened?" he asked, and, when she nodded and considered the towel she was holding, he offered his opinion. "No one was to blame, except that Mex. He maybe doesn't deserve the anger he's been getting ever since. Miss Hamblin, your father was dressed like almost anyone but a priest, and the greaser didn't see his offside so he had no way of knowing your father was unarmed. Sure, it was a bushwhack, but that Mex was trying to stay alive."

She stared. "You're making excuses for a man who tried to

murder him?"

"No, ma'am, not excuses. Just trying to let you see it as I look at it." He smiled tiredly up at her. "You make up your own mind. Just seemed to me you'd want to know both sides. . . . That outlaw's in enough trouble. When folks have been drinking over in *gringo* town long enough, they'll come over here, yank him out of bed, and hang him." He arose and struck dust from his trouser legs with a limp hat. "What did he tell you about how it happened?"

"My father? He didn't say a thing. We bathed him, bandaged him, and he slept through just about all of it. He has been so worn down lately, Mister Dennison."

He smiled at her. "I know. And it's partly my fault. You could tell him for me, when he comes around, that I sent a relay of riders up to Montoya to telegraph for a decent doctor . . . well . . . I meant to say for a professional doctor. With luck he'd ought to get down here by fast stage day after tomorrow." He kept looking at her as he dropped the hat upon the back of his head. "I expect you don't think much of what we did. I know Missus Gomez won't think much of it. To be right frank, Miss Hamblin, I don't think much of it myself . . . but I'll do it again tomorrow if I have to." He nodded and turned on his heel, spurs making a distinctive, richly musical sound as far as the end of the tiles, and even afterward when he stepped down into the pummeled dust on his way over to *gringo* town.

She was clutching the towel as though to strangle it.

Olivia paused in the cool corridor doorway to stand briefly, watching. She had seen John Dennison walking away.

Later, when they came together in the kitchen and the mission was settling into its depthless hush after this long, eventful day, Olivia said: "Your father spoke to me a while ago. He's asleep again, but, if you take this lemonade around, he should be awake again in a little while. Marie, John Dennison saved his life. That outlaw was aiming for a second shot after Father Eusebio fell. It was *Señor* Dennison who shot the horse thief." Olivia waited until the look on Marie's face had softened a little, then Olivia also said: "Your father said the man who shot him was not to blame."

Marie answered that quickly. "Not to blame the first time, Olivia. John Dennison told me that, and it sounded convincing enough, but he was going to kill a man he had already shot off a horse . . . and that's not his fault . . . that he would have willingly committed murder?"

Olivia nodded bleakly. "I feel exactly the same way. Marie . . . for now, until everyone is recovering, though, we can say nothing, can we?"

They looked steadily at one another for a moment, then Olivia did what Marie's father often did—she winked. Marie smiled and most of the rancor and the stiffness left her.

IX

Not until the following afternoon did they know which of the Mexicans had shot Father Eusebio. Marie, for some reason, had assumed it was the one with the broken leg, but that was not correct; it was the graying, round-faced very dark one who had been shot through the body and who seemed to be the least injured of them all. His name was Rey Sanchez and in both coloring and build he was typically low-caste Mexican—very dark, coarse-featured, with a forehead no more than two inches high and with a great mass of lank black hair growing across each temple. He was squat, thick, and ape-like in build, did not speak a word of English—or at least looked blank when anyone addressed him in that language—and watched both Olivia and Marie with black-eyed, snake-like intensity.

Olivia, whose experience was vast, told Marie, Rey Sanchez was a person to be watched, but, when John Dennison arrived in the late afternoon of the second day, he told Marie they would move Rey Sanchez to the jailhouse as soon as it was practical to do so, and that therefore she need not be overly concerned about the man.

The other Mexican was much younger, seemed to be in his mid-teens, and was unwilling to speak at all. He was mortally afraid and with some reason. He was surrounded by the very people men like Rey had been telling him for most of his life would kill him out of hand if they ever got the chance, and now they had that chance.

He had his broken leg in a splintered cast that precluded escape but otherwise he clearly would have made the attempt. Also, he was very weak, and that, too, would inhibit him. Meanwhile he thanked Marie and Olivia for everything that they did for him, watched everything and everyone with trepidation, and, when he heard that the priest was still alive and seemed to be improving, he smiled and seemed enormously relieved. Evidently he was pinning most of his hope upon Father Eusebio.

Those two Dennison riders were uncomfortable at the mission and insisted, when Dennison appeared late that afternoon, that he arrange for them to get back to the ranch, otherwise, weak or not, they were going to walk over to *gringo* town and bed down in the back room of the saloon.

Dennison agreed to send over a wagon and move them to the ranch. He smiled about that to Olivia and Marie while explaining how it was with men like these two. "They just can't get accustomed to having handsome nurses, and being flat out in a church. Well, it's a mission, but to them it's still a church."

When Olivia fixed John Dennison with one of her frosty, black-eyed stares, he made a small gesture of self-defense, still smiled, and said: "Missus Gomez . . . personally I'd ask nothing more, if I was wounded, than to be here. It's just that people are different."

He went to see Father Eusebio and Marie went with him. The day was waning. That small, high and very narrow window in the room let in a diluted form of rusty sunlight mingled with bluish heat haze.

Father Eusebio was flat on his back. Olivia insisted on it despite his objections. She also insisted that he drink boiled beef broth, regardless of the hotness of the day, and otherwise kept him on a water diet with limited amounts of lemonade. When he said something about all this to John Dennison, his daughter swiftly defended Olivia, and both men gazed at her. Then Father Eusebio smiled a little, softly.

"Wonderful woman," he murmured without specifying which one was the wonderful woman. Then he said: "John . . . what about the talk?"

Dennison answered without hesitation. "They are going to lynch him."

"Where is Jim?"

Dennison looked steadily down at the man on the bunk. "Jim Young won't be in town, Father."

Father Eusebio stared. "Just like that?"

Dennison nodded.

Marie knew what they were discussing, and, while she had formerly been in favor of whatever punishment was meted out to the man who had shot her *padre,* this callousness, this matter-of-fact, very calm, and deliberate discussion of the disposal of a human life by an illegal hanging made her feel cold all over.

The priest said—"It'll be up to you to stop them, John."—and Dennison shook his head. "You were out of it after he shot you off your horse," explained Dennison, "so you don't know he raised up to shoot you again when you were lying unconscious and unable to move. I saw him raising up and aiming, Father."

"You're the one who shot him, then?"

"Yeah. And, Father, I know how he felt and why he did what he had to do with that first shot. But to shoot a man who is already downed, unarmed and out of it. . . ." Dennison shook his head.

Marie was gazing with disbelief at the handsome cowman. "Mister Dennison . . . out on the patio you said for me to understand . . . you said Rey Sanchez probably did not deserve the anger he was getting. You defended him, to me, and now you're calmly sitting there, telling my father he will be hanged and you don't mean to do anything to stop it."

John Dennison turned slightly. "And when you knew how Sanchez had tried to murder your father with the second shot, you were ready to approve of whatever happened to the man. Miss Hamblin, all I tried to explain to you out there was that we live by range law not book law . . . not very much book law anyway . . . and it's better to be able to understand things like this than it is to just close your eyes and rush in with a hang rope in your hands. Someday maybe we'll have better law on the low desert. Right now what we have is the best for us and for our times." He waited a moment, half expecting Father Eusebio to interject, but the priest was watching his daughter's reaction to this and said nothing, so John Dennison added a little more to what he had just said. "You're new here."

She snorted. "New here? Does that make injustice different?"

John Dennison arose and looked momentarily at her father before nodding and stepping as far as the door before saying: "I got word back. That doctor I wanted to import is out of the territory. There's none other as good nor as specialized, Father."

The priest smiled. "John, I appreciate what you tried to do. It was generous and noble, but as far as I can see none of us are going to need special care. I'm certainly not going to. The bleeding's stopped and I feel better . . . weak but better. What I need, I think, is time."

Dennison walked out without another look in Marie's direction. In the corridor he encountered Olivia who was bearing a tray to Father Eusebio. Dennison smiled and she almost smiled back. Before ceasing to block her way, he said: "Being busy helps, *señora?*"

"It is the only thing that really does help," she replied in swift Spanish, and went past.

He got out to the front of the old mission, out upon those hundred-foot-wide, low stone steps in front of the chapel where his horse was tethered in roadway dust before Marie caught up. He turned at the sound of her swift, sharp footfalls over stone. Then he braced himself, hat in hand, and watched her approach. She was the handsomest woman he had ever seen.

"*¿Señorita?*"

She said a trifle breathlessly: "I need a favor, Mister Dennison."

He stood gazing at her. She was taller than most women, and she had the glow of health and vigor. He sighed. "Whatever you wish."

"Don't let them do it. Don't argue with me. Please, Mister Dennison, don't let them do it. My father just now said you were the only person who could stop them if Constable Young would not be drawn into it." She returned his gaze without blinking. "I'll never ask another favor of you."

He seemed to want to say she had no idea how much of a favor she was asking. Then he swung and glanced out where two curly-headed Mexican boys were standing in respectful admiration of his fine black horse and the silver-mounted bridle and saddle. One of them was the nephew of Olivia Gomez who Marie had spoken to concerning the passing of his old grandfather, but Dennison did not know it.

She stood in silence, waiting.

Then he turned back and found her eyes unwaveringly upon

him. He nodded. "I said . . . whatever you wished." He turned
on his heel and went down to the horse to untie it and turn to
lead it on foot over in the direction of *gringo* town. He walked
slowly and with his head lowered in thought. She felt she
understood his dilemma. Another time, perhaps with less criti-
cal stakes, she might have impulsively run after him to release
him from her charge. Now, she felt pain for him, and she also
felt another emotion.

Olivia appeared in the chapel doorway, classically pale and
erect, great wealth of shiny black hair piled high and handsomely arranged.

Marie went slowly back into the coolness of the building.

She wanted to attend to the injured survivors. The young
Mexican, who she saw first, finally started to talk—it was like
releasing floodgates. He told Marie of his poverty, of the squalor
of his childhood, of the fight, of other fights. He also told her he
was certain he would not leave Fort Triumph alive.

The pair of wounded cowboys from Dennison's riding crew
were together when she found them. One could walk well
enough to be in his friend's room when she came around with
lemonade. They were friendly but they were clearly unhappy at
being where they were and glad to be leaving. She listened to
their veiled complaints and smiled non-committally, and then
left them to go down to where her father had finally been allowed to sit up. Olivia was just leaving as Marie arrived.

She told him of exacting the promise from John Dennison.
He did not seem very pleased and that made her feel as though
he wanted to reproach her, except that she did not know for
what—meddling, perhaps? Intruding where women had no business? Forcing a promise from a man who obviously found her
handsome?

He finally said—"How is Rey Sanchez?"—and she had to
admit that she had neglected the border jumper without really

meaning to, or maybe she had subconsciously meant to.

"When I'm able, I'd like to go to his room," her father told her.

She thought she understood; her father wished to make his understanding and forgiveness known. As she thought of Rey Sanchez, though, she thought of a man who would accept the priest's forgiveness with the sly craftiness of someone who would simply want to use people. It was uncharitable of her to think that way, but there it was—that was her intuitive and instinctive reaction to the Mexican brigand.

She said nothing and leaned to make certain her father was well braced in back, and, as she drew away, their eyes met. He said: "You wonder about Olivia and your father."

For some reason she blushed wildly and swung toward the far wall to become busy with something else, angry with herself, until the blush subsided, then in a tone of practiced calm she said: "Dad, everyone down here is different. I wonder about them all." She turned back to face him. "John Dennison, I think, most of all. He seems so rational and calm and wise . . . and yet, he sat right there talking about giving a man's life away as though it were a stick of wood."

"Sweetheart, it's not just down here. People are the same everywhere. What makes the difference is their environment. Back East you call for help and policemen come at once. Out here, the law is basically the same but with the differences made mandatory by this totally different environment. . . ."

She said: "I understand. Well, I'm *trying* to understand any-way."

He kept looking at her, his thoughts still upon the topic he had broached earlier. "And, Olivia, my dear . . . ?"

She could afford tolerance here very readily. Mainly because he was her father, who she loved very much—more now that she was with him than before—and also because she loved

Olivia, who was so different, but so gentle and loyal and so—well—tolerant and understanding in her own very different way. She smiled into his questioning eyes. "Maybe after you have recovered . . . ?"

"Now," he said, with a trace of sudden firmness.

But she could not discuss it now. For one thing, she simply did not know what to think about their relationship. For another thing, she did not want to make judgments or assessments, perhaps because she was instinctively fearful of what she might come up with, but whatever it was, as she stood looking down into his sunburned face, she shook her head.

"Please, Dad, I just don't know."

His expression underwent a gentle change. He seemed perfectly willing to accept this, for the time being, although moments before he had seemed almost stern in his demand. He could of course have helped her arrive at her judgment but it was clear that he was not going to do it. She was willing to believe his personal integrity would not permit him to say things that would most certainly influence her opinion.

As she left the room, in troubled thought, and nearly collided with Olivia, she decided that no man with his basic honesty could be other than ethical in all things, including his relationship with Olivia. Then she raised her eyes, saw the guarded look in the older woman's glance as they passed in the cool, gloomy corridor, and her doubts flooded in again.

The dilemma had not seriously influenced anything thus far, and with those injured men it did not seem Marie would have the time to become very introspective now, either. Shortly after sunset that handsome *vaquero* arrived with a ranch wagon and took away the pair of injured range riders. She and Olivia went out with them, accepted their bashful expressions of gratitude, and stood a while in the softness of a blessedly cool early evening.

It was the first time in days there seemed to be any awkwardness between them, and Olivia's habit of being quiet when she had nothing to say in particular abetted it.

Then she shattered that unique condition between them by saying: "Marie, I am going to need help with Rey Sanchez. He is dead."

She stared.

Olivia shifted her shoulders a trifle in the manner of someone with ingrained fatalism, and turned to lead the way.

X

Father Eusebio would have gone at once, but Olivia would not allow it, and right now she was undisputed ruler of the old mission, so Father Eusebio had to make his analysis by guesswork. Rey Sanchez, he told them, must have been hemorrhaging internally very slowly but without let-up since being shot. In simple terms he had bled to death internally.

At least that was what they all had to believe, and in fact it was exactly what had occurred. There would be no *post-mortem* examination; not only was it considered barbaric and sadistically ghoulish by the church, but among low-desert people, and most Mexicans elsewhere, the cause of death was never as influential as its arrival. If a man such as Rey Sanchez had died . . . well, God had willed it and cutting his body open would neither change God's will nor bring him back. A dead man was dead, that was all there was to it.

Father Eusebio understood perfectly. To a great extent he concurred, but having studied both medicine and surgery now for many years, mostly from old books by candlelight, he had developed a physician's deep interest in both life and death, so he speculated from his room, asked Olivia a number of pertinent questions, and, when she told him she had arranged for men from Mex town to come and make the grave, Father Eusebio had another crisis to consider. No one had been buried inside the old mission's walls in perhaps fifty years, and certainly no renegade or horse thief, ever.

Marie was in the room when Olivia leaned and softly said: "Father, people speak of equality while we are alive. . . . I have never believed we were equal . . . alive . . . but I certainly see us as being all the same when we are dead."

Marie's father gazed at the handsome older woman. Marie turned aside and became busy because it seemed to her that watching the look in his eyes and the soft, gentle little quirk down around his mouth was like eavesdropping.

The gravediggers from Mex town worked at the site selected by Olivia and did not so much as mutter about putting this brigand in consecrated ground.

Marie went back to the room of the young Mexican to explain, but he already knew and rolled his eyes at her when he said: "Poison, *señorita?*"

She was shocked. In Spanish she demanded to know where he had developed any such ridiculous notion and he rolled his eyes toward the small window in the wall. Beyond, she could hear metal spades striking small stones where the diggers were working. That added to her surprise. "They believe he was poisoned?"

Maximillian Sotelo, the youthful brigand with the broken leg, simply said: "They were discussing it, *señorita.* Rey Sanchez to them was a very bad individual. I am also a very bad man to them."

She explained how Rey Sanchez had died and the youthful border jumper seemed to accept fatalistically her version without evincing any genuine belief in what she had said at all. It was exasperating not to be believed. For Marie, it was a fresh experience. She pulled up a little bench and sat beside the cot, but, before she could start her argument, Olivia appeared in the doorway. Marie responded to Olivia's beckoning hand, promising Maximillian Sotelo she would return.

She returned all right, but not as she or the youthful Mexican outlaw, or anyone else in the mission, would have expected.

Olivia led the way to the *ramada*. Northward the perspiring diggers were at work up to the waist of each man, and digging deeper. Uniquely enough that was exceptionally deep, rich earth out there, not sandy or stony or leached out and gray. It was the kind of soil that only required adequate water to grow anything, but Olivia, who had lived in Mex town all her life already knew how fertile the earth was. She also knew how useless it was to have rich soil and not enough water, so, while she watched the diggers and spoke to Marie, she seemed to expect nothing different up where those men were sweating at work.

"One of my nephews came around a short while ago, Marie, to carry a warning . . . the men over in *gringo* town are beginning to get organized."

Marie faintly frowned. "For the hanging?"

"Yes."

"It will be a disappointment to them that Sanchez is dead."

"Marie, they will hang the other one."

The young woman stared. "Maximillian? But it was Rey Sanchez who shot my father."

Olivia's expression did not change. "I know that." She turned back from watching the gravediggers. "Marie, this is not your world down here. Understand, then, that to drunk townsmen and range men from *gringo* town it will not matter. Only he must have the look of a Mexican. They will hang him. If not Sanchez, Sotelo, if not Sotelo, someone else." Olivia shrugged, then reverted to English to say: "If John Dennison stops them, I will be very surprised."

The implication was clear; John Dennison would most likely be *with* the lynchers. Marie disagreed. "He promised me to help . . . to prevent something like this, Olivia."

She shrugged black-clad shoulders and did not speak for a moment. "Well, Father Eusebio and I talked. He said we must hide the young border jumper."

It was an idea that had not occurred to Marie, and now she saw the boundless opportunities. "Where, Olivia . . . here in the mission?"

The older woman thought so. "If we try to get him away"— she pointed to the diggers—"if they don't see us trying it, someone else will. Nothing happens here that eyes don't see it. There are some monks' cells down under the mission in a stone room that adjoins the wine cellar. They are dark and damp." Olivia shrugged eloquently. "But they are preferable to a hang rope."

Marie thought of the youthful Mexican. "He will be frightened half to death."

Olivia did not dispute this. She did not even discuss it. Whatever she might have said was interrupted by the arrival of someone from the *gringo* town Marie had not seen since her first week on the low desert. It was the husky gunsmith, Will Emerson, and he was gravely smiling at both women before he got close enough to greet them in English, then to ask if he might see Father Eusebio.

Olivia was smiling. She gave permission as though there had never been anyone else to give it, and, after she had escorted the gunsmith to the corridor, had pointed out the correct room, she returned to Marie and said: "What we need to know is whether they will come for the youth in daylight or after dark. I would think after dark. Most of the lynchings I've seen and heard of happened long after nightfall. Usually on a moonless night."

Marie, thinking of the gunsmith, said she thought she could find out from him, if in fact he had any idea. Olivia was lukewarm, but she assented, and, as Marie returned indoors, she went up where the dripping gravediggers were now up to their shoulders. She inspected the grave with the calm wisdom of someone who had done it before, then went to get a large pitcher of their precious lemonade. After she had departed, one of the Mexican laborers leaned upon his spade handle and said: "Such a pitiful waste, that woman being a widow."

The other man shrugged. "She has only been one a few days. What would you wish . . . that she rush forth and embrace another man immediately?"

"Yes, if I were the one," the first Mexican said, grinning as he spat on his hands before taking his friend's place down in the hole. Only one man could work there at a time.

Marie waylaid Will Emerson in the gloomy long corridor as he was departing, after having spent a quarter of an hour with her father. The meeting, as a contrived accident, was rather expertly carried off. At least the gunsmith thought so, but he was hardly an authority on being waylaid by beautiful women.

It also turned out to be an unproductive ambush. Will Emerson strolled the long cool tiled patio with Marie discussing all the small things she brought up, and, when she got around to hinting at a lynching, he gazed blankly at her.

"Why would anyone want to lynch the one who didn't shoot Father Eusebio?"

She knew from this that he could tell her nothing. The next thing of course was to recruit him, and that was also easily accomplished. He promised to let her know the moment he picked up anything over in *gringo* town that had to do with a lynching.

He did not seem averse to lynchings; he just did not seem to know there was talk of one now. Then he told her how the puppy was growing, and she related her father's reaction. He nodded; he had just come from talking about that, and other things, with her father.

He allowed awkward moments to come into their conversation—little interludes when neither of them spoke, he, in particular, because he had moments of being tongue-tied in her presence.

It reminded her of her first beau many years earlier back East. She felt amiably affectionate toward the gunsmith. There were certainly times when it was better to have an honestly uncertain and unpracticed suitor—and this was absolutely what he would have been with just a little encouragement—than to have the other kind of male friend.

Finally he departed and turned once to wave. She waved back, a harmless thing to do except that, when a man was as obviously enamored as Will Emerson was and evidently had been since their first meeting over in town, the slightest show of just plain friendly manners was liable to an incorrect interpretation.

She went to her father's room. He related the gist of Emerson's visit, which had been more like the duty of a friend or the compassionate concern of an old acquaintance than anything else. Her father told her what she had discovered by herself: Will Emerson knew nothing of any lynch talk. He also told Marie she and Olivia had better hide the youthful Mexican before dusk, and, also, they had better get the other one buried. Then he asked her to help him get out of bed and she refused, a little breathlessly because she had expected nothing like this. He said he would officiate at the burial of Rey Sanchez. Instead of arguing, Marie went swiftly in search of Olivia, found her on the *ramada,* holding a wooden tray upon which were two empty cups and an empty lemonade pitcher. Marie took the tray and sent Olivia to argue with her father. Ten minutes later, believing Olivia might need support, Marie went soundlessly down the shadowy old stone corridor and turned in at the doorway—then froze.

Olivia was leaning gently. Father Eusebio was lifting his head. The kiss was so gentle and tender. . . . Marie turned away and walked in a slight daze on down to the farthest small doorway leading into the chapel. There, she looked in, saw the small, dark figure of an old woman crouched before the altar in black, head completely covered, then slowly turned back, never afterward quite certain she had really seen that humble old petitioner at the altar.

Her innermost reaction was not one of despair, of anguish that her celibate father and Olivia Gomez, the very recent widow, loved, because Marie was not a Catholic and had not been raised in an atmosphere where ministers did not marry. However, she knew the rules as well as did most other people, and it was this that troubled her now. She felt that her father was violating his oath—something like that. She also felt that it was awfully unfair for his faith to put that kind of burden on him. But perhaps most of all, it bothered her to think how he must feel, how he must view his own particular fall from grace.

And when he had asked her what she thought of his relationship with beautiful, ascetic Olivia Gomez, all she could do was stand like a fool, begging to be excused from making a judgment.

She turned back, walking slowly up the long corridor. Olivia had departed. Her father was lying with his profile foremost, with his eyes fixed upon the narrow shaft of light coming through the vaulted high east-wall window. He had no idea his daughter was in the doorway until a sixth sense warned him and he turned to face her, and to smile gently.

"Are you sorry?" he asked. There was an implication, a suggestion that fitted perfectly with her foremost thoughts.

Since she was confident he could not know she had seen him kissing Olivia, that was not what he had just meant. She did not really know what he had meant by that question, but, regardless, she shook her head.

His next statement clarified everything. "I'm glad, Marie, because it's always worried me that, if you ever came here, you'd be disappointed and anxious to leave."

She stepped farther into the room, smiling gently. He was indeed a handsome man. Gray and wide-eyed—distinguished, that was it. Her father was a distinguished-looking man.

"It's a fascinating place, Dad, not only your work and the mission, but all the different kinds of people . . . and . . . well, the desert, too, what I've seen of it. And Olivia, who is so knowledgeable."

"But different, Daughter?"

She leaned to look at his bandage. "Is it too tight?"

His eyes twinkled their strong irony. "Are we ever going to be able to discuss her, Daughter?"

She leaned, kissed him squarely on the mouth, then pulled back and straightened up. "There is nothing to discuss. I think she is wonderful. You evidently think so, too. So she must be, mustn't she?" Marie smiled. "Anything else . . . Dad . . . is, well, more your concern than mine."

He watched her steadily as she spoke, and now, when she seemed to hang fire while searching for more words, he returned her gentle smile.

"Just one other thing," she told him. "I approve . . . whatever it is, I approve of it." She went over to the door. "Would they really come over here and try to hang this young Mexican? Really, Dad?"

It required a moment of adjustment before he could reply to her short question. "I don't really know whether they will or not, Marie. If they do, I want you and Olivia to help me out of this bed."

She neither agreed nor disagreed. She winked, turned, and headed in the direction of the kitchen to find Olivia and perhaps to help get the Mexican youth with the splintered leg down into the cellar beneath the old mission. Maybe Olivia would believe it was too early in the day, or maybe she would believe the lynchers would not actually arrive, but, whatever she thought, it seemed to Marie that getting Maximillian Sotelo down there early might be good strategy.

It never once crossed her mind what her own fate might be if she braced a band of hard-drinking lynchers.

XI

Olivia was perfectly agreeable. The reluctant individual was Maximillian Sotelo. Not because he objected to being protected by a pair of women, nor because he preferred remaining where he was to face the lynchers, but because it was very painful for him to make it down into the dungeon area below the old mission, and, once they got him down there and he could see no second way out, he told them in Spanish he was trapped in the cellar. They told him that if the lynchers arrived, and wanted him, instead of Rey Sanchez who was being buried out back, they could certainly take him away from the mission if he remained upstairs.

They promised to bring him something to drink, and a half hour later Olivia took a little watery wine down to him, along with two candles. He had been praying. Olivia said nothing. Once he was aware of her presence, she spoke very little to him. Even when he volubly expressed himself, both hands working for emphasis, she was cool in look and manner.

Upstairs, she mentioned to Marie that, even if they saved the Mexican, they would probably only be doing some other people north of the border a disservice. "Once a renegade, always a renegade," stated Olivia, and, at Marie's look of reproach, she simply shrugged as though to imply that being older, having spent more time in the low desert, and knowing more of men,

Mexican marauders especially, Olivia was the one who knew best.

Marie had a little trouble adjusting, first to John Dennison's bizarre ambiguity, and now to a similar ambiguity in Olivia Gomez. But she did not waste much time dwelling upon any of this, for, as time passed, the more distant did any actual serious trouble appear.

She helped Olivia prepare a meal, even went out back to watch Olivia pay off the gravediggers, and to stand afterward in somber admiration of the excellent way they had buried Rey Sanchez. The mounded earth had been perfectly rounded and smoothed down. Rey Sanchez not only slept now among the law-abiding, the orderly, the decent, and devout old-timers of Fort Triumph, he also was the latest recruit to their ranks.

The longer Marie stood gazing over there, the more it was borne in upon her that something Olivia had said sometime back was sound and valid. She had said people were not very equal in life, but, when they died, they most certainly became equals. She could not imagine any of the other dwellers there in the ancient cemetery objecting.

She turned and went back inside, although the closing day helped the coolness out back where the *ramada* was so that it was equally as cool and pleasant out of doors as it was indoors. Actually the heat had not been noticeably unpleasant today, in any case. Perhaps because Marie had not had a chance to think about it during the course of all the other worries and responsibilities that had filled her life this past twenty-four hours. Nor was the day ended, although she would have been justified in believing it was certainly approaching an end.

She went into the dungeon below the mission to take food to the Mexican youth. He was grateful. Evidently he had been reconsidering all that he had been warned against with respect to *Yanquis*. He was friendly with Marie, which he might have been in any event since he was a young man and she was a slightly older but very handsome woman.

Later, when she returned to the kitchen and found Olivia gone, and guessing about where the older woman might be, she went down to her father's room just in time to hear Father Eusebio say: "You know how they talk."

Olivia came right back. "No one knows better how much my people gossip . . . but this time they don't have to gossip do they . . . it is the truth."

Father Eusebio saw his daughter fill the yonder doorway and flicked a warning glance toward Olivia, then smiled and offered his hand.

Marie crossed over, grasped it, placed it gently upon the edge of the cot, and studied his handsome, rugged face. "You look almost well enough to be up," she said.

Olivia sighed, shooting Marie a reproachful glance. Evidently Father Eusebio felt well enough to be up and around and Olivia had been adamantly opposed to it. Then Marie had come around.

The younger woman smiled feebly at Olivia and turned again toward the bed. "Almost well enough, but I can see indications that you aren't that well. Not really."

Her father laughed. Even Olivia nearly smiled. She felt for Marie's hand, lightly squeezed it, and let go as she leaned to readjust covers and punch the pillows she had finally allowed Father Eusebio to have. From one side, Marie had no difficulty seeing how her father sought and briefly held the dark glance of the older woman leaning above him. Marie blushed.

Someone outside stepped onto the tiles with ringing spurs. Olivia cocked her head, sighed, rolled up her eyes, and went quickly from the room. When Marie would have followed, her father held up a hand to detain her. Within moments it became clear why he had asked her to remain in the room.

Olivia allowed the booted, spurred individual to come up to
her; she did not go forth to meet him. It was part of a practiced
strategy evidently, because the man was almost directly below
the high, narrow window in Father Eusebio's room, when he
said: " 'Evenin', ma'am."

It was the village constable, the man John Dennison had said
would not be in town. Marie and her father exchanged a look of
plain interest.

Olivia did not verbally respond but it was easy to imagine her
giving one of those curt little head nods as she clasped both
hands across her stomach and primly waited.

"I'd like a word with Father Eusebio," the lawman drawled.

This time Olivia spoke crisply. "He is resting. He needs all
the rest he can get. Constable, you can trust me with a message.
You have done it before."

The spurs rang slightly as though Constable Young were shifting stance, perhaps shuffling self-consciously as he answered.
"There's been some tough talk over in town today. Mostly I
figured it was the kind of talk men got a right to make when
there's been a horse raid and some shootin' by greasers from
below the line. Well, this afternoon range men came into
town . . . a few now and then . . . and this evenin' about sup-
pertime the talk's begun to sound a mite ominous."

Olivia stood erectly, looking stonily at the tall lawman. "And
you?" she asked in Spanish. "You are doing what . . . coming
over here to warn us? Splendid! And what else do you mean to
do, man?"

Jim Young, who had known Olivia Gomez a lot of years,
shifted again, making his spurs ring softly, as he spoke in a voice
of mild protest. "You know I always got plenty to do, and a lot
of it don't call for me to be hangin' around town, so I got to
ride out for a spell. It's my duty and I got to do it, *señora.*"

Marie put her hand to her throat. This was exactly what John

Dennison had predicted. She was stricken when she glanced at her father. But he was facing the window, intently listening as Olivia spat words that dripped venom. This time in English.

"Your duty, Constable, is to protect innocent lives. What duty calls you beyond town this night when you have just warned me they will come over here for the prisoners? Duty?"

She hurled that last word at him. But he was not very daunted because in reply he said: "It's up to me to decide, and I've made up my mind. Anyway, this Rey Sanchez is nothing but a lousy. . . ."

"Rey Sanchez is dead, Constable. Look yonder . . . that is his mound. He is buried under it." Her voice dropped. "All right . . . tuck your tail and run, and let those whiskey drinkers, those filthy talkers, come over here and dig up a corpse and lynch it."

Constable Young was silent for a long while. Clearly he had been stunned by the revelation that the man who had tried cold bloodedly to murder the priest of Fort Triumph parish was dead. He finally said: *"¿Señora, es verdad?"*

She raked him. "Have I ever told you anything but the truth? Are you so much a liar yourself you have to doubt everyone else? What do I care whether Rey Sanchez lived or died . . . except that he should die in His grace? Get shovels and dig him up! I don't lie, to you or to anyone else. Go get shovels and some of that range-riding scum and dig into the grave. Go!"

Her ire rolled off Constable Young like rain off a duck. He studied the fresh grave for a long while, still stunned. "No one told me," he eventually complained. "What did he die of? He seemed pretty good when we brought them in."

"He bled to death internally. How would you know what his condition was, Constable? Are you also a physician?"

Young had a limit and he had just about reached it. Whether Olivia realized it or not, she kept right on boring into him with biting sarcasm and clear, raw dislike. She said: "Ride out of town. Tuck your tail and run rather than have to try and face down the desert riff-raff. Leave it to a pair of women and a wounded priest!"

He reddened. "Missus Gomez, damn it all, I don't have to stand here and be talked to like this."

Olivia snorted. "Then go away, *jefe!* Go climb upon your horse and ride away. And stay away until the drunks and brutes and armed scum have done their worst. Afterward it should be safe to return."

Olivia turned on her heel and marched swiftly back up the interior corridor of the old mission. Her anger was such, though, that she did not return to Father Eusebio's room. She walked right on past and did not even slacken gait until she was entering the distant kitchen.

Father Eusebio showed a smiling, proud set of features to his daughter as he faced away from the east wall. "Go to her," he said. "Marie, I want you to know something . . . Olivia is by nature gentle. Strong as iron, but very gentle and soft and understanding. Go tell her you are proud of her. That I am also proud of her. All right?"

Marie departed without speaking, and down the tiles outside in the thickening soft gloom Jim Young's spurred boots made their soft echo as the lawman headed away.

Olivia was standing at the sink looking dead ahead out through the mightily recessed old windows into the shortening dusk distance when Marie entered the room and went over to lay a warm hand lightly upon the hotter, more rigid hand of the older woman. Marie said what her father had wished her to convey and Olivia turned and smiled. Then she shrugged as though putting it all behind her, out of her mind.

Marie said: "John Dennison told me he would help us."

Olivia's smile dimmed, but she kept her contrary convictions to herself and simply said: "If God is willing." She clearly had no faith at all in this source of aid.

Marie was not discouraged. She had known from the beginning that Olivia did not particularly like or trust John Dennison.

But they had to trust someone if this crowd of lynchers really materialized, and, if it amounted to very much, she and Olivia by themselves, even if they could prop up her wounded father, would be unable to stop them from perhaps ransacking the mission, perhaps doing worse. Drunken men who lived a harsh, celibate life out upon the exacting low desert, who suddenly found themselves confronted by a pair of handsome women, might decide on some variety of diversion from lynching, at least for a short while.

It made her flesh feel cold. She had known no fear up until this moment. Now she felt it, because now for the first time it was really borne in upon her that trouble was actually approaching. Heretofore, like most people, especially most women, she could be aloof and cool in face of peril because there was no clear, visual evidence that it was really coming.

The look on Olivia's face alone should have been sufficient reason to accept and to believe, but then the older woman also said what Marie had heard before. "They won't dig up Rey Sanchez. They'll hunt down the other one. Or they will. . . ." She looked steadily into the younger woman's eyes and gave one of those gentle little enigmatic, perfectly Latin shoulder shrugs.

"Do we just stand here?" Marie asked in a whisper.

A dog barked over upon the outskirts of *gringo* town, a perfectly harmless sound—any evening but this one. Another dog took it up, and the pair of stationary women listened, making out some kind of progress as other dogs picked up the sound, marking a route across from the upper end of *gringo* town of something, which could have perhaps been nothing more menacing than another foraging dog. Or it could be the stealthy approach of a mob of red-faced range men and townsmen with ropes in their hands, their hot eyes fixed upon the ancient mission several hundred yards distant as they stalked through the litter and débris of the starless, dark late evening.

Then the dogs ceased barking. The silence returned. Olivia picked up a small towel out of long habit and dried her hands—which had not been wet—and in her expressionless, strong way jerked her head for Marie to follow, and led the way from the kitchen out through several dingy, moldy-smelling old rooms to a distant, windowless little storeroom where four rifles, older than anyone knew with bell-flared muzzle ends, hung from rawhide thongs, and beneath them, also suspended by thongs, were three fairly modern Winchester saddle guns.

Marie accepted the gun handed her with no more idea of what to do with the thing, how to cock it or make certain it was loaded, or even how to aim and fire it, than the man in the moon would have had.

XII

It was a long wait. Except for the gun and the look of Olivia when they returned silently to the kitchen and lit two tapers, Marie would still have not felt that there was any actual imminence. The coldness of that blued steel though had a harsh way of forcing reality upon people, even ones who had never before even been close to actual fierce violence.

They took their weapons to the corridor outside Father Eusebio's room, propped them, then entered the room looking perfectly calm and innocent. Olivia lit more candles. Marie marveled at the way Olivia could act a part, while at the same time she was also doing a very good job of it herself.

They visited for a while, scoffed at the idea of trouble, and went back to the corridor, scooped up their weapons, and went down as far as the little doorway leading out to the dark and cool *ramada*.

Olivia, who had always impressed Marie as a self-sufficient individual, a strong person who was entirely capable of handling just about everything with her hands folded, her shoulders squared, her strong chin tilted, and her dark eyes dead level, did not really seem very different with the carbine in the crook of a bent arm now. She smiled at the younger woman and said: "I hope we don't have to fire these things." She did not elaborate and Marie did not ask her to. Marie felt the same way.

"Are we going to wait out here for them?"

Olivia looked down through the lengthy *ramada* to the darkness beyond the southernmost end before replying. "I don't know what we are going to do, child, except keep them from bothering your father . . . or finding their way to the cellar below."

Marie was agreeable without having the faintest idea how this could be accomplished. She held her carbine the same way Olivia was holding her weapon, but without any clear idea of why she held it like this or what she was really going to do with the thing.

Then she heard them coming! It was a dull, weighty sound; a noise made by booted feet crossing through inches of dun dust from the direction of *gringo* town. There was some talk, but not loud or consistent. Not at all as she had thought it would be, if they were indeed drunk. It was neither loud nor profane, just low and raspingly harsh, and venomous. Gradually the fear filled her until it was difficult to breathe. She looked over; Olivia had not changed. It occurred to Marie that this would be the stance, the expression, the demeanor, of Olivia Gomez on Judgment Day.

Over the increasing sounds of marching stragglers there

eventually also came the sound of horsemen on shod animals. To Marie it sounded as though the entire countryside was coming. Her fear could not increase beyond what it was so her other senses became more acute. She could distinguish harsh words, finally, and individual voices. Even the fragrance of the early summertime night was sharper, and, if she had looked up, each star would have stood out more distinctly.

Olivia did not change at all, neither in appearance nor position. She was watching that far lower end of the *ramada,* classical features settled in a look of fatalistic resignation.

A man whistled. It sounded like some kind of warning or perhaps a signal to other men. That occurred around front. Olivia sighed. "They are coming through from the chapel. Well, we are only two people so what else can we do but stay here and let them come up on all sides?"

Marie's throat was dry and her breathing remained shallow. Perhaps the Winchester should have imparted some sense of security. It didn't. She was not even conscious of holding it.

A heavy old oak door opened and slammed somewhere behind them inside the mission. Resoundingly strong footfalls echoed in a stone-flagged corridor, but at the lower end of the *ramada* Marie detected shifting shadows of stalwart men, so her attention became fixed upon this nearer and more tangible peril.

A thick, barrel-built man, whose stomach hung over his belt and who walked with the unique rolling gait of a seaman ashore, came steadily up the center of the tiled porch way keeping to the center of it. He was hatless, had a thick matt of coarse curly hair, and a salt-and-pepper beard to match. He fascinated Marie because he resembled a great spider.

Olivia, cocking her Winchester, caught that bull-built individual in mid-stride. He let his forward boot come down but did not take another step as he peered into the yonder darkness.

Behind this man several others halted. One rammed up into the rear of someone in front and the humped man swore.

Marie was slightly in front and to one side of Olivia. That bull-built man looked from one of them to the other, then shook his head as though he were annoyed by flies. He put Marie in mind of bulls she had seen bothered by gnats.

He said: "That you, Miz Gomez? Don't do nothin' silly now, with that gun. It ain't lady-like . . . a woman usin' a gun."

Olivia did not respond.

The bull-built man shifted position a little and looked elsewhere, as though wondering how many defenders there might be. "The priest up there with you, is he, Miz Gomez? Listen here, now. We come for the greaser who shot the priest. That's all. Now don't do anything you're goin' to be sorry you done . . . Miz Gomez?"

Olivia's voice did not sound loud enough to carry through the increasing noise of other converging lynchers, but it did carry. "The man who shot Father Eusebio died this afternoon. He is in that fresh grave north of the mission at the upper end of the old cemetery. You want him . . . go dig him up. You think I'm lying, go hunt up Laro Sanchez and Domingo Cardoza. They dug the grave and they put him down in it, and they covered him up."

The lynchers stood a moment in silence. Clearly this announcement had caught them flat-footed, but of course if any of them had chosen to visit the mission during the day, rather than spend all the time at the *gringo* town *cantina,* they would have known this.

From the rear doorway a soft, deep male voice said: "It's the truth. The Mexican who shot me died of internal bleeding and is buried out yonder in the old cemetery."

A man muffled a swear word, twisted to look around at the other men, then he said: "*Aw,* the hell with it. I already tol' you, if the Father didn't get kilt, what's the sense of goin' to all this work when we could be settin' back yonder at the cool bar?" This man shouldered his way to the edge of the crowd and went stamping his way back toward *gringo* town. He clearly did not have a genuine lyncher's motivation.

Another of them decided this was certainly likely to be more productive, and pleasurable, and turned to follow the first man, but none of the others was that easily turned aside, and it looked to Marie as though there were about ten of them still out there.

Olivia finally changed stance, but not to menace the lynchers further. She turned to see if Father Eusebio was still in the doorway. He was. She said in quiet Spanish for him to go back to bed, that he was an ill man. Marie saw her father's face as a pale oval. His glance back toward Olivia had that peculiar, gentle-soft expression she had seen him use toward her before. Even in that poor light. He did not respond but neither did he depart.

A range rider among the men on the *ramada* hit upon what would inevitably have happened. He pushed up and said: "Where's the other one? There was two greasers. One shot through and the other with a busted leg. Where's the other one, missus?"

Several other men took that up, muttering their identical demands.

Olivia said: "He is not the man you want. He is only a boy and he. . . ."

"Damned greasers all stick together," growled a large man, edging on beside the bull-built man. "Where is he . . . we'd as leave hang one as another one."

Marie saw the men get new motivation, saw how their expressions altered, became fierce again as they inched up menacingly. Marie lowered her carbine from instinct. The nearest men halted dead still. She had not cocked the weapon, but, still, a gun barrel at close range was able to inspire great respect.

The older man leaned around and Marie recognized him at once. It was the man who had brought her down here from the stage stop up at Montoya. Pete Redd. She saw his look of disapproval and said: "Mister Redd, I wouldn't have believed this of you."

Old Pete drew back behind another man and remained there. But he did not leave. None of them did.

From the corridor behind Father Eusebio a gruff, deep-toned voice spoke out. "Ain't no Mexicans in the rooms along here." This man pushed past and walked forth behind Olivia and Marie. There were four more of them who pushed out and also halted when Marie swung her gun barrel. These were the individuals who had entered the building from the chapel. They had not heard Olivia explain about Rey Sanchez, so someone, perhaps Pete Redd, told them now in a disgusted-sounding voice.

The gruff-toned man gazed past Marie as though she did not have a Winchester pointing at his middle. "Dead and buried?" he exclaimed. "*Aw,* they done told you fellers that to keep us from stringing that Mexican up."

"There's a fresh grave out yonder. I seen it earlier," a man growled, and immediately a second man said: "Yeah, but we still got the other one."

This thought was transmitted easily to the men behind Olivia. One of them, a tall, lanky cowboy, leaned and in almost totally accentless Spanish asked Olivia where the second outlaw was. She answered him in cold, biting English.

"Did you believe we wouldn't make him safe from people like you? Do you think I've lived in this town all my life without knowing what kind of predatory animals also live here . . . and walk upright?"

A drunk man snickered, appreciating how Olivia had singed

someone's hide, but evidently he was the only one who thought it was funny because the bull-built man came right back with a snarl.

"You're makin' us waste a lot of time, Miz Gomez. Them saddle guns don't scare us, neither. Now you'd best just stand aside because we're goin' to search the old church until we find that greaser."

Father Eusebio pushed up off the doorjamb. He was also an oaken man, thick and massive, but he was larger, taller, and therefore much thicker than the bull-built man. Ill or not he was an impressive sight in the little doorway as he said: "You're not going to violate a sanctuary. None of you!"

The large man standing with the bull-built man started forward. He had seemed incapable of making up his mind about what to do to a pair of armed women, but Father Eusebio was a man and he seemed to arrive easily at a conclusion about what to do to another man.

Olivia cocked her saddle gun and swung it to within two feet of the truculent man's stomach. He halted. So did the bull-built man.

Someone else swore with disgust and turned his back to go heading southward in the wake of those other two dissenters who had departed earlier. Other men closed up behind the menaced individual. They were all armed and there were probably some who would, in their cups now, shoot an armed woman, but from the north end of the *ramada,* where someone stepped up onto the tiles from the bean patch, spurs rang and Marie's heart jumped.

The men behind Olivia twisted to look back. So did the others, all but one man—the large stranger whose middle had been threatened by Olivia's gun barrel. He lunged, caught the gun, and struck it violently aside.

Without hesitation the mighty form in the doorway came

fluidly forward, there was a sound like someone breaking a tree limb across his upper leg, and the man with the gun barrel went down in a pile. His companion, the bull-built man, swung from the waist but he was not fast enough. Father Eusebio dropped him, too, but with a blow between the eyes.

Someone from back up the porch called softly. There were other spurred riders up there; they all hastened southward.

Marie felt someone graze her and whirled desperately to point her gun, but it was Father Eusebio stepping back to lean upon the rear wall after his lightning-like surprise attack. He had used up all his small reserve of strength.

The lynchers were moving, were fired up now for trouble, even the ones that had infiltrated from within the mission. But now it was too late. John Dennison and his booted, spurred range men were there, several with drawn six-guns, all of them ready to fight, and they were stone sober. Someone said—"*Aw, Chriz'!*"—and turned away.

Olivia looked long at Dennison, who either ignored her or was too interested in watching the lynchers to be diverted. She moved across, leaned the Winchester, took Father Eusebio by the arm, and turned her back on them all as though there was not a shred of peril, and led the priest back to his little room.

Marie saw the tightness leaving John Dennison, where he stood in front of his riders. She grinned, scarcely even aware she was doing it, and he slightly smiled back. Then he gestured with his ivory-handled Colt.

"Go on back to the saloon," he told the knot of lynchers. "You don't hang a Mexican tonight. Unless you want a gunfight about it. Go on!"

They got the bull-built man and his groggy friend back upright and, by supporting them on both sides, turned, and started trudging back the way they had come.

Marie was still gripping the saddle gun when John Dennison

gently took it from her and leaned it against the adobe wall.

The handsome youthful *vaquero* whose black-eyed admiration had been so abundantly evident when they had first met smiled dazzlingly at Marie, then took several other range men and strolled on down the *ramada* in the wake of the departing lynchers.

Marie felt behind her for the wall, and leaned.

XIII

Olivia made coffee for them all. She said very little, once she got Father Eusebio back to bed and had sat with him for a short while, holding his hand and smiling downward. She never seemed capable of losing all her inhibitions, of being a fully outward individual, when she was not with him, but none of the armed range men who accepted her coffee knew this, or would have cared very much, either, for that matter.

They were tough men, lined and bronzed and leaned down from hard work under a blasting desert sun. They were not all young men; in fact, except for one other youth no older than that good-looking *vaquero,* they were all men who could have been in their forties, but were probably more nearly in their mid-thirties.

Not one of them looked incapable of looking out for himself, and that included their employer, John Dennison, who took his coffee, took Marie, and went down to Father Eusebio's room.

He was flat out, exhausted and sound asleep. Marie leaned to pull a coverlet closer, then she and John Dennison went on down the corridor and out to the empty *ramada.* There was no indication that a gunfight had very narrowly been averted out here only about a half hour earlier.

There were stars, larger than ever, and a purple high vault curving from all the corners of the universe, hushed and warm. John Dennison teetered upon the edge of the patio and sniffed, then said: "Rain coming." He turned and glanced down at her.

She wrinkled her nose as he had done and nodded. "Yes, indeed."

That tickled him. "You're the nicest thing that has happened around Fort Triumph since I can remember, Miss Hamblin."

"The most frightened," she replied, avoiding his bold gaze but very aware of it upon her. "Will they try again . . . Mister Dennison?"

He doubted it. "Not if they have an hour of leaning at the bar. They didn't strike me as being dead set on lynching him anyway. Not after they found out the one they wanted was already dead." He stepped back closer to her in the dark shadow of the overhang room.

She liked his closeness. She liked his company and had liked it before. She remembered Olivia's steady gaze at him when the confrontation had been at its height. Olivia had said nothing and as usual there was no way to read her thoughts from her expression, but Marie had got the impression, back then, that Olivia had suddenly approved of him. It made Marie feel much better. She put a lot of faith in the judgment of Olivia Gomez.

Several of his riding crew came ambling out, also, to enjoy the night upon the long patio. He took her by the hand and walked northward up around the far corner where the bean patch was. There, with the faint distant sound of men's voices behind them, sometimes musically lifted in soft laughter, sometimes a muted blur of sound, she leaned in the darkness watching John Dennison's profile as he looked around, and seemed momentarily to be listening, before finally turning to say: "I thought you were going to ride out."

She remembered mentioning it, but there had been no real occasion. "One of these days," she murmured. "Early, before the heat comes."

He leaned looking down at her slightly tilted face. She did

not have to ask his thoughts, intuition told her as much as she would listen to, and the rest of it she simply turned off.

He said: "Where is the young Mexican?"

"Down under the mission next to the wine cellar. There are some monks' cells down there." He seemed far more interested in her than in what she had to say. Without looking at him, she got the impression that he hardly more than half heeded what she had just said. She did not directly face him.

It was like something she had never experienced before—and she was no young girl, either. It was impossible to define, to analyze, how she felt in his company.

Out of the clear he said: "The low desert is such a hard place to like, for folks who haven't pretty well grown up down here."

She remembered something Olivia had said—or perhaps it had been her father—but in either case she was sure he had not lived here all his life, so she said: "How long did it take you to like it?"

He chuckled. "Well, it's a little different with me. I make a good living off the low desert. That helps a man to like something . . . if he can make money out of it." His humor ceased. "Marie, how long are you going to stay?"

She had no idea, and, even if she'd had one, she might not have wanted to be pinned down about it. "A while yet," she told him, and finally turned slightly so she could see up into his face.

Somewhere down the rear patio a man sang out, his voice hard and demanding even in its echo, and that shattered a tremulous moment for Marie and John Dennison. He pulled himself away from her with visible effort, stepped to the edge of the porch, and looked down there.

"*¿Quién es?*" he called. "Who is it?"

For a moment there was no reply, then a rough voice sang out in answer. "Emerson. Will Emerson."

The range riders had sent the gunsmith up toward the north end of the *ramada* where John was waiting. When the gunsmith got up there, he had no idea Marie was around the corner. She was not visible when he said: "There's some rough talk over at the saloon. Seems some folks didn't like you siding with one of those Mex renegades. They're trying to talk up something more than just a lynching, John."

Dennison pondered a moment, then said: "Go down where my men are waiting. I'll be down there in a minute. And, Will . . . thanks."

Dennison waited a moment, until the gunsmith had departed, then turned back to face Marie. She had heard it, and had interpreted most of it, but this was not her kind of country, so there was still more conjecture than knowledge in it, when she said: "They are angry with you? They are going to try and make trouble for you now?"

He reached, took one of her hands, briefly held it, then, as he released it, he said: "There are always a few, Marie, no matter where you are. Sure, it went down hard with a few of them that I bought in on your side, so they'll try to make out like I was trying to save the Mex." He smiled gently. "I'll be back in the morning. All right?"

She was unsure about what exactly that meant, but she agreed with it. "All right."

He disappeared around the corner. She leaned, listening to the ring of his spurs. Later, she heard them all leaving the *ramada*, walking crisply southward. She had no idea where they had left their horses, or even if they had come over to the mission on horseback. All she knew was that the longer she stood there in the warm, magnificent night, thinking about him, the more disturbed and mildly uncomfortable and wonderfully upset she felt. She snorted. A woman of twenty-five feeling and acting like a girl of sixteen!

She moved finally, went down to the door leading into the corridor, heard voices in her father's room, went soundlessly right on past up to the kitchen where Olivia had cleaned up all the mess after those range men had had coffee there, and sought enough coffee to fill one more cup for herself.

Beyond the recessed back-wall window the stars were just as brilliant seen through wavy glass. The night remained as wonderfully magical. She turned with a sigh and saw Olivia in the doorway, gazing across the room. Marie smiled.

"The let-down leaves a person slightly weak in the knees," she said, and Olivia walked as far as a chair near the kitchen table to seat herself and to reach to trim a candlewick as though that was all she had on her mind. "They aren't through yet, Marie, they are organizing to make trouble for John Dennison." Olivia raised her eyes to the girl's face. "I wouldn't worry much if I were you."

Marie leaned and sipped coffee, trying to imagine just how much she really was worrying. Not enough, evidently, for it to trouble her. But she had something on her mind that was a different kind of worry.

"Do you think better of him now?" she asked.

Olivia was slow to answer but eventually she said her opinion increased favorably of any person who kept their word, and, if this seemed to be a guarded statement, indeed it was one, because in the very next breath Olivia looked up and said: "There aren't many unmarried men down here. John Dennison is also the most successful cowman."

Marie understood Olivia as she would have understood any other woman, when this kind of a topic came up. Olivia was either going to warn her away from John Dennison, or she was going to warn her to take plenty of time with her own feelings.

"It's a different life for you, Marie. We don't live as well down here." Olivia pushed the candle back half across the table before continuing. "It's a harsh world most of the time."

Marie finished the coffee and turned to put aside the cup. As she turned back, she said: "Olivia . . . I'm almost twenty-six years old." As a reproof it was mild, the only kind of reproof Marie would ever offer to Olivia Gomez, who she liked so very much.

The older woman continued to sit, loose and relaxed. "Well, I know something about making mistakes with men, Marie. I know how long a woman can be saddled with sorrow and bitterness, and how hard it is to fight back from those depths."

Marie crossed and impulsively leaned to kiss the older woman, then gently to trail a gentle hand across Olivia's shoulder as she left to cross over where another chair was at the other side of the rickety old table.

If there was a way for older people to prevent younger ones from making mistakes, evidently it had been a secret for centuries because young people were still making them. But not all young people. As Marie sat down, she said: "I'll be careful and take plenty of time."

Olivia showed a very faint little poignant smile. She should have been gratified, perhaps, but so many sterile, wasted years had been wrung from her in her own sad union that she simply could not cast all of it off. Moreover, it was not the temperament of Olivia Gomez to be light-hearted. That, perhaps, had come from her Spanish heritage. Marie thought it might also have come in part from too much of a dolorous religion, which was the only kind the old-time *padres* had dealt with.

Olivia arose, took down her scarf shawl from a wooden peg, and dexterously swung it so that it settled in part across her raven's-wing black hair and partly across her shoulders. "I'll take the chair in Father Eusebio's room," she told Marie, and waited a moment, but, instead of commenting, Marie arose and went down through the dingy corridor with her, left her at the doorway of the sleeping man's room, and, as she was turning, she softly said: "He couldn't do half of it unless he had you, Olivia."

The older woman stood in thought for a moment, gazing at the slumbering bear-like man. "I sin almost every day of my life," she whispered. "Marie . . . ?"

In a stout retort the younger woman said: "Not in the eyes of the God I know. Good night . . . God bless you."

She did not feel alone until she was back in the kitchen with the darkness dripping from rafter ends out yonder beyond the kitchen window. Then she felt not just alone, but a little frightened. They'd survived that face-down not more than three hours ago, and over in *gringo* town the drinking had gone on, with more and more trouble on its way. At least that was how she felt as she blew out one of the candles and, with the other one in her left hand, went down the stone corridor and out where those two old Winchester saddle guns were still leaning.

She took them inside, propped them against a door, then wondered whether or not she ought to go down into the dungeon before going to her room, to make certain the youthful Mexican outlaw was all right. He would be whether she went down there or not, because there was nothing for him to do but lie still and recuperate. They had fed him and had left an *olla* of water with him.

She wanted company, and that was something else she had noticed about people on the low desert. They were either just naturally self-sufficient or they developed the ability to be that way, but in any case they were much less gregarious than the city people where she came from.

Finally she went to her room, barred the door, put down the candle, knelt at the side of her cot to pray, and during that process she asked for understanding and tolerance for her father and for the woman he so very obviously loved and who so obviously also very much loved him, and, when she arose, she felt surprisingly better, as though every burden and difficulty had been taken from her. She looked up at the high, slit window, saw the stars out there as brilliant—more brilliant than before—and she smiled with gratitude.

Sleep came swiftly and she would have wagered good money she would not have been able to sleep until the wee hours. Evidently her experiences this day had drained away much more of her reserves than she had thought.

She was still sleeping in the sun-washed morning when Olivia called softly from the corridor, then passed along to the kitchen.

It took time to be presentable in a place where running water existed only in springs and a few very rare creeks and rivers. She did not get up to the kitchen to help Olivia prepare her father's breakfast until the job had already been done and Olivia was down with her father.

But there was someone else there, freshly shaved, scrubbed, freshly attired, and wearing an immaculate white cotton shirt. He smiled at her expression of astonishment. "Told you I'd be back in the morning," he said, arising with a coffee cup in his hand. "Olivia told me to wait, that you'd be along."

His smile was one of the most reassuring things in her life, lately. She smiled back. "Have you had breakfast, Mister Dennison?"

"Yes'm. And I have my top buggy out front to take you across the desert to my camp."

She stood at the stove with no appetite at all, but she forced herself to eat the food Olivia had left on a plate for her. With her back to him, she said: "What happened last night over in *gringo* town?"

"Nothing. I told you . . . there are always a few soreheads. There were five of them. When my men and I walked in, two of those five had to go home because it was very late. That's all.

That ended it. And Constable Young was there, finally. He helped batten it down. You can bring your Mex up from the cellar now. They won't come back for him or make any more lynch talk. . . . Marie, I sure do want to show you my cow camp."

She was uncertain but she did not allow him to see it. A cow camp did not sound like anything she much wanted to see, but, when she turned and saw the kind, gentle look on his face, she smiled. "I sure do want to see it," she replied, making her words a Southwestern drawl the way his had been.

He laughed.

XIV

They went across the desert with cool morning on all sides, with soft shadows on the leeside of things and with a sweet fragrance accompanying them all the full distance.

He showed her little bands of his cattle and twice they caught sight of speeding remudas of loose stock, heads up and tails high. He laughed.

"Broke horses every blessed one of them, but you cut them loose and pull their shoes, and you'd swear they'd never seen a human being."

He showed her an ancient adobe ruin, all that remained of a large, thriving Mexican *rancho* from generations ago; so long ago in fact all anyone knew now was the name of the Spanish family, since all else had been stamped out when the Indians had reclaimed their heartland.

He demonstrated a remarkable—for a man—knowledge of flowers, of all the various thriving bushes, mostly with thorns, of all the little animals they saw, and once he showed her two lizards performing an act of acquaintanceship. The darker and larger of the little creatures would flex both front legs, hoisting his scaly small body into the air while he simultaneously drew down a huge lungful of air. The effect was exactly as it would have been if the male lizard had been a fifteen-year-old boy. The female lizard pretended not to see, but she was clearly impressed. However, when the male lizard was confident and rushed at her, she turned with more agility and rushed away.

Marie laughed and John Dennison grinned as he drove on.

The cow camp turned out not to be anything at all like she had expected. A camp to Marie was a temporary place where people lived frugally and rather primitively. In the low-desert country a cow camp was a cow outfit, a cow ranch.

The buildings were large, massive, squat adobe structures with porches on all sides to protect the mud walls from eroding rains, but also to provide endless shade that in turn kept the interior of the buildings even cooler than they normally would have been.

It was an old ranch. Some of the structures had loopholes in the walls for forting up against attack. There were huge old cottonwood trees on all sides, and a blue-water spring, walled up now to waist-height to prevent animals and varmints from falling in and polluting the water, which had a respectable overflow, and this had been ditched away to a garden patch where three Mexicans were at work, when the rig wheeled into the big, shady old dusty yard.

Marie was too flabbergasted to speak. It was not at all as she had expected it to be. This place, in her eyes, resembled some ancient Moorish stronghold, some ancient fiefdom ruled by a proud lord, and in fact many of the old-time cow outfits of this low-desert country did indeed look and function that way.

They had borrowed in total the earlier Spanish notion and had perfected it, had improved upon it.

Three cowboys, including that good-looking young *vaquero,* were over beside a faggot corral where the dust was rising in the morning sunlight. There was another man over there, head and one arm bandaged. They were too interested in whatever was happening in the faggot corral to look around.

An older man the color of parched leather and with a single graying plait of hair between his shoulder blades was furiously punching a panful of white dough over in the shade of the cook shack porch. He looked around, looked long and carefully, then threw a flashing smile in the direction of the beautiful woman in the top buggy, and went back to kneading his dough.

A squat, frog-like man with silver hair was working at the shoeing shed. He, too, looked up, but his reaction was different. He simply made his brief assessment, lifted his hat in unsmiling deference to Marie, then went right back to his forge and his anvil.

She said: "It's like a village all by itself, John."

"Not as much now as it was when my paw founded it," he told her. "In those days you had to be self-sufficient. Sometimes it would be months on end before you dared ride away from your own yard." He pointed to those loopholes. "They fought off redskins, Mex border jumpers, and even a few bands of free-grazers."

She had no idea what a free-grazer was and had no intention of asking. Not now at any rate.

They left the rig over in front of the low old adobe barn where tree shade was as dense as early evening, and he walked with her across the yard to the main house, a low and very long expanse of massively thick walls and surrounding *ramadas*. Here, most of all, she thought of ancient Spain and the Moors.

The house was easily ten degrees cooler inside, and it had that unique silence most thick-walled adobe houses possessed. Sound, unless it originated within, could rarely penetrate.

He showed her large, oval portraits of his father and mother. She was surprised because his mother looked a little like Olivia. When he saw her staring, he said: "She was the daughter of Alejandro Montoya. Remember that old adobe ruin we passed and I told you about all anyone knew any more was the name of those old-time Spanish *rancheros?*"

She turned. "Montoya?"

He smiled. "You're perceptive, Marie. Come along."

She allowed herself to be led away, but, as she did so, she and the woman in the portrait exchanged a look. Her son, John Dennison, alas, did not resemble her at all.

There was a ballroom in the back of the house. She had never heard about the old-time ranchers being this self-sufficient, but in fact many were. The ones more wealthy, feudal, successful, and powerful—and very isolated—were.

He watched her reaction, then said: "One day, will you let me have a dance here for you?"

She was delighted with the idea. She was also becoming slightly wary; no man as busy with his far-flung interests as John Dennison clearly was spent as much time with a woman as John was spending, unless his interest was a little more than just—well—interest.

She evaded the question dexterously and took him out back with her to another of those full-length *ramadas.* Here, there was a carefully sculptured pool of blue water for birds to bathe in and drink from.

"My father used to say trees were not enough to make birds stay." He turned toward her.

She saw words forming, guessed how personal they would be, and stepped over to the little pond. "It is a separate world, John. Separate and private . . . I just simply had no idea . . . why do you call it a cow camp?"

"Well, that's what it is."

"No. Good heavens no, John. It's a wonderfully charming little private world."

"Marie . . . ?"

She faced him, willing finally, not to avoid him, finally willing to listen, to be told things she knew would forever alter their relationship.

"Yes, John."

"It's going to sound silly. I've only known you a few days,"

She smiled encouragement as she said: "You don't really know me at all. We've only been acquaintances, not even very close friends,"—then, fearful that she might have said too much, she broadened her smile—"but maybe all that other is for other people. Maybe some people don't have to go through the full gamut. Do you think they do?"

Before he could answer, that silver-haired squat man came around back to say calmly: "They're all shod, John. You still want to commence the gather this afternoon? Personally I figure dawn tomorrow would be better, but you're the boss."

It sounded to Marie as though the silver-haired range man was more than just a hired rider, and when John said—"Dawn'll be fine, Jared."—she was sure of it. Then John said: "Morgan, this here is Miss Marie Hamblin."

She did not remember him from last night but he clearly remembered her, because, along with a gallant little bow as he removed his hat, he said: "You sure looked right pretty out there on the mission porch holdin' that Winchester, ma'am."

They all laughed, and Morgan departed with twinkling eyes. She liked him instinctively. John said: "Range boss . . . my head honcho. You'd never guess how old he is. He's been on the place since I was a kid. Best stockman on the low desert."

She was sure of it. She was also sure that if Morgan hadn't arrived when he had. . . . She turned to look at her reflection in the turquoise water at her back. She said: "Some people just seem naturally to belong with other people . . . Morgan for instance."

She knew he was studying her profile in the shade and speckled, golden sunlight.

"What I was thinking about, Marie . . . what I had in mind to tell you." He cleared his throat. "Please don't leave just yet."

She was certain that was not what he had meant to say, but she answered as though no other thought had entered her mind. "I don't intend to. I like the low desert. Really, John. I realize I'm not supposed to, that most people don't, but I actually do like it. And besides that, my father is here. . . . John?"

"Yes."

"What do people say about my father and Olivia Gomez?"

That caught him totally off guard. He hung fire and finally said: "That's something else you'll learn down here. A lot of things are different. Folks . . . well . . . they've adopted a lot of Mex outlooks and habits." He shrugged.

"You're saying they know how my father feels about his housekeeper and they don't care?"

"Why should they? Father Eusebio is a great man. He is doctor, confessor, priest at graveside, savior at birthings, Marie . . . they just don't have the same puritanical hypocrisy down here. They never have had." He waved his arms as though wishing to leave here, to get off this subject.

She allowed him to walk her slowly completely around to the front of the house where the shade was paler because there was more raw sunshine out there.

Those men at the faggot corrals were laughing about something. There was less dust arising from within the nearest corral by now. John said: "They're making a rider out of a Mex chore boy . . . an orphan we found on the lower desert last year and brought home with us. Sixteen years old."

She felt pity. "It looks to me as though they're laughing because he got bucked off a horse."

John smiled. "That's exactly what happened, Marie, they never baby 'em down here. When the lad's twenty, he'll be a man in every way that counts." He faced her. "It's such a different world."

She understood his fears for her so she told him how she felt. "I can cope with it. I can handle it, John. If anyone had ever told me I'd have stood beside another woman with a rifle in my hands facing a bunch of drunken lynchers. . . ."

They went back down to the rig, climbed in, and turned back in the direction of town. They had scarcely cleared the yard before all those patently indifferent range riders came together over by the cook shack watching the buggy grow small. The men commented as men would always do, as men had every right to do.

The sun was higher now, there was heat on all sides, and even the soft brilliance of morning had subtly become something lemon-yellow in its overhead increasing malevolence. John Dennison would have hastened so she would not have to be out in it longer than was necessary but she told him heat did not really affect her all that much, and he seemed to relax over this scrap of information.

When they saw the roof tops, and soaring above them the great red tiled roof of the old mission, she remembered who she was for the first time since they had driven away.

It was like returning to a familiar world from an unfamiliar one, except that even her most familiar world on the low desert was not actually familiar. At least not really, it wasn't; she had only been down here a month, but, as they crossed the upper environs of Fort Triumph on their way to the mission at Mex town, she felt as though she were reëntering an ethos to which she had always belonged. It was a unique way to feel about something she was just now finally beginning to appreciate and to understand.

She went with John while he watered the horse, then loosened his harness and left him in tree shade over near the shed where

Father Eusebio kept his dapple gray.

It was while they were alone and apart, over there, that John Dennison said: "Marie, could I just speak out with you . . . could I be natural and free?"

She had no real misgivings. She was, like her father, a good judge of people. He was different and they would probably never be able to see things, some things anyway, the same way because their forming and sustaining environments had been different, but she knew this much about him already—he was honest and forthright and truthful. She nodded her head.

He finished with the horse and swung facing her. "I didn't just want to take you out to the cow camp for a drive. I wanted you to see how I live. I wanted to see if you could possibly be happy in a place like the cow camp. Marie. . . ."

Someone was crossing the gritty dust from the direction of the mission. She thought she knew who it was as they both turned, facing a fresh direction as Olivia appeared, cool-looking, faintly aloof toward John Dennison, perhaps slightly protective of the younger woman who had become more and more like the daughter Olivia had never had. Then she smiled at them.

"Father Eusebio is sitting on the *ramada*. He saw you arrive. We were going to have lemonade. . . ." Olivia's beautiful eyes drifted from one face to the other face.

"We'd love it," Marie said. "We'll be right along. Olivia? How is Maximillian Sotelo?"

"Constable Young came and we handed him over. He will be much safer locked in the iron *calabozo*." Her glance flicked past to John Dennison. "And no one seems to believe he should be hanged after all."

"And my father?"

"See for yourself," Olivia replied. "Come over to the *ramada*." Their eyes met and held; they both loved a man who filled two lives very much. Olivia added a little more, in a softer tone: "He will be fit again in a month, I think. He says he will and he is the only doctor. But we'll keep watch, no?"

They looked warmly into one another's eyes, then Olivia turned away.

John Dennison said: "One hell of a lady, that one." He felt for a hand and clung to Marie's fingers. "Can I try once more?"

She laughed softly, squeezed hard, then released his fingers.

"What I was going to say when she came along. . . ."

"John, it's not all that vitally essential right at this moment, is it? I mean . . . I want you to say it, too, but we're going downhill at a very fast pace without any brakes, aren't we?"

"Marie, I don't want any brakes."

She felt for his hand again. "I do, John. I can't just . . . well . . . react the way a man would. I'm not one." She watched his face. "Nothing really has to be resolved today anyway, does it?"

He loosened his grip on her hand, willing because she wished him not to press her, to be patient, but clearly not entirely exuberant.

They went over to the *ramada* and drank lemonade. She told Father Eusebio what his cow camp really was and what she had expected it to be. She also told him she was glad Maximillian Sotelo was safely in jail now, and that the troubles seemed to have diminished, and, when her father gazed past at John Dennison with a parent's knowing look, she blushed and turned to Olivia so that the older woman would come to her rescue.

Olivia understood and arose to return inside with the pitcher and glasses. She asked Father Eusebio to help her. When he arose to do so, Olivia glanced past his bent back at his daughter, showing no expression but clearly transmitting a personal message.

Marie, who was not stoic at all, nor even very fatalistic, smiled at the older woman.

John Dennison reached for his tobacco and papers to roll a smoke. He proved to be much more perceptive than Marie had expected when he said: "I don't see how a man ever wins if all women are like you and Olivia Gomez."

His eyes twinkled as he lit up and blew smoke into the still, hushed air of the ancient overhang.

A pair of mud nest swallows swooped low beneath the slanted roof, saw the people sitting there, and immediately fled back to the sunlight where they had nothing to impede escape. They then landed and fiercely scolded, waited a moment, and flew off together.

"Probably spirits from some of the old folks out yonder in the graveyard," John said, watching the birds disappear side-by-side.

She was a little shocked. "John, that's not religion, that's animism."

He nodded. "Yeah, the Indians believed in it." He looked at her. "What's wrong with it? Maybe it's not right, but who can be sure which religion is right . . . or if any of them are? So . . . the idea of you and me as a pair of swallows still being together around this old mission . . . is that so terrible?"

She smiled at him. No, it was not so terrible. In fact it was not terrible at all. She settled comfortably and with ease at his side. Their hands groped and interlocked and neither of them said a word as they watched that pair of swallows—or maybe another pair; they all looked alike—return to the ancient eaves and hover there.

The longer she sat relaxed like this and watched, the more she actually came to like the idea of those swallows having been together another time.

★ ★ ★ ★ ★

GUNS OF THUNDER

★ ★ ★ ★ ★

I

"Sobriety," stated O'Casey very gravely, "is a splendid thing, Slattery. Save me that last drop, it's a cursed dry country, for a fact."

Four hours back they had left the village of Acton through the broken hills with a fresh-day sun dulling the dark faded blue of their regimentals, and Acton wasn't much of a place, as towns went, even the towns of border-country Arizona, but it had a café, and a barn where they had their mounts grained, and it also had a saloon. Perhaps more than one saloon, but the nearest one to the barn had been sufficient.

"It's a cursed dull country, too," grumbled Pat Slattery. "Look around ye an' what's there . . . nothin', miles an' miles of nothin'. Sometimes tipped on end, sometimes flat an' infernal hot like now. Sometimes with the damned thornpinned chaparral so thick a man can't push through it."

"Don't hog the bottle, Pat, me lad. There now . . . that's better. An' the people. Did ye ever in ye're life see such a scruffy lot. Eyein' us they was back in that hell-hole town o' theirs like we was perfect strangers . . . like they never so much as laid eyes on uniformed gentlemen before."

"Border scum," Slattery agreed, and pushed a forearm across his face to squeeze off the sweat. He canted his head. The sun hung up there, smoke-hazed in the midday heavens, pale and brassy and hateful. All around lay the broken land. Shadows were all shapes, but thin and watery. There were few trees, mostly fat junipers, but there was brush—sage and chaparral, ocotillo, catclaw, and paloverde.

They flung away the bottle where a burro trail veered northwesterly below the looming onward clay hills. It seemed like a cañon and Pat Slattery said something about that.

John O'Casey was doubtful. He was also somewhat unconcerned. "Seven days I'll hand you," he said, casting a look around where the onward hills seemed to close in upon their burro trail. "Take any man ye wish, O'Casey, he says, and you got seven days to deliver the orders and fetch back the answer." O'Casey rolled his blue eyes. "Seven days, sir, says I . . . it's easy a ten days' ride, sir."

Slattery smiled ruefully. "As well reason with the captain as the lieutenant, John."

"That's a fact, indeed it is. So here we are comin' back a short cut to steal a day anyway." O'Casey threw back his head and laughed.

There were heat-hazed peaks stealthily marching down from the north. From the south the breaks got taller, brushier, rougher. Dead ahead to the west loomed a continuing run of those northward slopes, barren except for rockslides and an occasional juniper, and here and there narrow, deep-scored cuts where wintertime rains and springtime freshets had over the years carved out sluices of their own.

"Blasted hot in here," Pat Slattery said, opening his blouse, his face very red. "Are ye sure, John, the feller said to take this trail?"

"Sure as a man can be, me boy. Take the burro trail over against them brown hills, he says. Take the burro trail an' jus' keep follerin' it. It'll take ye through the hills on a short cut an' whittle a whole day off your route."

Slattery shook his head. Heat bounced off the slopes to roll back against them. It piled up in the pit of the cañon they passed through, moving in gelatine waves. "What a country to be pa-trollin' anyway," he growled, sweating copiously. "Why didn't the blamed Army just leave it to the redskins . . . what's it good for anyway, I'd like to know."

"You just give the answer yourself," replied O'Casey. "Red-skins."

"Naw. Ye're in ye're cups, John. Hasn't been any redskin trouble in five years now."

"*Ahhh*," murmured O'Casey, with a sly, knowing wink. "But that's how them red devils work, Pat me boy. They're tricky ones, they are. I been soldierin' out here since the war's end an' can tell ye for a fact, they're tricky."

Slattery's blouse turned steadily darker as they progressed through their cauldron cañon. The whiskey soured in his gut and sobriety came a little at a time. He was younger than O'Casey and not so leathery, and, also, he was not so blithe, either. He had been soldiering three years now and knew a box cañon when he saw one. Box cañons let you in, then gradually closed down on all sides of you, and, when someone deliberately directed you into a box cañon, he invariably had a reason for doing it.

Finally Slattery halted in the trail. Up ahead those sere, tan slopes stood straight up off the alkali earth. Right and left the darker soil of other hills pinched down. The burro trail petered out into dust near an alkali sink that at other times of the year held bitter drinking water.

"Why?" he murmured, twisting in the saddle to look back where the land lay more open and where their burro trail was still visible.

O'Casey's horse halted without any help from its rider. He turned solemnly to regard the back trail, too. He said: "What is it, Pat . . . red devils?"

"No. It's nothing at all."

There was a silence so deep in the cañon a man could hear the pull of arid breath into his own hungry lungs. Heat saturated the place in layers. O'Casey tilted his canteen. The water was warm and oily but it was wet. Sweat burst out afresh to darken O'Casey's tunic. He sighed, unbuttoned, and ran a freckled, hairy hand across his cracked lips. The sobriety was coming to him, also, but a lot slower, for O'Casey was a drinking man with a degree of strong resistance to this kind of heat. He was an old soldier. During the war he had once been a sergeant major, but had been broken back even before the war ended. Not that he wasn't a good soldier, but that was just it. John O'Casey was a soldier, not an officer. Not even a non-commissioned officer. He could smell out Indians and he could thin out a saloon full of civilians. He could shoot hard, ride well, scream like a banshee, and swing his dragoon saber like a Viking, but he could not accept the restraint that went with responsibility.

He had the reply to that message inside his sweaty tunic right now, and, if a man of flesh could deliver it, he would do it. He was a fighting soldier, a drinking soldier, a brawling soldier. He was everything an officer asked for in the men he commanded, but he was no more than that, so now he sat there sweltering, eyeing the solid bulk of those onward slopes with dull understanding that for some strange reason they had been directed into this hell-hole from which there was only retreat, and he hiccupped.

"Why?" Slattery asked again, slowly sweeping the landscape with his roving eyes. "Maybe the one who told you about this short cut was a joker, John. A man who has no likin' for soldiers." Slattery removed his rakish campaign hat, flung off sweat, and resettled the hat. "Whatever his reason, I'd like to have him in front of me right now for a minute or two. Short cut indeed!"

O'Casey's lowered dark brows shielded a testy pair of considering eyes. He looked here and there and finally said: "Pat Slattery, we been boondoggled, an' 'tis the heat, but just now I saw movement off there in the brush to our left."

Slattery turned. The movement of his head might have been a signal for the first gunshot. It came, flat-sounding in the gelatine heat. Slattery looked straight toward the sound of that shot a full moment, then he sagged out of his saddle without a sound and fell face down.

O'Casey, drunk or sober, was conditioned to instinctive action at the sound of gunfire. He went off the right side of his big government horse, tugging at his carbine. He was suddenly as sober as a judge. A faint wisp of smoke arose. Gunshot echoes went crashing around the cul-de-sac cañon. It was a tight and cruel moment. They could also be behind him. Without much doubt, if they didn't mean him and Pat Slattery to leave here alive, they would be down the burro trail, too, secreted in the brush.

"Pat," he softly called, sweat stinging his eyes. "Pat, lad . . . how bad is it?"

There was no answer from Slattery on the far side of their horses.

O'Casey strained to detect shape or movement. There was neither. He was too seasoned an old campaigner not to understand what this silence meant; they were stealthily stalking him. He considered. He could drop the two horses and fort up between them, which would at least give him a chance. But the moment he did that he would also deprive himself of a plausible retreat. A man on foot in this country wouldn't get far with his enemies mounted. He could run hard for the nearest brush, which lay upon the southward low slopes. But first he must determine how many of them were waiting for him to try that.

125

One or two, he would risk it. Five or six, he wouldn't stand a chance.

Finally there was a wild race back down out of the dead-end cañon, but it rankled that he would have to abandon Pat Slattery. He had never left a friend, dead or wounded, in all his years wearing the blue. It went against the grain now.

He couldn't wait any longer; they would be nearly around him on all sides by now. He never once wondered why, for that was the kind of a soldier he was. What possible benefit could be obtained from two dead troopers who had no money and little of anything else?

He aimed into the chaparral where that solitary earlier shot had come from, and fired. As before, the echoes chased themselves up and down their slopes, imprisoned, and afterward there was the leaden silence again.

They were closing in now, were saving their lead. He drew down a deep breath of the insufficient oxygen, checked his weapons, reset his battered hat, and stepped around the horse's rump. Ahead fifty yards lay the underbrush. He cast a quick look at Pat as he started. Pat's back had a rusty, scarlet shininess where a ball had hit in front and plowed right on through. Pat had been dead before he had hit the ground, the dirty devils.

He ran broken, clever at it, experienced to the cross-whip of the lead that finally came, and it did not occur to him that there weren't but three or four of them hidden and firing at him until he felt the wind smashed from his lungs, felt his legs turning to uncontrollable stumps, and then it was too late, for a burst of strange, flooding warmth swept upward from below and he fell, struck hard, bounced and rolled like a half filled grain sack, losing the carbine, and finally, where he halted on his right side, also losing his hat.

Darkness came in waves, and blessed coolness, too.

The firing was finished. Somewhere hastening boots struck

rattlingly over hard earth scuffing loose rocks to life. That was the last sound he heard. They were running up on him. He still thought of Indians when his last shallow breath ran out.

Two of them ran to Slattery and bent to rummage his tunic, his pockets, even his saddlebags. The other pair stayed with O'Casey. It was one of these that sang out, finally, holding up the sweat-limp envelope from inside O'Casey's tunic.

"Here it is! This one had it."

They all came together, standing above O'Casey, lean, sun-blackened, fierce-eyed men. One of them said: "Read it, dammit, don't just stand there lookin' at the envelope." Another one was eyeing the riderless horses where they patiently stood out there in the sun smash beside Pat Slattery. "If it wasn't for them damned U.S. brands, I'd trail those critters back down to Acton and trade 'em for something."

"Listen," muttered the man with the letter in his hands. "It says . . . 'Rifles will be delivered by common carrier under armed guard no later than Twenty-Second instant.' . . . an' it's signed colonel something-or-other, I can't decipher the writin', the sweat's done blurred it."

"Well we don't care, anyway," another one said. "The Twenty-Second, that's all we wanted to know anyway. The rifles'll be along on the Twenty-Second. Good. Now, let's get shed of these damned bodies an' get out of here."

II

At early dawn Captain Southern led his scout detail down out of the Pinals and across the dry wash country toward the post where a visible sprinkling wagon was ponderously going around settling dust. Ben Southern was a professional: a tall, sun-layered man with wide shoulders and lean flanks who on the trail sometimes reverted to what he had been during the war—a private soldier—and made an atmosphere that his troopers liked, understood, but never took advantage of.

No other officer at Camp Scott did it. No other officer at Camp Scott had risen from the ranks, for that matter, nor had come to command so much loyalty.

"Cap'n," Sergeant Tolliver said, chewing his cut plug with a steady rhythm. "The Mexicans say the colonel's mad to waste water like that, puttin' down the dust."

Ben Southern looked ahead where the faded sky blended against a writhing emptiness of dun desert. "The Mexicans aren't married to Colonel Noble's wife, Ned. Anyway, if Camp Scott's got nothing else, it's got a damned good well."

"I hope so," stated a lean, hawk-faced, dark-eyed trooper farther back, whose sleeves showed where chevrons had recently been removed. "I aim to soak in the tub at the laundry shed for two hours, just puttin' moisture back all this infernal patrollin' has dried out."

Southern smiled a lazy, tolerant smile, his gray glance lingering on the clutch of raw buildings up ahead. Camp Scott was the most ugly, desolate, demoralizing outpost he had seen in twelve years of border soldiering. What a rotten place to station a commandant who had a society belle for a wife. Sometimes it seemed that the War Department perversely did things like that just to see how rough it could make conditions. Well, this time it had succeeded beyond its wildest dreams, if, for a fact, it did do that perversely. Colonel Noble was a harassed man. He upon occasion drank too much, but Captain Southern and everyone else on the post, for that matter, understood.

It was a small post; two companies of the 4th Cavalry garrisoned it. Actually, since the last Apache battle years back, there wasn't a reason to maintain it anyway, but, as Ben Southern had reason to know, the War Department never acted in haste. He and the others had been making the same pointless patrols over the same depopulated Indian paths for several years now, and had never once encountered anything more formidable than an occasional furtive Mexican family creaking northward up out of Mexico in an ox-drawn *carreta* fleeing from their revolution-ravaged native land.

There were orders to turn these people back, or, if they offered trouble, to escort them to the Camp Scott guardhouse. But they never offered trouble and most of the time Ben Southern, Lieutenant Beecham, even the colonel himself on the few times he made the scouting trips with the troopers, ignored them. There was nothing more wretched, more thoroughly demoralized, than those gaunt peons fleeing their bloody homeland.

The flag hung lifelessly above the clutch of buildings. There was an acrid, metallic scent to the summer day. Where there was shade, it offered no succor; desert heat, particularly in midsummer, permitted no surcease from its savage brightness. After a while men in Arizona squinted their eyes. It became a lifelong habit. Women fought against it because it brought crow's-feet wrinkles, but the sun always won.

Lieutenant Beecham was near the gate when Southern and his patrol came along. He turned, a red-faced, heavy young man with pale eyes drawn out long and narrow. Elsewhere, troopers stood or moved, some down near the laundry shack, others across at the stables. Two of them listlessly walking sentry-go.

Beecham let Ben Southern get right up close, then said: "Indians by the hundreds, I can see by the way your men look it was a terrific fight." He didn't crack a smile or lift an arched brow. He had that kind of sense of humor.

Southern drew rein, lifted to halt the line, and stepped down. "Dismiss the men," he said to Sergeant Tolliver. To Lieutenant Beecham he said: "What a waste of vaudeville talent, sending you out here. How's the colonel?"

"Sober," replied Beecham, "if that's what you mean. And he wants to see you the minute you get in."

"You've been standing here since dawn with that breathless message, I take it?"

"No, Captain," said the boyish lieutenant. "Since last night." Beecham saluted, smiled, turned, and struck out after the listless troopers who were leading their animals across the parade.

Colonel Noble's command hut was in front of his quarters. It was a handy arrangement. Sometimes too handy, for the monotony could drive a man like Colonel Noble back to his parlor where the liquor was. But the Army was tolerant; drunkards were perfectly acceptable as long as they showed up for the monthly parade sober, got off their reports on time, and kept order in their areas. In Colonel Noble's perimeter each of these mandatory requirements was elemental; in fact, except for them—and detailing the pointless patrols there was nothing else to do. Or at least there hadn't been up until the time Captain Southern returned and was summoned to Colonel Noble's presence.

They were friends. Noble had requested Ben Southern when he had drawn the Camp Scott assignment. Southern had risen to brigadier general under Noble during the war. Afterward, with the customary cutbacks, they had both suffered. But actually, because they had been duty soldiers, they hadn't minded terribly. What had changed that, at least for the colonel, was the *ennui,* the deadly heat—and the colonel's lady.

Captain Southern washed up, smeared unsalted butter on his cracked lips, beat dust from his clothing, then crossed over to the little adobe building where the bored sentry stood below the lifeless flag. Colonel Noble was waiting, a rangy, raw-boned man with a noticeable saber scar down one cheek, an unnaturally reddened countenance, and a pair of cloudy blue eyes above a handsome dragoon moustache.

Southern saluted and said: "Sir."

Colonel Noble smiled. He was a handsome man; it wasn't hard to imagine a lovely Washington belle becoming his lady. "Anything?" he asked.

Captain Southern said. "No, sir, nothing. Not even any *mestizos.*"

"Well, I've got something for you, Ben." Noble held up some papers. "O'Casey and Slattery are dead."

Southern's looseness lingered but his gray gaze hardened slightly with interest. "Dead . . . ?"

"Shot, Ben. Slattery shot through the chest from in front. O'Casey hit four times in the body." Colonel Noble offered a letter. "It's from a sheriff down at Acton near the border." As Southern took the letter, the colonel clasped both hands behind his back and paced the length of the little room, about-faced, and paced back. "A cowboy saw buzzards and rode over to investigate. Evidently he expected to find a dead cow. Instead, he found where someone had buried two soldiers in shallow graves that the coyotes had dug out and had chewed upon. O'Casey and Slattery."

Southern put the letter carefully aside, picked up another paper, examined it, and also put it down. "The orders," he stated, not interested, "about the rifles."

Colonel Noble stopped pacing. His handsome face was still. "The orders," he echoed. "That's exactly how they came to me. Without any envelope."

Ben Southern faced the colonel, waiting. Over across the parade a man's voice rose in the heavy air, dropped, then faded away. There was a clock upon a mantel of Colonel Noble's office that endlessly ticked.

"No envelope, Ben," the commandant said again. "And two dead troopers."

Captain Southern's glance lingered thoughtfully upon his

colonel. "I see."

"You're going to Acton, Ben. Take Tolliver and Lee with you. Find out if . . . when the sheriff got those orders . . . they were in an envelope, and, if so, why he . . . or someone . . . opened them."

Southern nodded, saying nothing. The colonel's suspicion was sound enough. Rifles, particularly new Army carbines, were better than gold in the border country. Over the line in Mexico they were priceless. The particular rifles referred to in those orders were to be transferred, along with their accountability, from one Army post to another under escort. Mexican revolutionaries would risk a brush with U.S. soldiers to get their hands on those guns. It was exactly to avoid their falling into the wrong hands that they were being sent away from the border, up to Camp Scott.

"And, Ben, the three of you are to appear in Acton as civilians. In uniform you'd be a target, if there's something wrong down there." Colonel Noble made a small grimace. "Army blue doesn't seem to be any deterrent. O'Casey and Slattery were good men."

"O'Casey was a lifer," Southern said. Then, as though in recollection, he sadly shook his head. "I remember him from the wilderness, Colonel."

"And I," stated Colonel Noble, "from three courts-martial and at least twenty battles. O'Casey was a fine soldier. Upon occasion he was even a pretty fair man."

They smiled at each other. They recalled O'Casey perfectly.

"It's not our job, I know," Noble said, "but if in the course of your purely military investigation you should happen across the men who killed John O'Casey, Ben. . . ."

Southern said—"Of course."—and glanced at the letter again. "Acton, Acton. . . . If my memory serves me right, it's a cow town a few miles north of the border."

Colonel Noble went briskly to the desk, counted out some paper money from a drawer, and tossed it down in front of Captain Southern. "General services funds," he muttered. "Keep me informed if you can, Ben. And one more thing . . . I'll send word that the rifles aren't to be moved unless you authorize it from Acton, so when you finish the investigation, if you think I'm just unduly suspicious, ride on down to Fort Brown and escort the guns back to Camp Scott."

Ben Southern saluted, dropped his arm, and smiled. "Anything's better than the patrols, Colonel."

Noble also smiled. "Beecham will turn green with envy." He stuck out his hand. "Good luck, Ben, and keep a close watch. Tolliver and Lee are good men. I don't think there are better on the post for this duty."

Captain Southern left the office, halted out in the weighted heat, ran a glance around and back again. There wasn't a soul in sight except two limp sentries, one over at the main gate, the other pressing into thin shade behind him in front of the command post. He stepped forth to stride on across toward officers quarters. Halfway there he saw Sergeant Tolliver poke his head out a door to expectorate darkly.

"Tolliver, front and center!" he sang out.

The seamed, leathery face came completely through that shady opening, followed by Tolliver's lanky, dehydrated body. Ned Tolliver was an old soldier; he was one of those tough campaigners who could render junior officers helpless with a look or a very dry remark. He knew all the ways of being too polite, too punctilious, too correct, without ever being insubordinate. It was the Sergeant Tollivers who really ran the Army. They were wise to the ways of warfare and equally as seasoned to the lesser methods of campaigning.

"Sir," he murmured, halting to offer a respectful salute, brassy sunlight burning unnoticed across his faded shoulders.

"Get Lee, and the pair of you find some civilian pants and shirts," ordered Captain Southern. "Pick up three unbranded horses at the stables and rig us out with three civilian saddles and outfits. Tell no one what you're up to."

Tolliver's faded eyes got ironic. "That won't be hard, sir, since I don't know what I'm up to."

Captain Ben let that pass. "The three of us are on detached duty. We're heading for a town named Acton down along the border."

"Tonight, sir?"

"Yes, tonight."

"All right, sir."

"One more thing, Sergeant. O'Casey and Pat Slattery are dead."

Sergeant Tolliver's jaws gradually closed hard. His faded eyes gleamed behind the perpetual squint of lids. He said nothing.

"They were carrying orders about some surplus rifles, Ned."

"Shot, sir?"

Southern nodded and glanced over where Lieutenant Beecham strolled forth from his quarters and lounged back in the shade under a warped wooden awning. "We'll pull out right after retreat, Sergeant."

"Yes, sir. Lee an' I'll be ready."

Southern looked back. "You know my first name, Tolliver?"

"Yes, sir. I ought to. It's Ben."

"From now on I'm Ben, you're Ned, and Lee is Walt. Three civilians. Clear?"

"Clear as a bell, Captain."

"Meet you at the stables later," said Southern, and strolled on across where Lieutenant Beecham was lighting a black and crooked little Mexican cigar.

Beecham said: "The colonel mapping a campaign?"

Southern paused, before ducking on through inside, to say:

"Hadn't you heard . . . Arizona seceded from the Union." As he passed along, the younger officer exhaled a cloud of smoke and looked off where the lowering western sun was hanging over some sharp-toothed far-away crags.

"That's not such a bad idea at that. At any rate it'd keep us all from going crazy from fried brains in this lousy place." Beecham straightened up and started on across the parade toward the stables. Camp Scott was a poor place even for Army gossip, but if there was one place it could be picked up, that would be the stable area.

III

Sheriff Ed Mittan was forty-seven years old and anxious. He had spent many years in law enforcement work and was good at it, but he hadn't been at it so long he was bored and indifferent, which was frequently the way with lawmen.

Particularly he wasn't indifferent the day he arrived in Acton in response to a lathered messenger sent to him by John Fincher, the owner of Acton's general store, who was also president of the Acton town council. John was waiting at the Acton jailhouse, a stuffy little adobe building that was rarely used, and he had some things to show Ed Mittan: two filthy, bullet-riddled soldier tunics, campaign hats, an opened letter to the commandant at Camp Scott up north, and the disturbing recital of a local cowpuncher.

Sheriff Mittan had at once sent a letter, along with the Army communication, to Camp Scott. After that he had gone out to examine the spot where those two dead soldiers had been hastily buried.

There had been a fight, he saw at once. Actually more of an ambush. The Army was touchy about civilians shooting soldiers. Ambushing them was even worse. Ed Mittan did not like in the least bit the notion of the Army descending upon his territory

135

full of gorge and perhaps declaring martial law. He had a comparatively quiet country.

He went back to Acton and spent a couple of days asking questions. John Fincher didn't recall any strangers in town. No one had seen Mexican brigands passing across the range, which was fairly common as the fighting loyalists and *guerrilleros* down in Mexico chased one another, sometimes up over the international boundary.

"There'll be a pair of U.S. horses, saddles, and maybe carbines circulating around somewhere," Sheriff Mittan told John Fincher. He also unhappily told him the Army was certain to arrive in Acton.

"That's fine with us down here," Fincher stated. He was a portly man who perspired freely and habitually wiped sweat off his face and neck. "To tell you the truth, Ed, folks are gettin' a mite uneasy, what with those greasers down in Mexico bringing their cussed war so close to the border that sometimes they spill over. I tell you, we've needed soldiers down here for a long time."

Ed Mittan was skeptical about that but kept his own counsel. The border towns had, a few years back, prospered by having troops billeted among them. They sold supplies and livestock to the Army, they hauled its freight, and got fat off its wood contracts. Ed had always privately felt that the merchants, although joining everyone else in loud cries of relief when the Apaches had been vanquished, had actually been a little mournful at the end of the Indian wars in the Southwest, because the Army pulled out and all the free-flowing money pulled out with it.

"Be that as it may," Mittan told Fincher. "It doesn't look good, John, the Army having to come here because someone shot a couple of soldiers."

"Mexicans more'n likely," growled Fincher darkly. "They're

stealing horses and guns every chance they get. I tell you, Ed, if that revolution down there doesn't end soon that whole blessed country will collapse."

"As long as it collapses south of the border, it's fine with me," Sheriff Mittan said, and went over to the livery barn to inquire about anyone trying to peddle a pair of horses with the Army's neck brand on them. He drew a blank over there. Next, he visited the harness shop, but no one had either tried to sell a pair of McClellan saddles, or brought in any to be repaired.

He located the cowpuncher who had found the bodies and spoke with him again, but the rider could add nothing to what he had already said. Even the men who went out with a wagon to bring in the bodies for burial couldn't tell much beyond the fact that the soldiers had obviously been dead several days.

An old cowman named Parmenter, who knew the country, sidled up to Sheriff Mittan at the lunchroom down the road a few doors from Fincher's store to make an observation. He said two soldiers had been in Acton a few days earlier asking about a short cut through the hills northward toward Camp Scott. He also said that while he hadn't viewed the corpses, since there hadn't been any other soldiers around Acton in over a year, he was certain the dead pair were the same ones who had bought a bottle at the saloon, then had ridden off.

Mittan was interested but didn't get the point of all this, so he asked bluntly what Parmenter was getting at. "Simple," drawled the old cattleman. "Someone around town told them of a short cut . . . only it wasn't no short cut, Sheriff. In other words, someone deliberately sent them two lads up into that box cañon."

Ed Mittan considered that. It did seem logical, since anyone who knew the country well enough to give the troopers specific instructions on how to get into the place, also had to know that cañon well enough to know there was no way out of it except back the way they had come.

Mittan invited the cowman to sit down at his table and have some dinner with him. Parmenter sat down but declined the invitation to eat. He was a spare, lanky, old man as brown as a nut and sparse with words. "One other thing, Sheriff," he said, waving off the counterman. "Ain't been no Apaches skulkin' around in a long time. They's a few greasers slippin' around, but they got no grudge with the U.S. Army. So . . . who'd trick a pair of common soljers into that box cañon to ambush 'em?"

Mittan pushed back his plate, reached for his cup of coffee, lifted it, and patiently eyed old Parmenter over his cup's rim. "Who?" he asked. "You've got some notion. You've given this some thought."

"Everyone has, Sheriff, everyone has. Hasn't been anything like this happen in the Acton country in quite a spell. Except for the Mexicans kickin' up their big ruckus over the line, things've been too peaceful for a long time. Everyone's speculatin' on the murder of two soljers."

"And you," prompted Ed Mittan again. "What've you speculated?"

"Before I can answer that, you got to tell me what them two was doin' down here?"

"They'd been to Fort Brown down south and were on their way back to Camp Scott with a letter for their commandin' officer."

"This here letter . . . did it have to do with firearms, maybe, Sheriff?"

"It did."

"Figured as much. Used to be folks got killed just for money or maybe a fast horse or two, or for stickin' their beaks where they had no business stickin' 'em. But now, all of a sudden, it's guns. My speculatin', Mister Mittan, makes me wonder who, around the Acton country, wants to tie into a load of Army rifles."

Mittan's face fell a little. In a strained way he said: "That's nothing new, Mister Parmenter. Sure, they were shot over rifles. Well, not over rifles exactly, but over that letter they were carryin' because it listed a date when some rifles were goin' to be sent to Camp Scott from Fort Brown."

Parmenter's slitted eyes gleamed. "What date, Sheriff, what date?"

But Ed Mittan finished his coffee, put the cup aside, and shook his head. "We'll keep that part of it quiet for a spell," he said, pushing forward to arise. "Been nice talkin' to you, Mister Parmenter."

The old cowman said: "Not so fast, Sheriff, not so fast. A lot of riders were left off after the roundups. It was more'n one or two men dry-gulched those soljers, I figure, and most of the range men drifted on, lookin' for work, after they were paid off. I'd say it'd pay you to sort of nose around the ranches, Mister Mittan. Somewhere hereabouts, since it wasn't strangers 'cause none have been in town, there's a crew of men needin' money an' lackin' scruples enough, to be just who you're lookin' for."

Sheriff Mittan teetered a moment, then arose. "I had something like that in mind," he said, and walked out of the café.

Midsummer in the desert country was tolerable at dawn and dusk only. The rest of the time there was a smoky haze to the distances and a steady burning heat. No one, not even Indians or Mexicans who were inured by heritage and pigment to the fierce heat, moved around much during midday. For that reason Ed Mittan was interested when he spied three slouching riders coming down into town from the easterly roadway.

They were whipcord men, burned black and attired as most range men dressed, with low-slung hip holsters and scuffed boots. There was something about each of them that seemed to be shared by the others, and that, Ed Mittan thought, was odd, because by and large range riders were individualists if they were never anything else.

The one in the middle was a pleasant-faced man but with a deceptive toughness down around the mouth. He was slab-hammered and wide-shouldered, rode as a man rides who was born and reared in the saddle, and seemed to be one of those men who, without appearing to, saw everything that was happening anywhere around him.

Mittan paced along to Fincher's store. Acton was within Mittan's territory, but, because there was seldom reason to visit it, he rarely did. For that reason he needed someone familiar with local folks to identify those three for him. He hissed at Fincher and beckoned. When the perspiring merchant came over and stepped outside onto the shaded plank walk, Mittan jerked his head and muttered in a low voice. The three riders were coming straight down Acton's main thoroughfare by then.

John Fincher looked, squinted hard, and kept looking. He didn't know any of them. "Strangers," he murmured from the corner of his mouth. "Never seen a one of them before, Ed. Plumb strangers." Fincher cleared his throat and fished out a limp handkerchief to mop his throat. "Maybe you've got something, Ed. I got to admit they're a mighty tough-looking bunch."

Mittan said nothing but he walked away from Fincher as those three horsemen turned and ambled on into the livery barn. He built a smoke in the shade across the way, lit it, and lounged against an overhang post waiting for the trio of lanky men to emerge. They did, eventually, each one packing his booted Winchester and his bedroll, then struck out for the lodging house across the road. Mittan finished his smoke, killing plenty of time, before he strolled on over to the livery barn.

But disappointment, while part of every lawman's job, came hard over there. The three horses had unfamiliar brands on them. The three saddles were also foreign. Two had been made at Miles City, Montana, and one had been made by N. Porter down in Phoenix. Old saddles, sturdy and well cared for, but nondescript like the horses. The liveryman, like everyone else in Acton, knew why Sheriff Mittan was in town. He said: "Don't seem likely, if they was the ones, Sheriff, they'd ride into town bold as brass after killin' two soljers, does it?"

Ed Mittan didn't answer. He was an easy-going man, usually, but after John Fincher and old Parmenter, he was getting just a little weary of home-made detectives.

He crossed to the rooming house and checked the ledger. Each of the three men had given a different name and a different town of origin, which wasn't unusual; generally range men put down anything that popped into their minds when they arrived in town. It was a sort of cow-country joke to see who could come up with the most humorous or most outlandish designation on those rooming house ledgers.

Mittan went back outside, crossed over to the jailhouse, and entered the building. It smelled moldy so he walked around opening windows, and had his back to the door when a willowy shadow fell across the small room bringing him around.

She stood perhaps five feet six inches, which was tall for a girl, and there was a supple leanness to her. Her eyes were direct beneath neat dark brows and her mouth was slightly longer than most, but full and heavy and ripe. She was, Ed Mittan thought, while reaching up to drag off his old hat, uncommonly handsome, and although she wasn't more than perhaps twenty years old and he was well along in his forties, Ed was young enough to be appreciative and old enough to be solicitous.

He reached for a chair, saying: "Come right in, miss. I just opened up some windows to air the place out. They don't often use this building over here." He stepped back. "I'm Sheriff Ed Mittan."

She walked over by the chair, but didn't sit. She said: "Sheriff, I'm Alice Clark." She seemed about to say more, then paused, took a fresh tack, and said: "About those dead soldiers, Sheriff, maybe I can be of some help to you."

Ed lifted heavy brows. He had just for the moment quite forgotten the dead soldiers. Recovering, he motioned toward the chair. "Please sit down, ma'am . . . Miss Clark. I'd be proud to hear whatever you can tell me."

She still didn't sit, but she said: "I have their horses and saddles, Sheriff. The Clark Ranch is southeast of Acton, nine miles."

"I see. Well, Miss Clark, I'm glad to hear they strayed in an' you corralled them."

"They didn't stray in, Sheriff, they were led in. If you'd care to make the ride this afternoon, we can get down to the ranch before dusk and I'll show you the tracks. If you'd care to do that, we'd best get started right now. We can talk on the way."

"Yes," said Ed Mittan, interested in the horses, of course, but also curious about Alice Clark. She had a way of biting off her words as though commanding troops in the field. It intrigued him. "Your animal outside?" he inquired, and, when she nodded, he said: "Mine's at the livery barn . . . you just set in the shade, I'll be right back, ma'am."

IV

Ben Southern saw Sheriff Mittan ride off with the handsome girl from his upstairs bedroom. Walt Lee and Ned Tolliver were lounging upon beds in the same room, making sounds of deep pleasure.

Captain Ben called to them. "The law's riding out," he said, "southward." Neither of the others moved. "He's riding with about as pretty a girl as I ever laid eyes on."

Both Tolliver and Lee turned, sat up, stood up, and crossed to peer, also, from their window. Ben smiled behind their backs and reached for his hat. "Care to ride with me, or do you need more rest?"

Tolliver turned, his lower jaw gently massaging the usual cud of chewing tobacco. Walt Lee was just as impassive and thoughtful. "All ready?" Lee murmured, and, when Southern didn't answer, only reached for the door latch, Lee rolled his eyes around at Ned and also started out of the room.

They hired fresh animals at the livery barn and rode out, southward. Not a word was said until they had cleared town and there was no longer any shade.

"I'm right curious, Cap'n Ben," Tolliver drawled, sighting far ahead where a faint skiff of dust lazily hung in the dead-hot afternoon. "Is it the sheriff you're interested in, or the handsome girl?"

Southern smiled his easy smile. Despite his air of tolerance and his sometimes long silences, he was deceptively smart in his judgment of other men. Tolliver was no longer a young man— was in fact somewhere in his middle or late thirties—but he, too, was tempered in the ways of other men.

"Now, Ned," Southern said softly, "what can it hurt being interested in both?"

Walt Lee, equally as dark and leathery and savvy as Ned Tolliver, chuckled. But he said nothing.

They rode along until Mittan and the handsome, tall girl left the road heading southeastward. They stopped for a while, these three wily campaigners, to make certain the lawman and girl got far enough ahead so they wouldn't inadvertently glance back and discern by that everlasting telltale dust that they were being followed.

As they loitered, Ben Southern said: "Nothing else likely to hold the interest of Acton . . . and its lawman . . . beyond the killing of O'Casey and Slattery. I think we're following the right trail."

"A good-lookin' one anyway," muttered Tolliver, shifting his cud to the other cheek and straightening for a long look around. "How far's the border from here?"

"Not far . . . twelve, fourteen miles," answered Walt Lee. "I drew a tour of duty at Fort Brown years back. It's danged close to the line. In fact, back in them days, we used to sneak down and trade cordial gunshots with the Mexicans."

Tolliver spat. "They havin' a war down there in those days, too?" he dryly asked. "Seems to me that's about all those folks do."

Lee smiled. "The dust is settlin'," he said.

They rode on. The land turned rougher, more gravelly and sterile, humped and washed and inhospitable, as they progressed. "If this is cattle country," observed Ned Tolliver, "then no wonder folks got to rob travelers to keep body an' soul alive."

But the land subtly changed after several miles. It remained just as tilted and broken and eroded, but little green patches began to appear. Finally, where a low hill loomed, the three of them rode up atop it and Ned Tolliver grunted. A mile ahead was a ranch. The buildings were old and thick-walled, and arranged to withstand a siege, which was not unusual in Apache country, but what struck the three soldiers was the large green meadow that completely surrounded those buildings.

"Be damned," Tolliver muttered, squinting down there. "Sub-irrigated. Who'd ever think to find such a place in all this waste?"

Ben Southern dismounted, squatted like an Indian, and made a slow, left-to-right study of that ranch down below. Where three great old cottonwood trees stood was a small, adobe spring house. Elsewhere, there was a large, low, mud barn, a bunkhouse with exposed rafter ends, and, close by, the larger, main house.

"Old ranch," he told the others as they, too, got down and stood, looking. He might have made other observations, but a man walked out of the barn leading two horses. The girl was with him. He tied the animals to a rack and slowly, thoughtfully paced around them and back again. The distance was considerable, but Walt Lee said: "I reckon it wasn't such a waste of time after all, Ned."

Tolliver had no comment to make. He tugged down his hat brim and stood like a dark brown statue, just looking and slowly working his jaws.

Captain Southern stood up, dusted his knee, and cocked an eye at the late-day sun. Darkness wouldn't arrive for several hours yet, until about 9:00 in fact, which permitted them plenty of time to familiarize themselves with the countryside.

"Let's go," he said.

They rode eastward for several miles, then southward as far as the little whitewashed cairns of stone that marked the U.S./Mexico border, then due westerly until darkness began to tell, hazing the land with a hot gloominess, and halted where a mortared old stone trough stood beneath a ragged old tree. There, they tanked up their animals, sluiced cool water over their heads and shirt fronts, had a quiet smoke, and finally headed back in the direction of the ranch buildings. They were quiet, scarred men for whom the need of conversation was not a constant thing as it was with other, usually younger men.

Where that low, thick hill showed, darkly bulking on their left, they stopped again. The ranch was less than a mile ahead now. Southern sought, and found, a good place to leave the horses. It was a pair of spidery little paloverde trees.

"Carbines?" Lee asked.

Captain Ben shook his head. Where they were going, if any trouble came, it'd be close up; no need to burden themselves

145

with carbines.

They walked ahead, timing their arrival as they had been doing all afternoon to coincide with full darkness. They were successful; in fact, they were so successful that the low-roofed adobe barn jumped out at them even before they caught the scent of livestock.

There were some pole corrals along the north side of the barn. Evidently whoever had built these buildings had spent a lot of time hauling logs from the far-away mountains because there were no trees suitable for corral-making anywhere around Acton, which was all desert country. Inside those corrals were several horses. The men heard them long before they could discern their silhouettes.

Ben Southern paused. Men who had campaigned against the wiliest of Southwestern Indians learned something from their foemen, if they lived long enough. He waited a long time to be certain how the scent would drift in the stillness before going on. Horses, particularly bored, corralled horses, had a habit of becoming aroused over the smell of strangers. What he particularly wished to avoid was an impromptu meeting with the men at this ranch.

They got to the barn undetected, but it was too dark inside to make out more than which tie stalls held those two horses. While they were considering this fact, Walt Lee felt a familiar shape ahead of him and whispered to the others.

"Here are the saddles and bridles. Have a look."

They were McClellan saddles all right, with the familiar blue blankets and the bridles whose cheek-piece conchos had the letters *U.S.* clearly marked upon them.

Ben Southern went in beside each horse and felt up along the neck, tracing out scar tissue with his finger. The brands were there. He returned to Tolliver and Lee. "So far so good . . .

we now know where their horses are and who's been hiding them."

Lee said: "That girl? Ah, hell . . . a girl wouldn't kill Slattery and O'Casey."

Tolliver, speaking from a more cynical long lifetime of association, said: "How d'you know what that girl'd do? I've known plenty who'd have killed them two for no more'n they had in their pockets."

Southern got between them. "I didn't say the girl was totally responsible. All I said was we know where the horses are and who's hiding them. Maybe her husband or her pappy could tell us more."

"Or the hired hands," assented Ned Tolliver, but Walt Lee had an answer for that.

"What hired hands? Your eyes are used to the dark now . . . look around . . . do you see any other horses stalled in here or any other tack hanging from the saddle pegs?" As Southern and Tolliver looked, Lee crossed his arms and turned with them. When they completed their long look, they were facing the east where the barn's front opening was, and, also, they were facing straight into the double choked twin barrels of a shotgun in the dead-steady hands of a lanky silhouette whose details they could not otherwise discern because of the gloom.

"Drop 'em," the silhouette said briskly, and none of the three men mistook that meaning at all. Tolliver and Lee waited for Captain Ben to decide on their course. Actually there was nothing to decide; that slug gun twenty feet in front of them had made the decision. Ben lifted out his .45 and let it fall. Ned Tolliver grunted and did the same. Walt Lee sighed; he was the least concerned of them all.

"Come out of there . . . head for the main house, and, if you're tired of living, just act cute."

One of the greatest persuaders of all time was the shotgun. It was also one of the most sobering persuaders. Ben Southern strolled forth from the barn, turned, and headed at a slow gait on across where a lamp shown orange past several parlor windows. There was a way to break up this stand-off—as soon as Ned and Walt were past the door, whip around and slam the thing on that shotgun. Of course there was risk, but that wasn't what deterred him; he was curious. Since those U.S. horses down in the barn couldn't offer much help, perhaps the man with the shotgun could. At any rate, he philosophized as he walked into the lighted parlor, the night was young, he and his companions had no place else to go and nothing better to do.

He turned when Ned and Walt entered, and got a shock. It was not a man behind that scatter-gun; it was the girl, only she was taller than he had imagined. He unconsciously removed his hat. So did Walt and Ned. It was wasted gallantry. The girl's violet eyes, nearly black now, did not waver.

"You could've gotten away with it if you'd been a little smarter," she said from the doorway. "Even Indians weren't as crude as you three . . . they lay in wait all day studying the habits of ranch people so they wouldn't be surprised. Every evening I go down to the far corral where I've got a sick horse. If you hadn't been in such a hurry, you could've stolen them without my finding it out until morning."

"Stolen them?" murmured Ben Southern.

"Those cavalry horses you were standing by when I walked in on you. Or didn't you realize those were U.S. critters?" Her full mouth lifted a little at the outer corners. "After daylight came, boys, and you saw those neck brands, you'd have been a long way from here. It would have been difficult to explain where you got U.S. animals whose brands hadn't been vented, if you were seen. The Army is rather hard on horse thieves."

Ned Tolliver rolled his eyes at Captain Southern. Walt Lee was impassive, but his dark eyes shone with irony.

Captain Ben said: "Lady, this is very interesting. What are you doing with U.S. horses? I understand the Army's just as hard-nosed about civilians keeping its horses in barns as it is about men stealing them."

She kept her little mirthless smile. "The law knows I have them . . . you aren't frightening me. Within a day or two soldiers will get here from Fort Brown or Camp Scott to take them off my hands."

"How did they get here, ma'am?"

"Someone riding south in the night left them. I heard riders passing. It was very late. The next morning I went out and there they were."

Ben thoughtfully nodded at her. "Likely story, ma'am, but it'll be hard to prove."

She shifted hold of the shotgun. "Not so hard, cowboy. I was born and raised here. I know all the ranchers in this part of the southern desert. Sheriff Mittan can convince the Army I only found those horses." She put her head a little to one side, scanning Ben Southern skeptically. Her gaze altered, lost a little of its hardness. "Did I make a mistake?" she softly asked him. "Who are you men . . . what were you doing in my barn?"

Ben Southern didn't answer that, for he, too, was interested in this unique meeting. When she spoke, it was with the crisp tone of truthfulness. She also had the look of truthfulness. He turned, ignoring the scatter-gun, went to a chair, and dropped down, lifted his face, and made a long assessment.

She was handsome, although taller than average for a girl, and she had a sureness to her that was more inherent confidence than bravado. "Where are the menfolk?" he inquired. "Your husband or pappy . . . or the riders from the bunkhouse?"

"If you think I can't handle you alone. . . ."

"Lady, I wasn't thinking that at all. We're disarmed and you have a shotgun. A six-year-old kid could handle us three under these circumstances. I was wondering about the menfolk. This is a fairly large ranch."

"I live here alone," she said, throwing the words at him. "My parents are dead and Mex guerillas have just about cleaned me out of cattle." She got that little unamused lilt to her lips again. "If you three were looking for work, instead of trying to steal your way through life, possibly I could use you for a little while. At least until I've finished rounding up the last of my cattle."

Ben Southern gazed at Tolliver and Walt Lee. They gazed right back. Ben said: "Ma'am, you've just hired yourself three range riders." He got up. "And just for the record, we weren't trying to steal those U.S. horses."

V

The girl was uncertain, Southern saw that, and she was anxious about these three prisoners. It would do no good to try to persuade her they were not what she thought, but she had given Ben an opening with that remark about hired riders, so he exploited it by saying: "Suppose you go down and get our guns, miss, and lock us in the bunkhouse tonight. It'll settle things for you, if we're still here in the morning."

She seemed to grow more interested in Ben, which was perhaps the only reason she listened, for his suggestion offered no assurance, once the three of them broke out of the bunkhouse, they wouldn't come to the main house. She said: "Where did you leave your horses?"

He gestured westerly. "Tied in the brush yonder."

She lowered the shotgun. "Go get them and bring them to the hitch rack in front of the house, and, by the way, what are your names?"

Captain Southern guessed her purpose in having them fetch up their animals. One glance would tell whether they needed fresh animals badly enough to steal them or not. "I'm Ben," he said. "This is Ned, and this is Walt." He turned toward the door, reached for the latch, and halted when she spoke again.

"Ben, be careful when you come back."

She didn't mention their guns or the fact that she knew they would go re-arm themselves before going after their animals. He nodded, opened the door, and walked out into the warm, silvery night. They were halfway to the barn before he looked at Ned and Walt. He was grinning.

"She's not a fool," he told the other two, "keeping us under a gun all night, then hoping she could herd us to the sheriff up at Acton included taking a lot of poor risks. She's put the thing in our laps."

"*Humph,*" Tolliver grunted, fishing in a pocket for his tobacco plug. "If we were what she figures, we wouldn't go back."

Lee was thinking past the obvious. He said: "She knows that, Ned. That's why she let us go. An' I'll make you a bet . . . if we kept on goin', she'd be relieved. An' if we go back with our stock like she told us to, she'll be perched in there with the lights out, and her riot-gun primed and cocked."

Walt chuckled. "Got to admire a woman who thinks like a man and who's got her kind of courage."

Ben led them out to their animals and led them back again. They didn't ask him why he had volunteered to ride for the girl or why he hadn't explained to her who they really were, but Ned said, on the walk back: "I'm not sure this is goin' to lead us anywhere, Cap'n."

Southern's reply was succinct. "It's a start, Ned. We've got nothing else to go on . . . just the two horses."

"Yeah, but suppose that lawman she brang out here sends to Fort Brown for someone to come fetch the horses?"

"He won't. He's the one who wrote the colonel at Camp Scott about Slattery and O'Casey. He knows where they came from and where their horses came from. If he reports to Camp

Scott, the colonel will ignore it. He knows what the lady and her lawman friend don't know . . . that the Army's already down here investigating."

Walt was right. When they returned to the house, it was silent and totally dark. They tied their animals at the rack and stood a moment, waiting. When nothing happened, Southern, facing forward, said softly: "Ma'am, you forgot to tell us who we're working for?"

Her answer came evenly: "Alice Clark." She hesitated as though making a long study of both men and horses, then said: "Put them in one of the corrals. There's hay . . . fork some over the fence to them. You can see the bunkhouse . . . bed down over there and we'll talk in the morning."

Ned Tolliver, rhythmically chewing, said dryly: "Miss Alice, there any coffee in the bunkhouse?"

"No!" she exclaimed. "And there'd be no way to cook it if there was. You'll eat in the kitchen in the main house . . . if you're still here in the morning. Good night."

Ned mumbled low, under his breath, loosened his horse, and turned with his companions to head back across the yard. "No wonder she isn't married," he grumbled. "Got a disposition like a buffalo cow at calving time."

They put out their animals, strolled around looking in the other corrals, found two horses outside in other corrals—one stiff as a ramrod—then strolled back over to the adobe bunkhouse.

Inside, the place had that moldy smell that accompanies long vacancy. Walt found a coal-oil lamp. It smoked badly so they had to put it out, trim the wick, relight it, and adjust the flame. There were six wall bunks, two on each of the three walls. The front wall, with the door and two small grimy windows, faced out into the yard. There, they saw a number of initials carved into the adobe. There were even a few full names and the years those long-departed riders had worked on this range. Quite a number of those names were Mexican.

They had no blanket rolls along. "If we're going to stay here," Ned said, "one of us ought to ride back into town and fetch back our stuff, Cap'n."

Southern nodded. "Plenty of time for that, Ned. Tomorrow, maybe, but I've got a feeling in the pit of my stomach that, if just one of us walks out of here and goes down to saddle up, that cussed shotgun is going to meet us again." He looked over at the bunks with their exposed rope springs. "You've slept like a babe under worse circumstances, pick out a bed, and sack out."

They selected their beds but sleep was a long time coming. When Tolliver and Lee finally did drift off, Captain Ben lay a long time staring into the darkness. He had no plan beyond staying close to those two horses. Whatever developed must occur somewhere in the vicinity of the Clark Ranch. If he could pick up the track of those men who had abandoned the cavalry horses, it would help. Also, if the girl heard those men pass in the night, she might also be able to help. The one person he didn't believe could give much assistance was that lawman from Acton. He eventually dropped off.

The summertime desert sun rises very early. So do the people who reside in the desert country, for if there is work to be done, it is ordinarily accomplished before 10:00 A.M. After 10:00, and until sundown, the land writhes under a smoky haze of debilitating heat. The Indians, the Mexicans of the Southwest, and occasionally a wise outlander learn how to live compatibly with the summertime desert, but everyone else leaves it as fast as possible, remains to loathe it with a frustrated passion, or tries to challenge it. For the last there is only defeat; the desert country cannot be coerced.

Ben Southern was already out at the trough washing when

Ned and Walt came ambling up. Neither of them said anything. They washed and went along to care for the livestock, then halted in the doorway of the adobe barn to look around.

Nothing was much different in daylight than in dark as far as landmarks were concerned. Some bizarre fluke of an inscrutable Nature had engineered the underground irrigation of this green spot in the middle of as desolate a waste as any of them had ever seen before. A man had salted this soil with his sweat, too. There were fences and the massive-walled buildings. There was piped water and shade trees. The corrals were stout and horse-high.

"I reckon she comes by it naturally," mumbled Tolliver, meaning the girl at the main house. " 'Way out here, a man'd have to be out of his mind to take a stand, a few years back. Bad enough the cussed Injuns raidin' through, but this close to the line I'd guess he buried his share of Mexicans, too."

"Hell of a place for a cattle outfit, seems to me," confirmed Walt Lee. "If the redskins didn't stick 'em full of arrows, the greasers'd run 'em down over the line in the night."

Ben Southern also had thought these same thoughts earlier. Now he said: "He had to have a good reason. A man wouldn't even be exploring this far south of safety unless he had a good reason."

Ned Tolliver turned and gravely considered Captain Southern. "Ah," he murmured, "a damned renegade who had to stay away from Arizona law, and be close to the line in case he had to make a run for it. Well, well. . . ."

From the house came the girl's strong call. They saw her standing on the rear porch over there with an apron around her middle and her honey-blonde hair down over her shoulders in a cascading soft wave. She was wearing a fresh white blouse, rusty-colored split riding skirt, and high-topped brown boots.

"Bound to be a pistol under that apron," muttered Ned Tolliver. He gazed across the yard a moment, then waggled his head from side to side. "I believe she'd do it, boys . . . I believe, if she set her mind to it, she'd shoot a man."

Ben Southern stepped forth to lead the way. He knew what was on Tolliver's mind, and there thus far was no reason to believe otherwise. Still, he didn't think she had had a hand in it. Not because she was pretty, but simply from a practical standpoint; she couldn't hope to attack a convoy of rifles northward bound by herself, and, as far as he could see, there had been no other men on this ranch in a very long time.

She was there in the kitchen when they trooped in, pulling off their hats. She had her back to them and didn't turn away from her labors at the stove, but casually said over one shoulder: "Sit down . . . the coffee's on and the meat will be ready directly."

They exchanged looks; the shotgun was not in evidence and Ned was wrong about her having a shell belt under the apron. For some reason, she was not the least wary of them. They crossed to the table and dropped down, each of them in his own way puzzling this over in his mind.

She brought the food, set the coffee pot on the table, gazed professionally around, saw that everything was upon the table, then went to an empty place and sat down. The men, recalling civilian manners, passed each dish to her first. They said nothing.

"My brand is Circle C on the right ribs," she said, scarcely looking at any of them, her voice as brisk, as business-like, as before. "My range runs southward to the border, northward four miles, eastward and westward as far as you'd care to ride. But this time of the year you won't have to ride that far . . . when the bunch grass withers, the critters remember the big meadow and drift back toward home." She paused, raised her head, and gave each of them a long, solemn look. "Be careful . . . the Indians are gone but the Mexican brigands infest the southward range. And they aren't all . . . there are renegade Americans down here, too. It's pretty much open country . . . if you get shot, it'll be your own fault."

"Thanks," said Ned Tolliver dryly, pushing back his plate and drawing in his cup of coffee. "I thought we was just to hunt Circle C critters."

"You are. But this isn't the Acton country. Down here men have died by the score, and no one to this day knows whatever became of them, or even where they've been buried."

Ben said: "Why do you stay, if, as you say, they've just about bankrupted you . . . it's not that pretty a country."

She had her strong answer ready for him. "It is to me, mister. I grew up down here. I've never been bothered. Once, the Apaches got me years ago. They took me to their camp, fed me sugared squash, gave me a little doll, and brought me back in the night."

"The guerillas must like you, too," Ben said. "Or is it just your cattle they like?"

She finished eating without answering Ben, without even looking at him until she arose to carry her dishes to the wash bucket. Then she gazed at him, on over to Ned Tolliver, and said: "You're range boss . . . that suit you, Ned?"

He blinked. "Range boss, Miss Alice? Well, but I'm not much of a cowman."

"You're range boss anyway," she stated, throwing another arch glance at Ben Southern. "Time will tell how good you are . . . all three of you. Bring your dishes over and put them in the bucket. Today I'll ride with you until noon to get you started, then I've got to go into Acton about those two cavalry mounts. Let's go."

At the barn, when Walt Lee gallantly offered to rig out her horse, she declined and did the chore herself. Afterward, when they were passing down the southward range in a big swing that would eventually bring them northward, she pointed out landmarks, her broad-brimmed man's hat low across her forehead. She was something none of them had encountered in quite a spell—a self-sufficient woman. What made it more glaring was the fact that she wasn't over twenty-two years of age.

She rode as well as any man, and, when they spotted a little straggle of lean-flanked cows, she saw them first and went after them best. Ben Southern, who was no cowman, saw something that set him to thinking. Out of that little bunch of critters, eighteen in number, only four had calves at their sides, but at least ten more were bagged up. He raised a puzzled glance and caught Alice Clark watching him from beneath her hat brim. He said nothing, though.

They drifted the cattle on over to a fringe of grassy meadow and left them, then struck out northward. They were a mile away when she suddenly drew rein, placed both hands atop the saddle horn, and sat gravely considering her three hired riders. They looked right back.

"Range men, my eye," she finally said scornfully, glancing back and forth. "Walt, how many of those were wet cows?"

Lee put up a hand to pull at his chin. He didn't answer.

She looked at Ned. "Aren't wet cows usually found with their calves?"

Ned chewed without dropping his glance for almost a full twenty seconds, then rolled his eyes around and put them upon Ben Southern.

"You noticed," she said, also staring at Ben. "You saw there were only three calves and there were almost a dozen wet cows. Most men would have said something, Ben. Most range men would have been curious about where the other calves were."

He said: "I was curious."

"But you didn't say anything."

157

Ben relaxed in the saddle. She was a disconcertingly hand-some woman, even when her eyes glowed with dark disdain, as they did now. "Miss Alice, you're the boss. If you're satisfied your cows don't all have calves, then who am I to butt in?"

"I'll tell you," she softly said, swinging her head to include them all. "You're no more range riders than I'm the man in the moon. Outlaws, perhaps . . . renegades, maybe . . . but cowboys . . . definitely no."

"Fire us," said Ben Southern, but she raised her eyebrows at him.

"Fire you? Why should I do that? I need three men. They don't have to be top hands. I couldn't afford top-hand wages, anyway." She paused, turned slightly bitter again, and said: "I think it's better you're exactly what you are. At least you'll probably survive, and cowboys wouldn't . . . not on the south desert." She lifted her hand with the reins in it. "I'll leave you here. Finish looking for cattle and meet me this evening when I get back from Acton." She hooked her horse and loped away northward.

Ned began chewing again. Walt Lee tugged at his chin, look-ing after her. He said: "Cap'n, I never trusted intelligent females. You know why she rode out with us . . . just to satisfy herself we weren't cowboys. Well, she done it. Now you know what she figures? That we're three gun-savvy outlaws on the run."

Southern, looking after her through the dancing distance, pulled a rueful little grin and said: "Come on . . . if we don't find a few more head by evening, she just might put us up against a brick wall."

VI

They were lucky. They found seven more cows within the first half hour, but after that Ben led them back to the ranch in a long lope, heat or no heat. He explained to Walt and Ned that he wanted to find tracks before a wind came along and erased them, or before other tracks overlayed them. The three of them fanned out and proceeded from north to south. It was Ned who met with the initial success. He flagged in the other two and showed them his find.

"I'd say four of 'em, Cap'n. But back a ways there was five. Thing is . . . the fifth critter was being led. It's plain as day. And still farther off, but comin' down the same course, was another horse. I'd say that one was loose and following. Anyway, right here . . . see there . . . that's where two horses split off. Now then, Cap'n, look close. See how the calks dug in? Well, those were cavalry mounts. Look at the other four signs. No calks . . . just plain cowboy cold shoes."

They began riding down those four tracks. Once, where cattle crossed over, they had to waste nearly thirty minutes picking up the trail again. The four horsemen had skirted far around the Clark place, then veered off southeastward.

"Toward Fort Brown, is my guess," opined Walt Lee, where they halted, finally.

Ned said: "Sure, they'll go down there, maybe over to the line to one of the little Mex towns, and loaf. Take turns, maybe, ridin' up close enough each day to spy on the Fort Brown roadway that heads northward toward Acton and Camp Scott."

Ben agreed with most of this, but pushed on farther, even though the other two protested. "Miss Sidewinder'll be gettin' back to the ranch," mumbled Ned Tolliver anxiously, "and, if we aren't there, she's liable to raise hell and push a rock under it."

Ben straightened around and laughed. Ned looked forlorn. Alice Clark had the Indian sign on Tolliver.

They kept to that trail for three more miles. In some places it was scrubbed out. In other places it was as fresh as the day it was made, and always it angled southeastward, which was in the direction of the Mexican border and, also, less southward and more eastward, in the direction of Fort Brown.

"Hold it!" called Walt Lee suddenly, his words bitten off. "Yonder ahead of us crossing downcountry . . . riders."

They headed into the nearest thorny thicket and dismounted. The sun beat upon them unmercifully but they scarcely heeded this intense discomfort.

The riders were misty in the middle distance, heat haze and dark dust partially obscuring them. But there was one characteristic in the Southwest, hazed over or not, that definitely relegated all men into one of four categories—their hats. Soldiers wore beaver-belly colored campaign hats. Cattlemen, range riders, lawmen wore the traditional Stetson of the Southwest. Mexicans wore the exaggerated, huge sombreros of their native land, and Indians wore only headbands.

"Mexicans," said Ben quietly. "Guerilla raiders. I wish we had ten more men with us."

"Suits me that we haven't," muttered Ned Tolliver, wiping sweat off his face and throat. "There's at least thirty of 'em."

That was true. They were in strong force for raiders, and, also, when the bitter lemon-yellow glare struck through the dust, it wickedly reflected off gun metal and the brass casings of bullets worn exposed in bandoleers across each raider's chest.

"Rare bunch of cut-throats," stated Walt Lee, who, like his companions, had campaigned against such men as those invaders many times in past years. "How come the patrols from Fort Brown aren't out an' after that bunch?"

No one answered. Tolliver and Ben Southern were intently studying those horsemen. They were bronzed and lean and wolf-like. Their animals were tucked up, but, also, they were good quality horses. The kind of mounts professional raiders invariably used. One slim man in a short, sweaty *charro* jacket was smoking a crooked cigar. He seemed to be the leader. Just before the band passed along, a rider eased up and said something to the man with the cigar. He laughed and turned his head to call out something to the others. They all laughed.

"Very funny," growled Tolliver, expectorating amber and looking down his nose in powerful distaste. "They've got a real grisly sense of humor, those bloody-hand bucks. Cap'n, what you figure we ought to do?"

Ben neither answered nor looked around until the last guerilla had slouched past and the dust was beginning to settle along the back trail. Then he turned and said simply: "Let's get back to the ranch."

They rode slowly because the heat was a punishing weight for their animals as well as for themselves. It was late in the afternoon before they even came in sight of the buildings. It was evening before they skirted around to hit the barn from the west, and rode inside to step stiffly down and throw off their outfits. From a shadowy tie stall Alice Clark raised up and turned. She, too, was off-saddling.

"I thought you'd be in before this," she said, making each of them whip around because they hadn't been able to see her until she had risen up and spoken. She looked at their faces. "What's the matter . . . did you run into some ghosts?"

Ben Southern went back to off-saddling. "Pretty lively-looking crew of ghosts," he stated, and went forward to remove the bridle.

Alice came out of the stall, went forward a little distance the better to see his expression in the gloom, and said: "Oh? *Gringos* or *ladrónes?*"

Ben paused to gaze over at her. "Mexicans," he said. "Or are they all *ladrónes?*"

She came right back at him. "If there were more than five, they were *ladrónes* . . . outlaws."

Ned Tolliver cleared his throat. "Then they was *ladrónes!*" he

161

exclaimed with a strong nod of his head. "There were thirty of them."

She stood a moment, watching the three of them, then turned upon her heel, went as far as the doorway, looked back long enough to say—"Supper in a half hour."—and walked off.

Ben led his horse out to turn it into a corral. He stopped to consider her as she moved over closer to the main house. He was still standing like that when Ned and Walt Lee came along to turn out their animals. "Got somethin' on her mind," opined Walt. "I know women and. . . ."

"You know women!" exclaimed Tolliver witheringly. "Walter, you've never even seen one like her before, let alone know anything about them." Tolliver heaved a loud grunt, turned, and stalked away.

Walt looked at Ben with raised eyebrows. When Ben said nothing, Walt hitched up his shoulders and went hiking along in Tolliver's wake.

After they had cared for their animals and washed up at the trough, Walter made a smoke in the settling gloom of a hot dusk, lit up, and expansively exhaled. "Were they returning from a raid, I wonder," he softly murmured, thinking of those Mexican horsemen. "They sure didn't act like men who'd been in a fight."

"Their kind don't fight if they can skulk aroun' in the night for their dirty work," growled Ned Tolliver, slicing off a fresh cud from his tobacco plug. "What say, Cap'n . . . am I right?"

Ben shrugged. Speculation along these lines solved nothing and had a habit of dragging on endlessly. He led them over to the rear of the house and on into the kitchen, where Alice turned to look briefly, then went back to work at the stove. Her face was flushed from heat but she had, Ben had noticed, a way of appearing cool in spite of discomfort.

"Found a few more head," he said, stepping to a chair at the table and dropping down where he could see her profile. "But if you have very many head, they sure aren't on the west or south ranges."

"Or the east range," she said, without turning. "You forgot to mention that you'd ridden over there."

Ned looked at Walt. They both looked at Captain Ben. He was watching the girl's back, his face impassive but his eyes kindling with a hard, fresh light. He said sardonically: "You must've gotten back from Acton early."

She brought over two plates, one for Ned, one for Walt. She returned to the stove and turned her back upon them again. "What I went into town for didn't take long . . . Captain."

All three men looked up at her. She faced them, two more plates in her hands. She bored Ben with a flinty stare, saying nothing, just waiting. But he made no comment, so she finally took him his plate and returned to the far end of the table with her own plate, sat down, and said: "It was a good guess, wasn't it . . . Captain?"

Ben bent to eat, still silent. Ned and Walt looked from one of them to the other, expecting something to explode out of this. She was decidedly antagonistic while Captain Ben was patently being very careful.

"You weren't cowboys, that was very obvious, Captain. In Acton it wasn't hard to discover you weren't wanted men. Sheriff Mittan went through the piles of Wanted posters with me. He wrote the commandant at Camp Scott over a week back. The first new arrivals in town since the killing of those two soldiers rode down from the north . . . from the direction of Camp Scott . . . and even Sheriff Mittan said there was something that troubled him about you three when I described you. Soldiers. Three soldiers with the Army stamp on them as plain as day."

Tolliver was looking at her with profound respect. Walt Lee

was also impressed. Ben Southern ate slowly and only looked down the table when the silence had stretched to its maximum limit.

"It sounds like a crime, the way you say it, Miss Alice."

"No," she shot right back a trifle hotly, "but you didn't have to work so hard to fool me. I'm not a *ladróna.*"

He raised his brows, saying softly: "Oh? Well, that's reassuring. But if you were, it wouldn't be the first time a lovely woman was involved in the death of soldiers."

She started to retort, then stopped, abruptly dropped her eyes, raised them again, and said: "You . . . suspected . . . me?"

"You had the two horses, didn't you? There are two Army saddles, bridles, and blankets out there in your barn."

"But you tracked those men this afternoon."

"Yes," he assented, holding her attention with his steady stare. "But why did you spy on us, if you didn't have some kind of an interest?"

"Because," she threw at him, "I wasn't sure you three weren't the killers."

"There were four of them, ma'am."

"The fourth one could be anywhere, Captain. I didn't know any more than you did. I did know you sneaked into my barn in the night to look over those U.S. horses. I also found out your own animals are up at the livery barn in Acton and that the three of you checked into the boarding house . . . under different first names than you gave me. What would you have thought, Captain?"

Ben resumed eating. There was a hard little twinkle in his eyes. "Maybe the same thing you thought," he conceded. "All right. I'm Captain Ben Southern from Camp Scott. This is Private Walt Lee and that is Sergeant Ned Tolliver. Now you answer a question for me . . . why would those murderers leave the horses here at your ranch?"

"Sheriff Mittan has an idea," she said, her voice softening slightly toward him. "So they would be found down here and all attention would be diverted from some other place."

He thought on that a moment. "The only other place that could be of interest to the killers of Slattery and O'Casey would be Fort Brown, and no four men alive would dare attack Fort Brown without an awful lot of help. There are three companies of dragoons down there."

"And how many," she asked, "will be detached to ride escort when those rifles start northward for Camp Scott, Captain?"

He finished with his meal and leaned back. "Sheriff Mittan talks a lot," he murmured. "Who else has he told about the rifles, I wonder?"

"What difference does that make . . . the important thing is that the men you don't want to know are the ones who *do* know." She, too, settled back from the table.

Walt and Ned sparingly ate; they were too interested in this exchange to be diverted by food. Ben ignored her question and turned to gaze at Tolliver. "Unless," he said very quietly, "those guerillas we saw, who were also heading south toward the border, were on their way to a meeting with the four renegades who killed O'Casey and Slattery. In that case . . . everything becomes a lot clearer."

Tolliver rolled his eyes. "Thirty brigands . . . plus four *gringo* renegades . . . hell, Cap'n . . . excuse me, ma'am . . . heck, Cap'n, that'd be about the same number that'd escort the gun wagons northward."

Walt Lee, picking up the fresh train of thought, added another admonition. "Thirty-four guerillas hiding in the underbrush along the route would be the equal to a whole blessed regiment, against twenty-five or thirty unsuspectin' escort riders from Fort Brown. Captain, what's the answer?"

"It's simple enough," Southern said. "Those guns don't leave

Fort Brown until I send word to roll out with them. Those were my orders from the colonel before we pulled out, and he was to send a letter to the Fort Brown commandant to that effect."

Ned Tolliver heaved a mighty sigh of relief and reached for his cup of coffee. "Lord o' mercy," he breathed, and drank deeply before putting the cup aside.

But Alice Clark wasn't through. She said—"I should thank you for your trust, Captain Southern."—and stiffly arose from the table and left the room, her head high.

Walt Lee waited until they could no longer hear her footfalls, then breathed a quiet oath. "What'd it take to tame that one, I wonder, boys?"

They left the house for their after-supper smoke and quiet pre-bedtime conversation. They had fresh thoughts to occupy them, but they still had nothing tangible.

VII

The following morning Ned left the ranch bound for Acton. He meant to retrieve their own horses, fetch their bedrolls, and return to the ranch before nightfall.

Ben and Walt Lee rode the range to the northeast. Ben had some notion he wished to check out. Every now and then he would stop, turn, and keep a steady vigil on the back trail. But each time the land lay empty and dustless.

Finally Walt said: "Cap'n, if you figure she's spyin' on us, why not set a trap an' let her ride into it?"

Southern nodded. "We'll do that, Walt, but not just yet. I want to be over in the east a goodly distance first."

If Lee wondered at this, he did not let on. They rode until the sun was a half hour shy of its meridian—the heat was a breathless pall over the desert—then dipped down into a brushy arroyo and dismounted to wait. Each had a canteen and each moistened their lips. It was cooler in the arroyo because the sun only struck straight down into it for one hour at noontime, but it was also inhabited by scorpions and hairy tarantulas, and horned toads. There was even a sluggish, very deadly Gila monster waddling along, who cocked a lidless, fishy eye at them.

Ben was scanning the land on eastward when Walt Lee let off a soft little sigh. Ben turned back and walked over. Walt shook his head as though in disappointment and pointed southwestward where a rider was poking along.

"Got to have a damned good reason for ridin' out in weather like this, Cap'n," Walt said, lowering his arm. "A real good reason. What's her game?"

Ben stared but did not reply. The rider was still nearly a mile away; it was difficult to recognize either the horse or the person astride it. Still, this was a huge country. It wasn't impossible that someone else should happen along riding the same time of day and the identical direction he and Private Lee were riding, but it surely was unlikely. Coincidences of course happened, but not this perfectly.

He stepped back from the lip of their arroyo, frowning. It only made it harder to believe the things she had told them, to find her doing this tracking by stealth. The two U.S. horses in her barn, for instance; last night he had believed her simply because she had said how four riders had left the horses there. To clinch it, he had found the tracks of those four. But now, all of a sudden, it came to him that those four hadn't slunk by in the darkness, abandoning two Army mounts. They had left the horses there *with her full knowledge* for some purpose.

"Hey, Captain . . . she's topped out there behind a big bush."

Walt turned and leaned upon the crumbly bank beside Lee, looking back. The haze was increasing as the heat rolled up off the earth in sluggish waves. There was no sign of her. Walt Lee pointed out the particular big bush and the pair of them watched it for a long time before heaving up out of their arroyo and walking back.

She wasn't there. She had obviously detected something up ahead, had gotten in behind the brush for a while, then had mounted up, reversed her course, and gone riding back the way she had come.

Walt swore with strong feeling and mopped off sweat. Ben studied the tracks for a long time, saying nothing. They eventually returned, got astride, rode up out of their arroyo, and reined off southward. After they had covered a considerable distance and found a seepage spring where cottonwoods grew, where they watered their horses, Ben said: "Something's wrong here, Walt. She's good at reading signs."

"Well, what of that . . . she couldn't have known we were down in that arroyo waiting."

"I think she could. She made out the places back down our trail where I halted and faced around every once in a while to see if we were being followed. Well, from that a person wouldn't have to be half as smart as she is to figure out that somewhere on ahead there was a trap."

Walt Lee made a smoke and lolled in the breathless cottonwood shade. "I don't understand the half of what's going on," he said through an exhaled blue cloud. "Why not just go back and sweat it out of her? Cap'n, if there's funny business going on, she could be settin' us up to get killed."

Ben nodded and went over to his horse. "She could at that, Walt," he murmured. "She could at that. Since last night she knows who we are. If she's on the other side, she'd pass the word some way. If there's one thing border jumpers don't like, it's the Army. Let's head for home."

They rode through the bitter heat haze with eyes slitted and their interest upon the tracks of that horseman who had almost walked into their trap, but not quite. For almost two hours they went along, now and then commenting upon the tracks, now and then pausing to throw a long look out and around. It was during one of these latter times when Ben Southern reined up and grunted for Lee to do the same. They were by then not very far from the Clark Ranch.

"Rider," muttered Lee. "Say . . . that's Tolliver. I've ridden in too many formations and on too many details with him not to be sure of that."

"Two riders," corrected Captain Southern. "Wait until they pass through the brush and back out into open country again. You'll see the other one."

Southern was right. There were two horsemen. One of them unmistakably was Ned Tolliver. The other one, after concentrating hard upon the identification, they saw was Alice Clark.

Walt was nonplussed. "How come?" he mumbled. "She must've pushed that old pony to get northward and find Ned to ride back with him like this."

Southern said nothing. He was beginning to look worried. They rode along until the others saw them and halted. As they came up, the captain and Walt Lee simultaneously noticed something intriguing. Alice Clark's horse was dry as a bone; no one had run that animal. It wasn't even sweating as much as the horses Ben and Walt Lee were riding.

Ned Tolliver disentangled some lead ropes and passed them over, one to Captain Southern, one to Walter Lee. On the other end were their saddle animals. Also, Ned patted the bedrolls stacked like cordwood behind his saddle.

"Cuts off the breeze," he said. "But I'll pack 'em the rest of the way."

Until now Alice Clark hadn't spoken a word. Now she did, eyeing Ben and Walt. "You're quite a way from the ranch, aren't you, boys?"

Walt smoothly said: "Yes'm . . . and there just might be stray Clark critters over here, too. That's what you hired us to do for you, isn't it, round up Clark critters?"

She didn't answer.

They rode along through the shimmering, brassy afternoon without much to say to one another even after the ranch showed ahead, low on the sooty desert. Captain Ben was particularly taciturn. When any of the others spoke, he answered with a grunt if he answered at all.

At the ranch, the moment Alice Clark left the barn for the main house, Ben jumped Ned Tolliver. "Where did you meet her on your way back?" he demanded.

Ned raised his eyebrows. "Where? Why, she was just south of town when I come ridin' out."

"Couldn't have been," stated Walt Lee emphatically. "Ned, she done tricked you somehow. That gal was east of the trail where we met you, one hour back, an' she was trackin' me an' the cap'n."

Tolliver chewed a moment, gazed from one of his companions to the other, and slowly brought his bushy brows downward and inward. "What in the hell are you . . . ? Say, you boys been out in the sun all afternoon? I tell you, damn it all, Miss Alice was leavin' Acton about the same time I was. We met up not more'n a mile below town, southward. And that's a cussed ten miles from where she an' I met you two, and no horse livin' could cover those ten miles in the kind of time you are intimating she covered them in."

Walt got splotchy in the face. His dark eyes smoldered toward scowling Ned Tolliver. He opened his mouth to say something, but Ben Southern raised a hand.

"*Two* of them?" Ben asked, looking left and right, and dropped his hand. "Could there be two women?"

For a long time the others were quiet, studying this suggestion. Walt said: "Cap'n, you an' I both saw her. *She* was a woman. A regular female woman."

Ned Tolliver chewed and looked down his nose at Lee. "Most female women are *shes*," he muttered. "Say, Captain, just what the hell are we involved . . . ?"

"Ned, what'd she do in town?" Captain Southern asked.

Tolliver shook his head. "Like I told you, I met her south of town."

"But she was there the same time you were. Acton's not that big a place, Ned. If you'd looked around, you'd have seen her."

"Mebbe, Captain, only I went there to get the horses an' the bedrolls, an', when I left the ranch, she was still here without lookin' like she'd be anywhere else, so I wasn't expectin' to see her, and I didn't see her."

"All right, Ned. Then tell me this . . . what did she talk about on the ride back?"

Tolliver averted his head, spat, turned back, and said: "You. Mostly she asked questions about you . . . had you been on the frontier long . . . had I served under you in any fights . . . how old was you . . . where did you originally come from. . . . I damned near told her the stork brought you. I'm not much of a hand at talkin' about other folks." Tolliver shifted his cud, cleared his throat, leaned over to peer outside, straightened back up, and said: "Two women?" It had just hit him what Walt and Captain Ben were puzzling over. "What the hell kind of sense does that make?"

Ben straightened up. "None," he answered. "Let's go get cleaned up. She'll be callin' us to eat directly."

They sauntered over to the water trough, put aside their hats, peeled off shirts and neckerchiefs, and plunged tanned arms up to the shoulder in cool water. The westward sky was a blaze of scarlet brilliance where the sun had touched down and violently exploded without a sound, drenching the southward desert in dull, red-rusty light. Over at the corrals horses rolled and grunted, scuffed dust, and vigorously blew their noses.

Ben finished first, eased down upon the side of the trough to let evaporation cool his hide, and made a smoke that he lit with a match Walt handed him. "Interesting world down here," he mused without bothering to elaborate what he was referring to, sucked back a deep-down inhalation, and tilted his head to let the smoke rise back up again. "I think I'm going to have to ride into Acton, maybe tomorrow, and get some things straightened out with that lawman."

"Like does she have a sister," mumbled Ned Tolliver, groping for his salt-stiff faded shirt. "And what her background is . . . because I'm beginnin' to smell a rat."

Walt whipped his body sideways to hurl off excess water. "You could just walk in over there and ask her, you know. Just because she's pretty don't mean she couldn't tell the truth. It's worth the effort if you ask me. Before I'd make that hot ride into Acton, I'd sure give it a whirl."

Tolliver, in the act of buttoning his shirt, suddenly straightened around eastward. "Hey," he muttered. "Listen you two."

It was the soft, distant drum roll of approaching horsemen. In desert late evening and early dawn, sounds carried best. They all gazed off eastward. It was too dark, however, to make out dust, and, if there was discernible movement out there, that also was obscured by the fading, rusty light.

"Sounds like a big patrol," stated Ned, thinking as training and long-time environment had taught him to think. "Captain, sounds like they're damned near in company strength."

Ben said nothing. There was no mistaking the fact that those horsemen, whoever they were, had the Clark place as their destination. It took no great amount of thought to arrive at that conclusion, either; there wasn't another ranch anywhere around. All three of them knew that; they had ridden the range sufficiently the past few days to be certain of it.

Finally Ben said: "Those aren't troopers. Listen to them."

Walt Lee picked up his hat, dropped it atop his head, and turned toward the house. "Those danged Mexicans, maybe," he murmured, "If it's not troopers and not ranchers, then standin' out here like this could make targets of us."

Lee had scarcely finished speaking when they distinctly heard those oncoming riders split away from one another, fanning out. At once Ben Southern growled an order, turned, and started sprinting across the yard toward the main house where a solitary orange light shone from the kitchen. Ned and Walt loped along in his wake. They had a considerable distance to cover, and, because they had been too engrossed in looking and speculating, they very nearly did not make it.

The riders rocketed out of the darkness into the yard from three simultaneous directions. Several of them saw the running dark shapes heading for the house and called out. Guns exploded, flame lanced southward in the direction of the main house, and Walt Lee's hat suddenly took wing, soared far ahead, struck a *ramada* post, and fell like a gunshot bird. Walt jumped up and lit down running harder than ever. He passed Ned Tolliver and almost passed Ben Southern. What slowed him, what startled all three of them, was Alice Clark. She flung open the front door, stepped through, threw up her shotgun, and let fly with first one barrel, then the second barrel.

The noise was deafening. The muzzle blast, to one side of the racing men but still ahead of them, was blinding. And the sudden loud scream of someone back down the yard added to all the other confusion.

They made it into the house. Ben caught the girl's arm as he ran past and dragged her inside, too. Ned Tolliver slammed and barred the door, then sprang away from it as two slugs struck hard into the hardened oak.

Outside, one powerful voice was calling orders. Guns continued to explode out there. Somewhere a window tinkled.

Ben called to Walt: "Go douse that kitchen light and keep watch on that side!"

VIII

Alice brought them carbines and ammunition. She reloaded her scatter-gun, but when she would have sidled up to a window, Ben Southern urgently caught her shoulder, spinning her roughly away. "You get in front of me one more time," he shouted over the crash of joined battle, "and I'll give you what for!"

There were more than fifteen attackers, but how many more it was not possible to discern because the attackers were constantly moving. From the kitchen Walt Lee fired often, indicating some of them were sneaking in close. Twice Ben darted to the room. Both times Walt shook his head and smiled, indicating he didn't need any reinforcements.

It was a fierce fight. The attackers had come expressly for this purpose; there was no doubt about that. But what motivated them, who they were, or even why they had attacked the Clark place, was a pure mystery to Ben Southern. He didn't have much time for speculative thought, though; the attackers were bold and aggressive. Some of them were in the barn; others were over by the bunkhouse. The remainder of them were pushing the attack from out in the yonder darkness, firing and moving in closer and firing again. They seemed both sure of themselves and confident of the outcome.

There were a number of advantages for Ben and his besieged companions. He was a seasoned soldier and took fullest advantage of each one. In another place, where homes and barns were made of wood, it would have been relatively simple for his enemies to burn them out and shoot them down by the backgrounding fire. Here, where every structure was adobe, nothing would burn. Additionally the main house was a veritable fortress. Not only were the walls three feet thick—stout enough to stop a cannonball—but also each window was barred with steel—a legacy from Apache days.

Unless the attackers out there could get in close enough to poke their guns inside, they were still going to be pushing their attack come daylight, which was what Ben was praying might happen. If they were still out in the yard after sunup, no matter how many of them there were, they were going to be at a disadvantage, for the defenders could then see who they were and where they were, without having to be exposed themselves.

When Ned strolled over during a brief lull to talk, Ben told him they just might come out of this with whole hides if they could prevent the attackers from getting under the outside walls. Tolliver, the old campaigner, was undismayed. He went on out into the kitchen to see how Walt was coming along.

The parlor—the entire interior of the house—smelled powerfully of burned gunpowder. It was occasionally lighted with gun flashes, too. Bullet pocks showed up pale, here and there, where high-flying slugs had come through the smashed windows.

Ben was reloading when Alice Clark crawled up and knelt at his side with a fresh box of .30-30 shells. "They're getting the worst of it," she gravely said, gazing straight at him. "I'm glad you three turned out to be what you are."

He finished with the carbine and raised his face. "Wish I could say the same about you," he muttered, and twisted to listen. Outside, the gunfire had dwindled down to an infrequent solitary shot. "They're up to something." He started to rise up.

She put out a hand to detain him. "They're resourceful," she murmured.

He raised an eyebrow. "Are they? Maybe, when this is over, you'll tell us what this is all about."

She lingered a moment longer, then picked up her shotgun and sidled away without answering. He watched her briefly, wondering, but outside someone was snarling orders, which diverted him. Sometimes that angry masculine voice spoke flawless Spanish, sometimes flawless English. Ben knew enough Spanish to be interested—there was no accent, which was extremely rare. If a man matured speaking one language or the other, he invariably had an accent when he spoke the other tongue. That chieftain out there, or whatever he was, could have been Mexican or American; it was impossible to tell from his talk which he was.

But there was no mistaking his resolve. He was bitter over his losses and the ferocity of those who opposed him inside the house. He was also determined everyone in that house should die. Ben made out just enough of his orders to understand his determination.

Ned returned from the kitchen, impassively set a cup of cold, black coffee beside Ben, walked on over across the room where Alice was darkly silhouetted, and handed her a cup, too. She murmured her thanks, and Ned, still without a word, resumed his vigil near the door.

"How's Walt?" Ben asked.

"All right," Tolliver replied, peering past a splintered window jamb. "Whoever that bunch is out there, Cap'n, unless they don't care about their losses, they're damned fools to keep this up. If I was their chieftain, I'd haul off, lie out there in the brush, an' pick us off one at a time in broad daylight like Injuns'd do. This is crazy."

Alice said softly: "He knows what he's doing. He always knows what he's doing."

Both Ben and Ned looked over where she was gloomily silhouetted, neither of them saying a word, both their faces calmly, sweatily thoughtful.

It became totally quiet outside. Ben cautiously got upright to peer out. The yard seemed empty. Star shine lent an unreal, eerie softness to the lethal night. A man called out, his voice hard, his words clipped off short as though he were holding himself in.

"You men in there . . . come out! You've made a good fight. You've done all you can do. Now come out!"

Ned Tolliver muttered something indistinguishable, shifted stance, and dragged his cocked carbine along a wooden sill making the only sound. Ben pinpointed the sound of that voice; it was down by the barn.

"Listen, in there. You, too, Alice. You listen good. If you come out, all but one of you can ride off. If you don't come out, we'll storm the place and kill every damned one of you. Think that over. One stays and the other three can go free. Otherwise, all four of you die. You've got five minutes to talk it over."

Ben leaned his carbine against the wall. Ned, too, was beginning to look around where Alice stood, her face a pale oval in the darkness. Ben said: "Who is he? He knows you, Miss Clark. Who is he and which one of us does he want?"

She said in a rough whisper: "He wants you, Captain." She stepped out of the formless shadows and halted where she could see Ben and Ned Tolliver. "He knows who you are."

"Much obliged," growled Ben. "You've been busy, lady."

"No. It wasn't me. You couldn't have kept your identity secret anyway. He always finds things out. He won't keep his word, though, if you're thinking of walking out there to save the rest of us. He can't keep it . . . not now. If he let us go, we could reach Acton before he could take you to Fort Brown where he'd force you to give the order for the guns to be sent north."

Ben and Ned exchanged a glance. Tolliver lifted his shoulders and dropped them. He didn't understand how or why Alice Clark knew so much. Ben repeated his earlier question.

"Who is he?"

"They call him El Vengador . . . the avenger."

"Mex?" growled Tolliver.

She answered that quickly. "No. He's an American. He is . . . my brother."

Tolliver's jaws stopped grinding. Ben Southern gazed straight at her. After an interval of hard silence he said: "I see . . . things are beginning to make sense. Yesterday, when you said you were going to Acton, then you trailed us southeastward, I wondered. Today . . . I don't know how . . . but you trailed us again. Ned says you didn't, but Walt and I saw you."

"No," she murmured. "You saw him. It was a disguise. Don't ask me why because I don't know. Perhaps to make certain who you were. After he was sure. . . ." She made a little fluttery gesture. "He brought back his whole crew and attacked. Captain, he'll get those guns. He's been riding with the revolutionists in Mexico for two years now. He's one of their high officers."

"*Ahhh*," murmured Ned Tolliver. "A renegade." He avoided looking at the handsome girl, turned instead, and peered out into the quiet yard, jaws rhythmically moving again. "The worst kind."

Ben stepped back to scoop up his carbine. He had nothing to say, either, until he had also made a survey of the empty yonder night. Then he spoke almost casually to her. "He'll be the one responsible for killing two soldiers. You'll have known that. Why didn't you tell Sheriff Mittan?"

She faltered slightly in her whispered reply. "I didn't . . . have to. Sheriff Mittan knew."

Ben looked quickly around. "But he did nothing."

"Captain, you don't understand. There wasn't anything Sheriff Mittan could do. El Vengador has spies everywhere. That's why I said a moment ago he always finds things out. If the sheriff had gotten up a posse . . . if he'd gone down into the desert after my brother . . . he not only wouldn't have ever seen him, but, as he told me yesterday, El Vengador probably would have doubled back and hit Acton or some of the northward ranches."

"So Mittan sits and does nothing."

"No, Captain, he did something. We talked again today. He told me he was going to ride down to Fort Brown tonight, when it got good and dark, and warn the commander down there. Try and get the Army to join him in cornering my brother."

Ned Tolliver sniffed. "Some cornering job," he muttered. "I don't know where the sheriff is or the Fort Brown detail, ma'am, but I can sure tell you for a fact your brother ain't bein' bothered by either of them right this minute."

From the shadowy night over by the mud barn that same clipped, tough voice sang out again: "Time's up! Are you coming out or not?"

Ben didn't reply to the question. Instead, he called back, saying: "Answer a question for me, mister . . . how'd you know who was here with your sister?"

The answer was slightly delayed as though Alice Clark's renegade brother considered it briefly before replying. "No trouble there, Captain. Soldiers are soldiers. North of the border or south of it . . . they like to drink. For a few pieces of gold spent on liquor, they'll loosen up."

"That's no answer!" called back Ben.

The outlaw chieftain laughed. "All right, Captain, I'll make it plainer. There are three officers up at Camp Scott. A colonel, a captain, a lieutenant. Yesterday a spy sent me word that the captain and two enlisted men, one a tough old tobacco-chewing sergeant, are no longer up there riding patrol. That's all I had to know to be certain that fool Mittan had written your commandant his two messengers had been killed. Today, one of my men saw you riding out. Another one of my men got up a

179

disguise and trailed you to make certain. I'd have caught you then, Captain, except that, when my man got back and I rode up, you'd come back to the ranch. Any more questions, *Capitán?*"

"One!" exclaimed Ben Southern. "If you think you can storm this adobe house against three carbines and a shotgun, come ahead."

For another long interval there was silence. Ned rolled his eyes around at Captain Southern. From the kitchen doorway Walt Lee appeared. "Hey!" he called in a hoarse whisper. "I saw some of 'em ride out behind the barn on horseback, heading southward."

Ben nodded, told Lee to get back to his post, and stepped in closer to the shattered front window to look out. There wasn't a sound out there, and, try as he could, he could not make out any movement, either. It didn't stand to reason, after all his vaunted confidence, that El Vengador was pulling out. Unless. . . .

"Hey Cap'n," Lee hissed again from the kitchen doorway. "There's a rattle of riders comin' in from the east. You reckon it's more of them?"

Ben put down his carbine, crossed over into the kitchen, and halted near a shattered east-wall window to listen carefully. Renegades didn't ride with the clank of saber scabbards or with the measured cadence of horse soldiers. He stepped back, looked around the shot-up kitchen, and said: "Better put some coffee on, Walt. It's troopers."

Back in the parlor, Ned Tolliver had also picked up the familiar clatter. He was imperturbably whittling off a fresh cud from his cut plug when Ben returned. All he said was: "I reckon Sheriff Mittan made good time an' got through."

Ben nodded. Inadvertently he and Alice Clark, Ned and Walt, had given Mittan exactly the relief he needed; as long as El Vengador was occupied attacking the Clark Ranch, his men wouldn't be skulking the desert country between Acton and Fort Brown.

Alice Clark put aside her shotgun, walked over to Tolliver, and said: "I'm glad you were on our side." She ignored Ben Southern when she went on past out into the kitchen. Ned pouched the fresh cud into his right cheek, tongued it into position, and soberly eyed his captain.

"Odd thing about females," he said. "The smart ones always seem to favor us older, more mature men, Cap'n. You ever notice that?"

Southern didn't reply. He moved to the wall, picked up his carbine, passed around Ned to the front door, and lay a light hand upon the drawbar. Then he said: "Sergeant, I think we'll set a little trap for Mister El Vengador. I think I'll authorize the movement of those rifles from Fort Brown up to Camp Scott."

Tolliver ruminated and gazed at Southern and didn't respond until the sound of someone approaching from the east ripped out a sharp order for skirmishers to advance. Then he said: "Cap'n Ben, whatever you think of her, remember two things. Her brother would have killed her the same as he'd have killed us. An' one other thing . . . she's been on our side right from the start. She could've tipped him off . . . she didn't."

IX

The Fort Brown detail consisted of twenty men and Sheriff Ed Mittan. The officer in charge was a ruddy-faced 1st lieutenant with a fierce dragoon moustache that made him appear older than he actually was. His name was Lieutenant Charles Johnson. When he halted out front and gazed from the saddle around the yard, then to the four stiffly standing, silent people upon the porch, he gave that splendid moustache of his a hard tug, stepped down, flung the reins to an enlisted man, and brushed his hat in Alice Clark's direction with gauntleted hands.

"Pleasure to find you're still alive, ma'am," he said, then turned briskly toward Ben Southern. "Who are you, sir, and what happened here tonight?"

Ben answered dryly. "Captain Ben Southern from Camp Scott. The man on my left is Private Walt Lee. The man on my right is Sergeant Ned Tolliver. As for what happened here, Lieutenant, I think Miss Clark can answer that better than I can. I can't even give you an accurate accounting of their numbers, except to say there were more than a dozen of them."

"El Vengador!" exclaimed the Fort Brown officer, and turned. "Sergeant," he spoke out, addressing a lean, slightly stooped older man behind him. "Detail horse guards, then survey the place. Any dead ones you may find, have them dragged into the barn. Any live ones . . . patch up and hold under guard."

Ned Tolliver turned his head to give Ben Southern a droll look. At Camp Scott they weren't so full of spit-and-polish as this Fort Brown detachment and its officer were.

Sheriff Mittan walked up and stopped close to Alice. He murmured something low to her. She gave him a negative head-shake.

Lieutenant Johnson stowed the gauntlets in his belt, gave Ben a little salute, then glanced along the front of the house. "Quite a little battle," he said. "One thing you can say about these old desert ranches . . . they were built to withstand just such attacks."

Walter Lee said: "Coffee's on in the kitchen, Lieutenant, if you'd care for some."

Johnson's big white teeth dully shone beneath his moustache. "First pleasant thing I've heard all day, gentlemen," he boomed out. "Captain, after you, sir."

Ben stepped aside, saying: "No thanks, I just had a cup. But go ahead, Lieutenant, I want to talk to Sheriff Mittan anyway."

Walt entered the house with the lieutenant. Ben turned toward Alice Clark and Ed Mittan. Ned Tolliver planted his legs wide, leaned upon his carbine, chewed his cud, and watched the Fort Brown detachment criss-crossing the yard. There was one dead one not a hundred feet away—that was the first casualty, brought low when the renegade had been struck by Alice Clark's shotgun.

Ben and the lawman exchanged an appraising long look. Mittan said: "Well, I figured you three might be something other than what you made out to be, when you rode into town day before yesterday, Captain. There's a certain stamp the Army puts on its men."

Southern let that pass. "Tell me why El Vengador rides around your territory attacking ranches when he feels like it, Sheriff."

Alice's head snapped up. She gave Ben a bitter glance, but Ed Mittan spoke before she could say whatever it was she might have said. "Captain, the Army's down here, too, you know, and the Army hasn't nailed him, either." Mittan took in an unsteady breath, let it out slowly, then changed his way of speaking. "He doesn't raid ranches, Captain. His specialty is U.S. soldiers."

"Like O'Casey and Slattery?"

Mittan nodded. "Yes, sir. An' what makes it so cussed hard is that he's got about as many Yank renegades riding with him as he has greasers. They were the ones who steered your two Camp Scott messengers into that blind cañon, then massacred them to find out about the shipment of guns."

Ben removed his hat, wiped off sweat, resettled the hat, and said: "Something about that affair intrigues me, Sheriff . . . why did he leave the opened letter about the guns on those messengers?"

"Can't say, Captain. I'll tell you what I think. I think if it'd been El Vengador himself, he wouldn't have done it so crude-like at all. He'd have gotten those two drunk, let 'em pass out, read the letter, stuck it back into their pockets, and no one'd ever have been the wiser . . . until the wagons with your guns rolled out."

"I see."

"It's only a guess," stressed the lawman. "He had some fellers spyin' in Acton. They saw the soldiers, heard or guessed they were from Fort Brown, figured they were couriers, and you know the rest of it." Mittan stopped speaking, gazed at Alice, and, when she nodded, he said: "This El Vengador is as venomous as a sidewinder. I've known of him for a long time, Captain, but, until day before yesterday when I met this young lady and listened to her story, I had no idea he was an Arizonan. I always sort of figured he had to be a Mex."

That lean, stooped Fort Brown sergeant ambled up, grounded his carbine, and saluted. "Cap'n," he drawled, "there's three dead ones. Two was laid out in the barn, the other one was nigh cut in two with a scatter-gun. All three are Mexicans. You care to look at 'em?"

Ned Tolliver straightened up. "I'll go," he said to Ben. "Chances are we wouldn't know 'em anyway, Cap'n."

As Tolliver and the other non-commissioned officer strode off, Alice said: "It's all over anyway. He won't get your guns now."

Sheriff Mittan glumly nodded his head in sober agreement. Ben Southern said nothing. He eyed the other two for a length of time. He could understand the girl's mood, but Sheriff Mittan seemed equally as gloomy even though he now knew who had killed Slattery and O'Casey.

"Tell me about your brother," he said to the girl.

She answered softly without looking at Ben. "He left home six years ago to run mustangs in Mexico. He came back occasionally but only stayed over night. And he changed. He always was wild and . . . well . . . cruel, in some ways. But the

last time he came back, he was a stranger to me. That was when
El Vengador began coming into prominence. I didn't know. . . .
One time he told me. At first I didn't believe him, but the last
time he came by I knew it was true. He was dressed like a
Mexican . . . the men riding with him were mostly Mexicans.
There were eight or ten Americans, too, but they weren't range
riders, they were gunmen."

"But why did he leave those two U.S. horses here?" Ben
asked. "Why would he wish to draw the Army's attention to this
place?"

She hesitated a moment before saying: "I wasn't sure. In fact,
Captain, I didn't think he'd do that. Of course the Army . . .
and the law . . . would come down here."

Mittan spoke up as the girl's voice faded. "He did it on
purpose, Captain Southern. He wanted us all to know who had
ordered those soldiers apprehended. I've never met El Vengador
face to face, but I'm plenty familiar with the way he operates.
He wants people to know who he is . . . he wants them to
tremble in their boots at the sound of his name."

Ben scowled. "He deliberately set his own sister up like this,
knowing there'd be trouble? What kind of a . . . ?"

"Cap'n." It was Tolliver coming across the yard with
something in his hand. Ben broke off from what he had been
saying to turn half around.

"Cap'n, this was on the one that stopped the buckshot." Tolliver handed over a money belt, the kind usually worn under a
man's clothing. It had four separate compartments to it and
was shiny from long use. Ben opened the compartments. Three
of them held currency, some Mexican *pesos,* some U.S.
greenbacks. The last compartment held several carefully folded
Wanted posters, all from Arizona, all listing outlaws wanted for
cash bounties. As Ben spread out the posters, Tolliver said:
"Four, Cap'n. Four murderers." Ned turned to Mittan. "How

many men were involved in the killin' of O'Casey and Slattery, Sheriff?"

Mittan, bending to scan those flyers, said: "Four or more, Sergeant, and, if you're thinkin' what I figure you are, you just might be right, only that buckshot feller they dragged off from the middle of the yard was a Mex."

"Sure," agreed Tolliver dryly. "Look at the amount of reward ridin' on those four heads, too, Sheriff. To a Mex from south of the line that'd be a fortune. If he could turn in those four and collect, he could buy himself a ranch down there some place and sit back the rest of his life."

Ben pocketed the folders. "Evidently El Vengador doesn't have all Mexican patriots riding with him," he said. "I think you've got it figured about right, Ned."

Lieutenant Johnson came forth from the house accompanied by Walt Lee. He looked out where his men were lounging, drew forth his gauntlets, and, as he tugged them on, he cocked an eye at the paling heavens. "It'll be daylight before too much longer," he stated, dropping his head and facing Ben Southern. "You folks had better ride along with us. We'll make a scout down along the border, then head on back to Fort Brown. It might not be a good idea to remain here." He said all this to Alice. As he finished with the gloves, he signaled to the stooped, lean, old sergeant over by the barn. "Mount 'em up!" he sang out. "Captain Southern, you coming along?"

Ben shook his head. "I want to do a little scouting of my own," he said. "But we'll call in at Fort Brown within the next day or two, Lieutenant. We want to get those rifles sent up north as soon as possible."

Even Ned Tolliver's eyes widened at Ben's last remark. Sheriff Mittan, Alice Clark, the lieutenant stared. Walt Lee was as startled as the others, but he at least had the advantage of knowing Captain Southern, so he recovered from the surprise first, stepped around the people on the porch, and walked on down to where Ned Tolliver stood. He mumbled something; he and Tolliver turned, and went hiking on down toward the barn.

"You'll be joking," Lieutenant Johnson said.

Ben didn't answer. He said: "Sheriff, if you're going back to Acton, I'll look you up tomorrow, if I can. There are a couple of things you can do for me."

"Yes," murmured Mittan. "I'll head back right now." He turned. "Miss Alice, maybe you'd best go with the soldiers. You don't think your brother'll come back here and neither do I. But, for a fact, he never does what folks think he'll do, so it'd be a lot better if you. . . ."

"No," she said. "If you're going back to Acton, I'll ride with you."

Mittan rolled his eyes toward Ben as though seeking support, but Ben ignored him. Over across the yard where the Fort Brown men were leading up their horses, he could see Tolliver and Lee rigging out their own animals. Without another word he strolled down where the activity was and went after his own animal.

Lieutenant Johnson got astride, left his men over by the barn while he rode up to the house, pulled at his moustache, and disapprovingly considered Alice Clark. "Ma'am," he said, "we have facilities for womenfolk at the fort. I'd be proud to have you go back with us and I think it would be best."

She thanked him and declined. He nodded a trifle stiffly, whirled, went back to his troopers, raised an arm, dropped it, and loped away through the cool pre-dawn with a little skiff of dust jerking to life beneath the hoofs of his company's horses.

Sheriff Mittan, watching, cleared his throat. "We might as well get riding, too," he said to her, and started down off the porch.

At the barn Ben Southern, Tolliver, and Walt Lee were

saddled and bridled. They swung up over leather as the leathery old lawman and the handsome, willowy tall girl came along. Southern was adjusting his reins when Mittan called over, saying: "Be careful, Captain! Be damned careful. He wants you worse than he wants anything else, right now. Remember that, because, if he gets you. . . ." Mittan didn't finish it. He went on over where two horses stood with their heads over the corral looking out, and reached for the gate.

Alice waited until Ben was turning his horse. "I'll put the Army horses out in a corral where they'll have feed and water, Captain. When you get around to it, you can get them."

He nodded down at her, swung, and led off in a loose gallop westward. Tolliver and Lee each gave her a gallant little hand salute, then loped out of the yard in their officer's wake.

The moon was gone now; the stars were beginning to fade. In the west where some far-away low hills jutted against a turquoise sky, there was a faint golden glow. Dawn was close.

Ben kept his mile-eating gait for a long while, but he altered course as soon as he was beyond sight of the ranch and traveled southward on a wide, angling easterly sweep until he came upon a score of fresh horse tracks. Then he slowed to a loose walk and followed the sign.

"It'll go arrow straight for the border an' on over into Old Mexico," opined Ned Tolliver. "Mister El Vengador got a scare thrown into him last night when that Fort Brown detachment come up."

"Say!" exclaimed Walt Lee garrulously. "Why does he sport a name like The Avenger? What's he got to avenge, anyway? Seems to me he's got the countryside eatin' out of his hand."

"Those Mex renegades pick out fancy names like that," Tolliver stated sagely. "Didn't you ever notice that? There used to be one over in New Mexico called The Scorpion. In Texas they had one called The Lion. They say it gets 'em recruits."

Ben rocked along taking no part in this conversation. He had his narrowed eyes fixed hard ahead upon the vague distances where Mexico lay, across an invisible line in the middle of nowhere.

What kind of a man threatened to kill his own sister, then actually tried to do it?

X

The border was marked by little piles of whitewashed stones piled into cairns every few miles. Once, some politicians had suggested fencing it, but everyone had laughed about that; the border between the U.S. and Mexico was one thousand miles long. In the end, a joint commission had supervised the erection of the little white stone cairns.

By the time Ben Southern and his silent, rust-colored companions got in sight of the first cairn it was dawn. The tracks they were following didn't hesitate. They plunged straight on over into Mexico. So did Ben Southern, Ned Tolliver, and Walt Lee.

The land didn't change for some little distance, but eventually, where a sluggish river the color of chocolate ran past in its shallow and oily way, there was some greenery. There was also a small band of dark horsemen. They wore the brown short jacket and high-crowned sombrero of Mexico's rural constabulary corps—the *Rurales.*

Each man had two bandoleers of bullets looped, criss-cross, over his chest. They were on foot in the underbrush when Ben first spied them. He immediately gestured and dropped back into hiding. *Rurales* were hard men; under Mexican law they were obliged to arrest all trespassers from over the line who rode armed and in numbers. Also, according to Mexican law, they were supposed to deliver those arrested to the nearest village judge, but, if the horses were good, the guns and ammunition valuable, the money in the pockets worthwhile, a prisoner could not count on living ten minutes after being apprehended.

Ned Tolliver stepped in beside Ben and Walt, reached forth to pry apart their shielding chaparral, and gazed ahead, jaw gently moving. "What are they doin'?" he asked.

No one answered him. No one knew what the Mexicans were doing. There was one officer and eight men. They had detailed a horse holder closer to the river while the others passed in and out of the underbrush. Finally the officer called exultantly, his men converged, and the three U.S. soldiers heard the word: "Dead."

Ben eased off. "El Vengador must've lost one more man. But he didn't die until they got down here."

Ben was right. The *Rurales* dragged a corpse out of the brush, indifferently plundered it for money or valuables, then heaved it into the river with low growls. They were not angry at the dead outlaw; they were disgusted that someone else had already taken the man's guns and valuables.

For a while longer the *Rurales* lingered, poking here and there, then at a barked order from their *teniente* they mounted up, headed for the river, and went splashing on across. They were mostly bearded, very dark, lusterless men, heavily armed and unsmiling. The Texans and others would make fun of Mexican *Rurales,* but no one who ever ran afoul of them was amused. Ben knew about them, too; he let them get well away before mounting up to continue his tracking, and even afterward kept an eye cocked on their distant dust.

One thing gradually became clear. Those *Rurales* were also trailing El Vengador's band. There were hardly enough of them to attack the renegades, but they were masters at the ambush.

Ned Tolliver finally said: "Cap'n, the odds keep buildin' up. There's those *Rurales.* They outnumber us. There's this El Vengador character. He outnumbers everyone else. It's sort of like three separate packs of wolves on one another's trails, and we're the least pack. If either side scents the other, we're goin' to be in the middle."

Southern agreed with Ned's reasoning, but he did not change course, so Tolliver said no more. He and Walt rode along, though, with their eyes never still. The southern desert country, north or south of the line, held the secret of many a shallow and unmarked grave.

At high noon with the heat like smoke and visibility limited because of this dense haze, the two sets of separate tracks suddenly turned and headed straight up northward again.

"Be damned," muttered Walt Lee. "Headin' for the line again."

That's exactly where the tracks led, but it was several hours before Ben saw another pile of those whitewashed rocks, and, when he got close enough to be able to see up into Arizona again, the sage and chaparral suddenly parted to allow *Rurales* to step forth, carbines in hand, black, hawkish faces frozen into a wary, unpleasant expression.

Ben halted. On either side of him Walt and Ned also drew rein. The tracks they had been following passed right on up past the pile of stones back into Arizona again, but evidently the Mexican rural policemen had halted south of that invisible line.

The Mexican lieutenant walked up. He, too, was an unsmiling, fierce-looking man, but clean-shaven and about Ned Tolliver's age. He had his gloves off, his huge sombrero tipped back, his ivory-butted six-gun holstered but readily accessible.

"*Señores,*" he murmured, gazing from one *Norteamericano* to the other. "It is a busy place, this part of the land. You are only travelers, of course." He showed very white teeth in a mirthless small smile as he said this, settled his black gaze upon Ben Southern, and waited.

191

"That's right," agreed Ben. "Travelers heading back into Arizona."

"Of course," murmured the lieutenant. "Other travelers crossed ahead of you an hour ago. Could they have been friends?"

Ned Tolliver snorted, looking disdainful. The *Rurale* swung for a lingering assessment of Ned, then seemed to relax a little.

"I see," he quietly said. "They were not friends. Tell me, *señores* . . . do you know who those other men were?"

"El Vengador!" exclaimed Ben Southern. "El Vengador and his brigands, Lieutenant, and you were trailing them, too."

This time the officer's little smile was warmer. "It is the truth," he stated. "And you . . . you are also hunting them? But only three of you?"

"To keep them in sight, and with any kind of luck to maybe get one good crack at them, Lieutenant," Southern explained. "But more than anything else, to learn what trails they use in going and coming."

The Mexican felt inside his short, tight-fitting embroidered jacket for a cigar, lit it, exhaled, and fixed Ben Southern with a steady black gaze. "I am Epifanio Garcia," he said. "This is my section of the border to guard and patrol. But one has difficulty, *señores* . . . in Mexico there are warring factions. One does not know from day to day who is in power and who is not. But you are fortunate today, because my men and I are loyalists. Otherwise, of course, we would kill you because you are also opposed to El Vengador. But as I've said, today you are in good luck." Lieutenant Garcia stepped aside and waved with his cigar. "Go. But be very careful. If we saw your dust approaching, it's possible El Vengador also saw it. *Señores*, do you recall how the Apaches roasted captives? Well, believe me when I tell you El Vengador has some of those red devils riding with him."

Ben urged his horse ahead. He saluted Lieutenant Garcia as

he went past and got back a salute and a villainous smile. The other *Rurales* stood like menacing statues, only their eyes moving as Ben, Ned, and Walt Lee crossed over into Arizona and kept right on riding. A mile farther along, Walt shook off sweat and said: "*Phew* . . . there's got to be an easier way to serve the Lord, Cap'n. Back there I was tryin' my dangedest to remember some prayers, and couldn't think of a one."

Ned said dryly: "If they'd been hostile, you wouldn't have had time to say one anyway." He looked at Ben. "You satisfied about whatever made you want to ride down there?"

"Plumb satisfied," Ben replied. "I wanted to make sure El Vengador hadn't given up after being chased off last night. The way he cut down into Mexico to make certain the Fort Brown column wasn't chasing him, then the way he swung around and rode right back up into Arizona makes it fairly obvious. Ned, El Vengador isn't giving up. He still plans to get those rifles."

"And you still plan on havin' them start out for Camp Scott?"

"As soon as we can reach Fort Brown and I can see the commandant," Ben stated emphatically. "You think I'm crazy, Ned?"

"Respectin' your rank, sir," muttered Tolliver, ". . . a little crazy."

Walt Lee chuckled. They grinned at one another and kept on riding.

They left El Vengador's tracks six miles northward, picked up other fresh sign going westward, and followed it until they were in sight of a quadrangle of low, massive-walled adobe buildings that Walt Lee said was Fort Brown. The sun was beginning to redden, to drop down the hazy sky. There wasn't a breath of air stirring anywhere and neither was there sufficient oxygen available to prevent a kind of stultifying drowsiness. What troubled them even more was their lack of rest for the past twenty-four hours.

"We'll be able to let down at the fort," Ben told his companions. "By tomorrow morning we ought to be ready to head out, feeling chipper."

"For Camp Scott with the gun wagons?" Ned asked.

Ben said: "For Acton, Sergeant. Camp Scott's still a day or two ahead of us." That was all he told them, and, while it did not appear to bother Walt Lee in the least, this withholding information, it clearly did not sit so well with Sergeant Tolliver. He rode along chewing and looking austerely miffed. But he said nothing.

They arrived at Fort Brown at "Retreat", halted their horses at the gate, and waited until the ceremony of lowering the colors had been completed. They saw Lieutenant Johnson among the other officers. They also saw the tough and capable ranks of leathery troopers, more than enough of them to chase off El Vengador or anyone else who came down here looking for trouble.

Afterward, Ben handed his reins to Ned and strolled on across the parade to the commandant's hutment, there to meet the officer commanding, Brevet Colonel John Hardin, who, as it turned out, was also a mustang Regular—an officer who had risen from the ranks as opposed to officers who had graduated from the U.S. Military Academy.

Hardin was a Southerner; he was also a soft-spoken man with eyes like steel balls and a build like a Sioux—tall and wide-shouldered, spare and iron-hard. He listened to Ben Southern while standing upon the tiny porch of his Fort Brown command hut chewing an unlighted cigar and watching his men being dismissed. He didn't really look at Captain Southern until Ben finished speaking.

"Some of that," he then said, "I've heard before, Captain. From Lieutenant Johnson. As for El Vengador . . . we know him here at Fort Brown. We damned well know him." The tanned, blunt jaw clamped down hard on Hardin's cigar. "As for sending the guns up to Camp Scott . . . I have your C.O.'s orders to release them when you say to do so, but I'm not sure you're using good judgment. Those damned weapons could very well make the difference south of the border. I reckon you realize that, don't you?"

"Yes, sir. I also realize those rifles may be exactly the bait you need to get a sight on El Vengador. He wants those guns very badly. So badly he'd try to kill his own sister to get them. I think, Colonel, that for once you won't have to chase El Vengador . . . I think for once he'll be chasing you."

"I understand," Hardin said, unbending a little, stepping to a little railing and perching there with the sultry, dusky sky at his back while he slowly ran a close look up and down Ben Southern. "I know how you're thinkin', and I approve of it . . . up to a point. But let's suppose he gets those guns, Captain. You got any idea where that'll put you and me . . . and your commander at Camp Scott for authorizing this thing? Back in the ranks, Captain."

Ben said: "I've been there before, sir."

Hardin removed his frayed stogie, looked soberly at it, then heaved it away. "So have I," he murmured, almost wryly smiling. "But I'm not very anxious to return. All right, Captain . . . your commandant seems to have faith in you. Lieutenant Johnson said you fought a good fight at the Clark Ranch, too. I'll listen . . . what've you got in mind?"

"Removing every firing pin from the rifles, Colonel, before we pull out of here in the morning, northward bound for Acton."

Hardin's keen glance lifted. "Go on," he said. "That's surely not all of it."

"No, sir. Send one of my men out tonight with the firing pins. He'll ride to Acton, stir Sheriff Mittan into gettin' up a posse, leave the pins in town, and ride back with the armed civilians. I have just the man for it . . . Sergeant Tolliver, an old campaigner, Colonel. He'll take Mittan's men southward in the night, get them aligned between Fort Brown and the border before sunup so when El Vengador's spies see the wagons pull out down here, they won't also see any dust except the dust we make."

"The gun wagons will be the bait," said Hardin, groping for another Mexican stogie inside his tunic. "You'll be with them, of course, along with the escort. Where'll I be with my troopers?"

"Twenty riding guard, Colonel Hardin. As many more as can be packed inside, put into the wagons. But none of it to be done until ten minutes or so before we ride out."

Hardin stuck the cigar between his teeth and began chewing it. He made no attempt to light the thing. "You're saying I've got spies among my men, Captain," he stated. "Is that just a guess?"

"Yes, sir. Something El Vengador said at the Clark place last night makes me think he's got some pretty good contacts in this south country."

"I don't believe it, Captain. Not on this post."

Ben didn't push the point. All he said was: "You use Mexicans for wood hauling, for freighting, for other chores."

Colonel Hardin stood up without comment, chewed his cigar a moment, then said: "Come on . . . I'll show you where the guns are. The sooner we get to pulling firing pins the better."

As the two officers moved off, Ned and Walt Lee materialized out of the dusk and fell in behind them at a respectful distance.

XI

Colonel John Hardin was a field soldier. Most frontier officers were field soldiers. If there were posts, camps, and stations where commandants could be less active, it was not on the frontier, for which reason most of the commanders along the border were mustang officers—men willing and able to pitch in with the fighting or, as in this case, with the rendering useless several hundred Springfield carbines. He sent for two other officers. One was the same Lieutenant Johnson who had led the Fort Brown detachment to the relief of Ben and the others at the Clark place the night before.

Counting Tolliver, Lee, Ben Southern, Colonel Hardin, and his two subordinates, there were six of them working by lantern light in the adobe shed near the stable area where those surplus weapons were stored. Ben said nothing about needing more men in order to complete the job in time for them all to get some rest, and John Hardin made no such offer of more help.

The actual chore of removing firing pins was not much of a job. What took infinitely longer was breaking out the weapons one at a time, then repacking them in the crates again. There was very little conversation; Colonel Hardin worked with his coat off, with a gnawed cigar between his teeth, and with experienced hands. Because there were several hundred of those guns to be made useless, when the final bugle call of the day sounded, near 10:00, they had worked over only about half the guns.

The colonel went himself to fetch back some coffee. While he was gone Lieutenant Johnson asked Ben Southern what was in prospect. All Ben said in reply was that Johnson would be given his orders by Colonel Hardin. After that mild rebuff, the men worked on in the feeble light, saying nothing to one another.

At midnight they had the last carbine packed, the last of the coffee finished, and two heavy little bags of firing pins for all their efforts. That was when Ben explained to Ned Tolliver what he wanted the sergeant to do. Ned listened, looking dour, but he made no comment about losing more sleep; he simply hefted the two bags, looked at John Hardin, and said: "If you've got a big, fresh horse, I'll be able to use him, Colonel."

They went over to the stable, rigged out Ned's beast, walked with him to the guarded gate, and waved him on through. It was then a little after 1:00 A.M. On the stroll back to the command hut Colonel Hardin said: "I didn't think it'd take this long. Captain, your man's going to have to ride hard to reach Acton, get that posse activated, and get back down here before sunup."

They passed a shadowy sentry at the hut and went inside. At the door Ben turned to Walt, saying: "Get some rest, you've earned it. And, Walt, just in case, when he lights out in the morning, ride out ahead, and scout the desert, then meet the wagons."

Lee nodded, threw the other officers a salute, turned, and walked away. Colonel Hardin gazed after him, shrugged, and said: "Discipline's a grand thing, Captain. I recollect during the war the excellent discipline of General Lee's army of North Virginia." He paused, chewed his cigar, then smiled. "And they lost the war. Well, gentlemen, I've got a nightcap inside, let's go in."

Except for the occasional singing out of a sentry or the measured cadence of a guard making his rounds, Fort Brown was darkly hushed and still. The night was cool and pleasant; the only time men could decently rest in the desert country during summertime was between midnight and 5:00 in the morning. The sun arose at 4:00 or 4:30. After that there was no more than another cool hour before the deadly heat came, with its haziness and its venomous yellow light.

The moon was up there, but little more than a symbol. Most of what light shone out over the dead emptiness beyond Fort Brown came from the stars. Somewhere out in the vastness was El Vengador with his deadly crew. They were the ones who knew this land. Including their leader, they had grown up in the southern desert. Others might perish, might go out of their minds searching for shade or water or settlements or food, but not the brigands who rode with El Vengador.

The people who knew the desert learned to live with all its variables, but, especially, they learned to live with the killing summertime heat. They drank sparingly, moved without haste, rested frequently, and survived. Also, they knew all the treacheries of the land and in time learned to emulate them. There were those who said, because the desert was flat, enemies could be seen miles away, but the troopers who patrolled this land as well as the cattlemen who ranged it knew better. In lieu of hills and trees and arroyos, desert outlaws used camouflage. More than once, unsuspecting freighters or travelers suddenly had the earth underfoot roll back to disclose murderous brigands who had lain under six inches of itchy sand until the opportune moment arrived.

Private Walter Lee had been campaigning in the Territory of Arizona for several years now; he knew precisely what to look for when he slipped out of Fort Brown the following pre-dawn, and he had an advantage—the poor light.

He hadn't been gone a half hour when Ben Southern strolled over to inquire of the sentry on the gate if he had ridden out. The sentry confirmed this and Ben strolled on over to the stable area where several cursing troopers were harnessing teams to a pair of light supply wagons, bitter over being routed out for this chore ahead of "First Call".

Colonel Hardin came through the stable without his customary Mex stogie. He was freshly shaven and scrubbed, wore a belt gun, and lugged a booted carbine, but he had no saber, which in fact the Army on the frontier had just about abandoned. Hardin watched the swearing troopers a moment, then moved over beside Ben to say: "Going to be hotter than the hubs of hell today, Captain. I've ordered two extra barrels of water stowed inside the wagons. They'll deprive us of two or three men, but the horses will need water and lots of it before we reach Acton." He cleared his throat. "*If* we reach Acton."

Lieutenant Johnson came hastening along buckling his gun belt. Out beyond the stable a bugler cut loose. Off in the east there was a steadily widening band of dazzling light.

"Good morning, sir," Johnson said to his colonel.

Hardin nodded, mumbled, then more distinctly said: "Pick the men, Lieutenant. No recruits. Twenty to ride, twenty more inside the wagons. Ten to a rig with two on the seat . . . carbines and pistols, filled loops and extra ammo. See to it."

Lieutenant Johnson saluted, whirled, and went briskly back the way he had come. Colonel Hardin groped inside his tunic for a stogie, offered one to Ben, got a negative head wag, and began chewing. "I got a piece of shrapnel in the lungs one time," he said conversationally. "The surgeon told me smoking would aggravate it, so I stopped smoking." He smiled and went on chewing, drifting his tough glance on around where the troopers, no longer swearing now, were backing the horses on each side of the wagon tongues to be hitched up. Beyond the barns there was the hard ring of booted feet assembling, the bark of orders for alignment, then "Mess Call".

Lieutenant Johnson returned at a trot. Around him, and also behind, came the men he had selected. Ben Southern turned to appraise them. There were no greenhorns amongst them; each man was lean and layered nearly black with desert patrolling. Hardin saw the way Ben was looking as the soldiers headed for the wagons or split off, heading for the corrals and their racked-up saddles.

"They'll do," he said quietly, his Virginia drawl more noticeable because he was speaking slowly. "I've got my share of both . . . Yanks and repatriates. That's one thing about the frontier, Captain . . . no old feuds out here that linger and sometimes wind up in saber fights out back of the barracks."

Lieutenant Johnson walked off. Ten minutes later he returned leading a pair of horses. One of them wore the range outfit Ben had acquired up at Camp Scott before heading southward. The other animal was for Colonel Hardin. As each man reached for his reins, they heard the sentry at the gate sing out a high challenge, then the gate creaked open and a horsemen loped through. Ben paused, thinking it would be Walt Lee, but it wasn't, and John Hardin, mounting, said: "Just a scout I sent out, Captain, to make certain the road's clear for the first few miles."

The soldier loped up, looking dusty, and reported. He had gone three miles upcountry and had spotted nothing. Hardin dismissed the man, straightened his reins, chewed his stogie, and said nothing until Ben also got astride.

"Hardly expected it to be otherwise, did we, Captain?" he drawled.

Ben didn't answer. He was watching the troopers form. The mounted ones were aligned by that same stooped, skeletal old sergeant who had been at the Clark Ranch with Lieutenant Johnson. Another sergeant, short and burly and red-headed with an Irish brogue thick enough to cut with a knife, was urging the dismounted cavalrymen to make room in the wagons as more and more of them clambered up inside.

Someone said it was going to be hotter than hell inside under that canvas. The Irish sergeant agreed that it was and offered the suggestion that, since every man jack of those troopers was going to hell or at least purgatory soon enough, this would constitute a splendid means for them to become oriented in advance.

Lieutenant Johnson passed the orders to Colonel Hardin who commanded the column to form on the wagons and move out. It was obeyed smoothly. Off in the east a huge yellow disc glided up over the dusty edge of the world and at once that blessed coolness seemed to lose its good softness.

They went out through the Fort Brown gates, bearing northward. The road was distinguishable only because it had two gouged-out ruts and wound in and out to avoid the cacti, brush, and what passed for trees on the desert, but otherwise, because the land was all flat anyway, it differed none at all from the rest of the countryside.

Ben rode up ahead with Colonel Hardin. Lieutenant Johnson was back in the rear with a detachment of five troopers. From time to time he would trot up one side and down the other where the balance of the men rode. It was an unnecessary undertaking because each soldier riding alongside the pair of light wagons was a veteran at this kind of escort duty.

For an hour the dust, the increasing heat, the abrasive sounds of leather upon leather or steel tires pulverizing gritty sand, was all. Now and then someone would sing out. Lieutenant Johnson's advance vedette came loping back midway into their second hour on the trail, with Walter Lee. As soon as he had seen Lee back, the trooper reversed and loped ahead again.

Lee came in on Ben Southern's far side, wheeled his mount, and threw Ben a salute and a shake of his head at the same time. "Nothing, Cap'n. Nothing to be seen up ahead for as far as I went . . . maybe four, five miles. Off to the east there's not a fresh track of any kind. To the west I found fresh sign aplenty, but it was all headin' south for the border, so I reckon that'd be Ned and the posse men from Acton."

"How many?" asked Colonel Hardin, leaning from his saddle.

"Quite a bunch, sir. Maybe twenty-five of 'em."

The colonel straightened up, chewed thoughtfully a moment, then twisted to strain backward through the rising mustard-colored dust. "Maybe he'll spot that posse," Hardin mused aloud, referring to El Vengador. "Maybe we pulled all those firing pins for nothing. If he's spotted us . . . which I'm sure he has by now . . . he'll add the escort numbers to the posse men numbers, and possibly get some sense."

Ben and Walt Lee exchanged a look but neither of them said anything. Colonel Hardin straightened around, spat, wiped sweat off his face, and peered ahead for some sign of his advance vedette. A moment later he turned and said: "And maybe not."

They rode with the heat steadily increasing. From within the wagons muffled curses were audible now and then, where there was ample water for the sweltering troops but where the cramped quarters as well as the totally breathless atmosphere made the trip pure torture. Colonel Hardin commented on that once, but, since there was no way to alleviate the anguish of those men, the subject was dropped.

They had been out of the fort several hours, were well beyond sight or sound of it with the heat deceptively lulling them, when the vedette came jogging back down toward the column with an upraised arm, his face pink and flushed, his blouse nearly black from sweat.

Colonel Hardin raised his free right hand without calling out. The column ground down to a dusty halt. Lieutenant Johnson walked his horse up from the rear. Ben heard Walt Lee mumble something under his breath but did not ask what, because the vedette came up, halted, and saluted, then said: "Colonel, there's a damned army lined up across the road in front of us . . . sir."

Hardin's brows dropped menacingly down. His gnawed cigar jutted. "What kind of a report is that?" he growled at the vedette.

"A true one, sir," stated the tough-faced dragoon. "If you'll ride up a mile with me, I'll show you. That's as close as I got, an' it looks like at least two hundred horsemen sittin' up there, barrin' the road. And, Colonel, they're Mexicans. Or at least two-thirds of 'em are because they're wearin' Mex sombreros and got their bullet belts crossed over their chests Mex style."

Hardin didn't lift his black scowl but he turned his head toward Ben. "Well," he said harshly, "care to ride up and inspect a greaser army with me, Captain?" He didn't await an answer but hooked his mount and loped away. The vedette cast a glance at Ben, then also turned. Ben was the last one of them to go galloping up the road. Lieutenant Johnson remained back with the wagons and the mounted escort. He dragged in a corner of his big moustache and gnawed it, looking up where the dust of those three loping riders lifted overhead.

XII

Where the vedette halted, finally, Ben and John Hardin reined down and silently sat their saddles. The scout had not exaggerated. A thousand yards up ahead athwart their road to Acton was the largest mounted body of armed Mexicans Ben Southern had ever seen, outside of Mexico proper.

John Hardin swore and clamped down hard on his cigar. "The guts of him," he growled. "That's a damned rebel regiment from south of the line. The guts of the man who's commanding them, coming up into Arizona like this!"

A horseman up among all those dark, motionless, watching riders, detached himself and started walking his horse southward. At once two men rode away from the others, one on each side, and accompanied the foremost horseman.

It was the rocky-faced vedette who identified that rebel chieftain. "El Vengador," he said thinly. "Colonel, I've seen him this close before. It's El Vengador as sure as I'm sittin' here."

"Which might not be for long," stated Hardin, easing off the little leather tie-down that held his six-gun from falling out of its holster. "If he thinks he's goin' to ride over us, he's got another guess coming."

Ben was both curious and interested. He hadn't yet quite formed much of an opinion of the notorious renegade; all he knew for a fact about the man thus far was that he was cold-blooded enough to see his own sister killed, that he was not a Mexican, and that he was one of those most deadly of all outlaws—a renegade.

When El Vengador got close enough, Ben got a surprise; he was just as dark-skinned, dark-eyed, and dark-haired as the two Mexicans riding on either side of him as his bodyguard. There was none of Alice Clark's clean, fair looks to this man at all. In fact, if he hadn't been told differently by those who knew, he would have sworn El Vengador was a Mexican.

The man was tall and willowy, like his sister, but right there any similarity ended. Also, he had a fierce, savage look to him that put Ben Southern in mind of a man whose inner spirit was impaled upon spikes of cruelty.

El Vengador halted thirty feet in front of them, draped both hands atop his immense Mexican saddle horn, and studied Colonel Hardin first and longest, then Ben Southern, and finally Walt Lee and the mounted vedette. "You have a strong escort," he said in perfect English, and reached up to tilt back his huge sombrero. "I thought you'd have more though, *Coronel.*" He paused to consider the canvas-topped light wagons. "You have brought me the rifles. I'm grateful for your effort."

"The rifles are back there," said John Hardin coldly. "If you care to, renegade, come an' try taking them."

"I will," replied El Vengador. "Of course I will. And I see in your faces you are surprised. *Coronel,* did you think I wouldn't come, or did you think I'd only have twenty or thirty men with me? No, *amigo,* I have respect for the U.S. Army . . . at least for the frontier Army."

"You have led these Mexicans into an overt act of invasion," Hardin said. "Even if you get the guns, you'll never get much chance to use them . . . as soon as I'm away from here, I'll notify every military post between here and. . . ."

"*Coronel,*" broke in the dark horseman, "what makes you think you'll ride away from here?" El Vengador gazed down where the armed escort with Lieutenant Johnson was sitting, sweltering and waiting. "If I raise my left hand not a one of you will ride away from here. That's the idea, *Coronel.* By the time anyone finds your carcasses, we'll be over the line with the wagons. As for invading Arizona . . . don't worry about it. I've had these troops hiding out down in the desert south of the line for ten days now for just this purpose. Let the official Mexican government take the blame."

The renegade turned his head slightly and regarded Ben Southern again, more intently and curiously this time. His dark glance was absolutely without mercy. His lips were a bloodless gash along his lower face. Thinking back to what this man's own sister had said of him, Ben agreed, but thought she hadn't told it all; whatever her brother had once been, he was now a ruthless killer, a cruel spoiler, and it wouldn't matter to him who he murdered or which side of the line he ravaged.

El Vengador said: "You are the *capitán* from Camp Scott. Too bad we couldn't meet at the ranch last night. You are responsible for the loss of five of my men."

"Four," corrected Ben softly.

"Five, *Capitán.* Another one died of his wounds this morning. For that we have some pitchwood splinters to ram under your fingernails and set afire."

"Then," said Ben, "you'd better get at it, Mister Clark, because we're wasting time sitting here just talking."

Ben's right hand was lightly resting upon his thigh near the holstered six-gun strapped there. El Vengador noticed this. He also noticed the look of pure contempt upon Ben's face. He said: "It's been quite a while since anyone called me Mister

Clark, Captain. My sister must have liked you to talk so much."

"What kind of a whelp would try to deliberately kill his own sister?" asked Ben stonily. "Even wolves don't kill their females."

El Vengador shifted slightly in his saddle. He glanced down where the wagons were again, appraising the mounted soldiers down there. It seemed as though he was no longer interested in either Ben or what Ben had said. But when next he spoke, it showed that he hadn't overlooked Ben's last remark.

"Captain, we grew up in different worlds. I'm not an Arizonan . . . I'm a Mexican."

"You," growled Colonel Hardin, "are nothing but a filthy renegade jackal, Clark. That's all you've ever been. Now go on back to your men and either attack or get over the line where they'll stomach your kind, I don't give a damn which, but we're going on."

The brigand chieftain's dark gaze settled upon Hardin with a sulphurous stare. "Bravery won't save you, Colonel. Neither will those troopers with the wagons. You didn't expect a rebel regiment, did you?"

"I should've," retorted the wrathful colonel. "I should've known you'd be afraid to try it with equal numbers."

El Vengador sighed and sat there stonily considering the colonel. For a long while he said nothing at all. He seemed neither anxious to start hostilities nor particularly interested in what he conceived of as the only outcome of such a fight. He was, Ben thought, studying him closely, one of those men who were totally without emotion; when El Vengador killed, he did not do it out of the love for fighting most killers had. Neither did he appear ruffled by the powerful scorn he had been shown by his enemies. He was cold, Ben told himself, as cold as ice and as impersonal, too.

Then he dropped his verbal bombshell. "Colonel, there is no way out, but, if you will send those wagons ahead to my men,

I'll settle for leaving you and your men bound and on foot. You probably will die here even then, though, because you see . . . that posse from Acton is chasing a detachment of my men who are deliberately leading it off to the west." El Vengador smiled a cold, absolutely humorless smile.

Ben had no clear idea what John Hardin's thoughts were, but he knew what struck him: if El Vengador had an element of his brigand band leading the posse away, that meant the desert was crawling with Mex bandits. The more he turned this over, the more it became apparent that even with their men concealed inside the gun wagons, El Vengador had overwhelming superiority.

"If," stated Colonel Hardin harshly, "you want these guns, you can come and get them, and, when you try it, Clark, I hope you're out front." The colonel started to turn his horse.

El Vengador let him almost complete the movement. "Hardin," he said, "I want the guns. I aim to get them. It's up to you how I do it, but let me tell you one of the facts of life. When you rode out this morning and left Fort Brown stripped of men, you just about ensured the death of the men with you as escort, and also the ones you left back at the fort. When I'm through here, I'm going to hit the fort . . . I need lead and powder, too, Colonel, and anything else you happen to have stored back there."

John Hardin said: "You're insane. Clark, you'll have the whole blessed U.S. Army down on you. You'll cause war between Mexico and the U.S."

El Vengador nodded. "You're probably right," he said. "I prosper durin' wars, Colonel. Now make up your mind . . . the guns without a fight or the guns with a fight. I don't care which."

Colonel Hardin turned and gestured for Lieutenant Johnson and the foremost dragoons to lope on up. Until they arrived, he did not tell the guerilla chieftain what he had in mind. Ben

Southern thought he knew. He didn't know John Hardin but he had known his share of mustang colonels just like him; if El Vengador got those guns, he was going to pay heavily in blood for them.

There were nine troopers and Lieutenant Johnson behind Hardin, also facing the guerilla leader, when Colonel Hardin said: "Go back and clear those Mexicans off the trail, Clark. Clear them out of Arizona because I'm going through them, and, when I reach Acton, I propose to notify the Army Area Headquarters of your invasion of U.S. Territory with armed Mexican insurgents."

El Vengador kept watching John Hardin without saying a word for a long time before he lightly lifted his shoulders, dropped them, and turned his horse to ride back the way he had come. His two bodyguards also turned and rode back in strong silence.

Ben Southern, gazing far ahead where the balance of that Mexican command was, felt his heart sink a little. There would be no mercy shown in the coming battle. Even had El Vengador's men been so inclined, their *comandante* would not be, and, as always with Mexican armies, it was the *comandante* who established patterns of behavior.

"Captain," said John Hardin to Ben, "you will command on the west side of the wagons with the men from inside each rig. Use rifle crates as breastworks, and, if the horses go down, use them, too. Some of the men can stay inside the wagons for sniping."

Hardin swung toward Lieutenant Johnson, urged out his horse, and the three officers started back. Johnson's enlisted detachment fell in behind. From time to time as they approached the wagons those enlisted men twisted to gaze back. None of them spoke but, obviously, that was an awful lot of Mexicans to be taking on with no more men than they had.

Ben was surprised the Mexicans did not attack as soon as their chieftain returned, but they didn't. He thought, under reversed circumstances, he would have struck hard before Hardin's command got set and ready.

They made their dispositions for battle; Hardin and Ben Southern divided the men, half to each side of the roadway. Lieutenant Johnson was with the colonel. They even had time to make their defenses out of rifle crates and saddlery. The disposition of dragoons was excellent. In order for the Mexicans to breach their line, they would have to charge them head-on, then leap the barricades. They might accomplish it, Colonel Hardin bitterly told Ben Southern, but only a brigand chieftain with no concern for his men would force such a fight.

They waited. The Mexicans also divided, some riding easterly around the forted-up *Yanquis,* some riding westerly in the same circling fashion. It was a probing ride that brought them in close enough to see how their enemies were protected. It was also done slowly, very leisurely, in order to give the defenders a good long look at the forces and the firepower arraigned against them.

"He's seasoned at this cat-and-mouse business," growled John Hardin, watching the Mexican guerillas. "But he's made the mistake of a lifetime today, Captain Southern. It's one thing for a few scruffy Mex raiders to cross the line . . . they're nothing more than outlaws. But bring a part of one of those Mexican Route Armies up into U.S. Territory and attacking U.S. troops . . . that's fatal."

Ben watched El Vengador. There was no denying it—the man, with his lean, bronzed appearance, looked like the stuff legends were made of. He gestured and called forth in perfect Spanish, making final dispositions. Ben Southern looked and waited and wondered: *Were all legends like this one . . . handsomely colorful to look at, utterly unprincipled and ruthless in action?*

Lieutenant Johnson walked over, halted, and pulled hard at his moustache while he silently squinted out there, too. "He may take us," he said to Ben. "But I don't believe he'll ever make the grade back at the fort. Granted he has twice, three times as many men, but the fort has stout walls . . . and artillery. He'd lose over half his command trying. If he's just half as coyote as I'm beginning to think he is, he'll know all that."

Southern looked briefly at the lieutenant, so busy with his military exercise he was overlooking something a lot more immediate and certain—his own violent death at the hand of those brigands forming to attack out there—and walked away.

The dragoons were ready. Colonel Hardin was ready. Even the professionally clinical lieutenant was ready. But Ben could not find Walter Lee. He went among the horse holders and peered inside the wagons. He went among the men, looking, and dropped low behind their improvised barricades. Still he did not find him. Lee seemed to have vanished.

Ben started around front where the colonel was in position at the foremost barricade, pistol in hand, gazing straight out through the shimmering sun smash where the Mexicans were beginning to move out. He intended to ask if Hardin knew where his man was, but in the face of imminent conflict the loss of Lee suddenly paled into insignificance, so Ben took a position, drew his six-gun, and also waited.

The Mexicans were walking their horses but that fooled no one. Like Indians attacking forted-up wagons, they would walk their horses to conserve them to the last moment, then raise the yell and charge. Each guerilla was holding up his carbine. Each one was concentrating fully upon the wagons. The sun beat down unmercifully making men and animals profusely sweat even though they were entirely motionless.

XIII

They charged from a distance of a hundred yards or about as soon as they came into gun range. They split apart, one segment whipping on around to come in behind the wagons from the west, the balance to bore straight down upon Colonel Hardin's force.

The Fort Brown troopers held their fire to the last second and fired only after their commanding officer leveled his pistol and knocked a guerilla out of his saddle. It was a volley of lead and deafening gun thunder and dirty smoke that erupted. The Mexicans vanished out there; one moment they were straining ahead, the next moment the second rank, much farther back and also much weaker, was visible through gunsmoke. A great wail rose up from the attackers. Around on the west side of the wagons the same thing happened again, but, where Captain Ben commanded, the Mexicans were stunned and, after the first powerful volley, turned and sped away. They had obviously been informed by spies of the twenty-five mounted dragoons riding escort, and had expected no more than ten or twelve of these dismounted cavalrymen to be forted up on each side of the wagons. When twice that number volley-fired, the resultant devastation and confusion was more than adequate to inspire consternation. The Mexicans raced back around where El Vengador and several other men stoically sat their horses out of range, watching.

John Hardin's exultant voice rang out among the men at the wagon camp. "Hold your fire! Save your powder, they'll be back to collect the rest of it. Every alternate man go for water and hasten back so the others can also get a drink. Captain Southern?"

Ben stepped through the wagons. Colonel Hardin was holding out an unstoppered canteen with a death's-head grin. "It's bad luck to drink a toast in water, Captain, but what more bad luck can befall us? Go ahead, have a drink."

They sipped water, leaned in wagon shade, and watched El Vengador's reforming horsemen out there where the heat was a blasting, shimmering source of noonday torture. Ordinarily this time of day, Mexicans crawled into the shade and napped until the worst heat passed. Not today.

Colonel Hardin chuckled. "That was a surprise, when you also volley-fired with twice as many men as they thought you'd have." Around them the troopers were moving back and forth between the barricades and the wagons where the barrels of water were. Lieutenant Johnson passed, saluted, and kept on walking. It amused Ben Southern, this matter of military propriety even at the edge of annihilation.

"I lost a man," said Ben. "No, not in the fighting. That private soldier I brought with me from Camp Scott."

"Ahh?" murmured John Hardin, turning. "Lee? That enlisted man you called Walt Lee?"

"Yes, sir."

Hardin considered the obvious thought and turned as he slowly gazed out and around. "An old campaigner, I take it," he said, and, when Ben confirmed that, Hardin said: "Well, in that case desertion's out . . . which leaves only two alternatives. I think we can eliminate one of those right away . . . goin' over to El Vengador . . . so that leaves. . . ." He brought his eyes back around. "You know him better than I do, Captain . . . do you think he can make it?"

Ben had no clear idea one way or the other, so all he said was: "It depends on the desert . . . and the greasers. Walt did a stretch at Fort Brown he told us, a long time back, so I'm banking on his knowing the desert. But as for El Vengador's cutthroats, I don't know. I hope he makes it, though. I also hope, when he does, that Sergeant Tolliver doesn't waste any time brushing past the other Mex brigands with Sheriff Mittan's posse and getting down here."

Colonel Hardin took the typical view of this. He said dryly: "How will it look, Captain . . . a strong detachment of U.S. soldiers saved by civilians?"

Ben shot the answer straight back. "A lot better, Colonel, than it would look if the U.S. soldiers got massacred and, in so doing, let a band of Mexican insurgents run off with two wagonloads of U.S. Army carbines."

Lieutenant Johnson called out: "Into the lines, men, into the lines!"

Ben gazed out where the dark and large-hatted horsemen were beginning to break up, were commencing to ride around at a respectful distance, all strung out and with their carbines held upright.

"Running attack in a circle," said Ben. "Indian style this time."

Colonel Hardin uttered a contemptuous epithet. "He's going to fool along here and get whipped by God, Captain. I thought the much-vaunted El Vengador was a better tactician than this. With all those men he could over-run us in one strong charge."

"He lost a few the last time he charged, Colonel, and, also, his men got a surprise when the soldiers who'd been in the wagons turned up full of fight, too." Ben watched the Mexicans. "I think they're playing it cautious this time. These surprises can whittle them down and they know it."

"We're fresh out of surprises," growled John Hardin, "except one . . . guts. Go back to your post, Captain."

Ben stepped back through the wagons to where his dismounted men were crouched and waiting, their blouses clinging with sweat, their faces dark red and shiny. A corporal, with a tipped-up Irish nose, freckles, and a mop of fiery hair pushing out from beneath his campaign hat, said: "Captain, what'll they be tryin' now, sir?"

"Indian attack riding around and around, kicking up a big dust and hoping, by throwing a lot of lead, they'll hit a few of us." Ben paused where this man and several others crouched. "Where did that trooper of mine from Camp Scott go?" he asked, not too hopeful of an informative reply.

One of the enlisted men removed his hat, shook off sweat, dropped the hat back down, and said: "After help, Cap'n. I covered him when he belly-crawled out there while them greasers was forming up to charge around the other side. He got away fine."

"On foot?" Ben asked incredulously.

"Yes, sir. He said he'd catch him a Mex horse as soon as a few saddles were emptied." The enlisted man slowly, almost lazily, grinned up at Ben Southern. "He struck me a feller who'd do just about like he said, Captain."

There was no more time for talk; Colonel Hardin sang out, calling the men to become alert, and, around where Ben Southern was, the first of the loping Mexicans made his appearance, dodging and ducking as he rode, bending low with his carbine held one-handed. He fired. Behind him came more of them. The gunfire swelled again; this time the troopers fired back at will. Volley-firing was useless under El Vengador's new strategy.

The dust arose to sting the eyes of the defenders and to burn their throats. Gunfire was endless. It was impossible to tell whether any of those saddles were being emptied or not. When several of his men called out, saying they were running low on ammunition, Ben went to a wagon, got more, and returned with it.

The fight was stubbornly prosecuted by both sides, but the Mexicans, for all their superior numbers, could not quite force themselves to face the unrelenting, deadly fire of Colonel Hardin's veteran warriors. Not even when El Vengador appeared around on the west side, gesturing and shouting indistinguishable orders through the smoke and dust and crashing gunfire.

Ben, sensing El Vengador's angry impatience that the defenders had held out this long, and wishing to inspire even more respect in his Mexicans, went down his line calling for the men to increase their firing. When they shot him quizzical looks, he bellowed at them.

"Shoot! To hell with whether you hit anything or not. Just throw enough lead to keep those Mexicans scairt. Shoot!"

The soldiers shot as often as they could, until it sounded like an entire regiment was forted up around the pair of light commissary wagons. It became so smoky no one could see ten yards away on the west side. The only way they knew El Vengador's desperadoes were still out there was by the fierce return fire. It wasn't any more accurate than the fire of the blinded defenders was, but it was just as lethal if anyone should poke up a head to find out.

This second attack lasted a full half hour. The Mexicans eventually turned their spent horses over to horse holders and skirmished through the smoke on foot, several hundred of them attacking the wagons from east to west, but the defenders, with better cover, picked off a number of the bolder and more reckless of the attackers, and this had a dampening effect upon the others.

Finally the attackers began to withdraw. They were given no order to do so. At least Ben Southern heard no one call for them to drop back. He thought they were breaking off simply because they could not, despite their best efforts, breach the defensive works. He could also imagine how furious El Vengador must be by this time. Between forty and fifty troopers holding off an entire guerilla regiment; something the brigand chieftain hadn't considered at all possible when he had earlier told John Hardin to give up the guns or be wiped out by El

Vengador's great numbers.

That stooped, cadaverous sergeant ambled up as the gunfire dwindled, mopped his leathery, dark brown face, and said: "Cap'n, them greasers must be second run. I've fought Mexicans from Louisiana to California and don't never let nobody tell you they can't fight or that they won't fight. But this bunch out here. . . ." The sergeant sadly wagged his head. "Second run. Probably a bunch of dirt farmers recruited by that leader of theirs."

The sergeant walked on past, heading for the water barrels. Colonel Hardin stepped through, saw Ben, and went over to him. "Mister Avenger doesn't have much choice left," Hardin said. "He tried a divided charge and it failed. He tried an attacking surround and it also failed." Hardin paused to watch Ben's men going and coming after water before he said: "Hit us on either my side or your side, head-on, with every man he has in one big crushing charge. That's all he has left."

Ben tried to see the sun but that choking dust was too thick so he fumbled for his watch. It was past noon. He wondered where the time had flown. Hardin got a canteen and returned with it. Ben didn't drink. He pondered over what the stooped sergeant had said.

Out where the dust was beginning to thin down a little could be seen Mexican horsemen walking their animals back and forth. To the northward one of the defending troopers called for Ben, and, when he got up there near the tongue of one of the commissary rigs, with John Hardin at his side, the lanky enlisted trooper said: "A feller on a sweaty horse just rode in up there where them dudes is gathered around that chieftain of theirs. He come in fast and commenced wavin' his hands like a madman and hollerin' long before he even got close."

They leaned in bitter sunshine, peering out where dust nearly obscured the Mexican leader and several men with whom he was talking. Suddenly El Vengador roared violently at the men around him. He flung his clenched fists into the air and fiercely shook them toward the forted up soldiers around Colonel Hardin's wagons. Then, without any additional outbursts, El Vengador jumped onto his horse and called for the others to do likewise. They did. They whirled and broke up, riding left and right down the line of resting soldiers, calling out sharp orders.

Ben strained to hear. So did the colonel, and the enlisted men standing over there with them near the wagons, but the distance was too great, the Spanish words too slurred and dust-muffled. But eventually all the brigands got astride, and to everyone's total amazement, they broke out southward in a quick rush without making even one more, departing pass at the beleaguered Fort Brown troopers.

No one immediately spoke or moved. Even the crouching soldiers in their sweltering position around the wagons, under them, inside them, or lying nearly prone behind the rifle crates. It was unbelievable that El Vengador with all those heavily armed insurgents would withdraw simply because he had been twice repulsed. And yet that was obviously precisely what he had done.

Colonel Hardin put one of his strong black stogies between his teeth and chewed hard. Ben Southern walked out past the nearest barricade straining to hear. He thought perhaps Walt Lee had gotten through, had found Ned Tolliver with Sheriff Mittan's posse, and was leading them back. But all he heard was the sullen, dissipating drum roll thunder of El Vengador's inexplicable retreat.

That stooped and dehydrated sergeant walked out, too, beyond their barricade. He said: "Cap'n, the colonel says mind yourself . . . them greasers are famous for pullin' sly tricks, an', if you get too far out here, they just might come chargin' back an' get you alive."

Ben nodded but was unimpressed. In the first place he could distinctly hear all those rushing horses still careening southward toward the line. In the second place, since El Vengador had got terribly angry over whatever had caused his withdrawal, there wasn't much question concerning the authenticity of the retreat.

"Hey," murmured the sergeant, cocking his head, "listen off there to the northwest, Cap'n. Sounds like they're comin' back."

Ben listened and said: "Not unless they've got wings, Sergeant. They went straight south. This must be the Acton posse. You'd better go find the colonel and tell him to pass the order to hold all fire."

As the sergeant hustled back toward the wagon, Ben turned also to walk back. He wasn't convinced at all those approaching riders were the posse men. El Vengador hadn't impressed Ben as a liar, and he had said he had more men out on the desert. He hoped with all his might it would be the Acton posse, but he prudently went back behind the barricade all the same.

It was a bad fifteen minutes for them all. Even after the riders were visible it was still a bad time, because dust obscured friend and foe alike. Added to the smoke haze from midday summertime heat, the dust hung bitterly in the breathless air.

"Captain!" called Colonel Hardin, coming around the foremost wagon where Ben was standing. "You recognize those men out in front yet?"

Ben waited a full minute before replying because until then, as the swarm of horsemen came out of the desert, he wasn't certain. "Yes, sir, I recognize them. One of them is Sergeant Tolliver and the other one is Walt Lee."

Hardin looked and made a caustic face. "That man, Lee . . . you should either have him shot on the spot for desertion, Captain, or you should see to it that he makes corporal for gallantry in the face of the enemy, I'm not sure which."

Lieutenant Johnson came up dark with sweat, his splendid

dragoon moustache hopelessly wilted. "Colonel," he said, "there's an awful lot of them for a civilian posse."

Hardin had evidently already noticed this, too, because he said: "Never look a gift horse in the mouth, Lieutenant. Now send out horse holders for them and have the barricades set aside." As the junior officer moved to obey, John Hardin turned and said: "Captain Southern, sir, by God, there are an awful lot of them. But it still doesn't make sense. El Vengador still outnumbered us. What can you make of it?"

"Nothing, sir," replied Ben, and went striding out where Tolliver, Walt Lee, and Sheriff Mittan were stiffly dismounting.

XIV

Walt Lee made a wry face as he saw Ben Southern approaching, and became very busy with the rigging of his saddle. Ned Tolliver, looking gray with fatigue but resolute, threw Ben a light salute. But it was Sheriff Mittan who actually took a couple of steps forward and thrust out his hand at Ben. As they shook and while Ben gazed around at the number of armed posse men, mostly cowmen and their riders, who had come down here with Sheriff Mittan, the lawman said: "Sort of took us by surprise, hearing from Walt Lee that the ones we were chasing weren't the main bunch, Captain. Just how many of them were there?"

Ben said he wasn't sure but that he would guess perhaps two hundred of them, not including the ones who had been used to bait the posse men. Ned Tolliver scowled over that estimate. Some of the posse men standing close by, listening, looked interestedly skeptical.

"Then why did they run out?" asked Mittan. "There aren't enough of us to scare them if they're as strong as you say."

Ben had no answer to that. He sent Tolliver and Walt back to the wagons where Hardin's Fort Brown troopers were getting ready to roll again. He asked Sheriff Mittan to detach a couple of his best men to scout southward and make certain El Vengador wasn't up to some kind of a trick, and finally he suggested that the Acton posse, instead of riding along with the wagons and their trooper escort, ride up ahead in a strung-out line, like vedettes, just in case.

When the cavalcade eventually started forward up the little crooked road again, that's how the men and wagons traveled. Lieutenant Johnson brought up the rear with a strong guard. The troopers inside the wagons had the canvas covers rolled half up the bows permitting a little air to come and go. John Hardin and Ben Southern rode at the column's head. Far out, up through the smoky heat haze, rode the men from Acton.

It was a long afternoon. Tolliver gave up his saddle, crawled into one of the wagons, and instantly fell asleep. Walt Lee and Captain Ben had a little discussion, the conclusion of which was that in the future it would be much better if Walt waited until he was asked to go for help.

Sheriff Mittan returned once, after they had been under way over an hour, and reported his scouts had gone as far south as they had dared, and the only thing they had seen had been an immense dust banner perhaps a mile long and at least a mile deep. They thought they had heard a battle raging but had not gone any closer to make certain since, if it was a battle, it was going on well across the line into Mexico.

After Mittan loped back up where his posse men were, lethargically doing their duty as forward skirmishers, Colonel Hardin said: "So that's what made him pull out like that . . . angry and in a big rush. Federal Mexican troops on his trail."

Ben agreed, then said he would like to see the battle. John Hardin was rueful about that. "It'd disappoint you, Captain. Mexicans don't use tactics or battlefield strategy. They charge in howling, hack and shoot and blast away until someone gives, and, if one side is stubborn, then the other side howls and hacks its ways out of the fight. More like a mêlée than a battle. The only Mex soldiers worth a damn are the mounted ones. Mexico is a nation of horsemen, Captain. Unless you're an excellent horseman down there, you're nothing."

They wore away the afternoon, made two rest halts and two water halts, then sighted Acton on ahead. Walt Lee loped up from the rear to tell Ben Southern that Tolliver had said the sacks of firing pins were locked in the safe at Mittan's office.

They entered a town enormously curious about them. Evidently Tolliver's dusty, haggard arrival the night before, and the subsequent recruiting of Ed Mittan's posse, had put Acton into a frame of mind that bordered on warfare. Men were everywhere with their rifles and carbines. Over in front of the gun shop men stood, thick and watchful. Elsewhere, armed men patrolled or watched, or just stood in little clutches, talking.

The greatest number of men congregated down at Ed Mittan's jailhouse where the posse was disbanded. There, Sheriff Mittan and the colonel from Fort Brown were subjected to shouted questions. When they related what they knew, especially the colonel who told of being under attack by Mexican guerillas, the townsmen profanely called on Hardin to lead them south in retaliation.

It was during the height of this acrimonious dispute, the townsmen insisting, the colonel refusing, that Walt Lee stepped up and plucked at Ben Southern's sleeve, turned, and pointed over across the road near the hotel doorway where Alice Clark stood in late-day shadows, looking as cool as she somehow always managed to seem even when the mercury stood well up into the sweltering heights in Acton's thermometers.

Ben caught Walt as he turned to fade out in the crowd. "Go get Ned," Ben ordered. "Treat him to a bath at the hotel, a big supper at the hotel dining room, then sack him out in a genuine bed upstairs. He's earned it. Get two more rooms, one for you and one for me, then get plenty of rest yourself. We'll be pulling out of Acton for Camp Scott in the morning."

Walt Lee looked dumbfounded. He said: "Cap'n, the Fort Brown escort won't go with us beyond Acton, sir."

Ben said: "I know that, Private Lee, and now, in case you thought what we went through today was bad, you just might be proven wrong. Assuming, of course, that El Vengador comes through his battle below the border. He'll be after us harder than ever if he does, Walt. He'll lose men and also guns down there, but most important, in order to get recruits, he'll be obliged to arm them. That's all . . . Private Lee."

Walt got the strong emphasis on his lowly rank. Captain Southern had discussed that particular point as far as he proposed to; the subject was closed. He turned and went away in search of Ned Tolliver, who was awake in one of the wagons, sitting dispiritedly atop a rifle crate. When Walt poked his head through the slit in the tailgate canvas, Ned looked out at him with watery, bleary eyes and said: "Go away, will you?"

Lee's answer was short. "Get down out of there. Cap'n Ben says you're to get a bath, a supper at the hotel, and a gen-u-wine bed at the hotel because we're rollin' out for Camp Scott come sunup . . . without no escort."

Tolliver lifted his head. He badly needed a shave, his eyes were red from dust and sun smash, his face was burned dark and peeling. He glowered out at Walt. "Does he figure those Mexicans'll get back up here, Walt?"

"He says maybe they will. Depends on whether they win their battle below the line. Anyway . . . yes or no . . . we're rollin' out in the morning, so come along with me. You need rest and so do I."

Still, Tolliver sat in there glowering. Finally he yawned and stretched and heaved up to his feet. At once his head came painfully into contact with an ash bow and Ned Tolliver swore with aggravated feeling as he made his way out of the wagon, got down beside Walt in the softening late day, and looked around.

Mostly the townsmen and range men had drifted off. There were still a few leaning upon their rifles here and there as though guarding the commissary wagons or just standing there in the hope Colonel Hardin and Ed Mittan would emerge from the jailhouse office and call for another posse.

Walt and Ned made their way across toward the hotel. They halted upon the outside plank walk while Tolliver lifted his head like an old hound dog, and sniffed. He seemed to lose nearly all his earlier lethargy.

"Walt," he said, "there's a saloon up the road there. Did the cap'n say anything about you standin' me to a drink?"

"No," answered Walt Lee, "he didn't. But that don't mean I can't stand you to a drink. Maybe two drinks."

They left the hotel entrance pacing up through the settling dusk side-by-side, tough, dehydrated old campaigners with a healthy thirst.

"Funny thing about tiredness," stated Ned Tolliver as he held open the spindle door of the saloon courteously so that Walt could pass on inside first. "It leaves a man in a twinklin', under the proper circumstances."

"You're not tired any more?" asked Walt.

Tolliver shook his head solemnly. "Never in my life felt less tired an' more dry."

They went to the bar. There was a crowd in the saloon but it was still a mite early so the bar wasn't crowded. They called for two belts of rye whiskey and afterward asked for glasses of ale to wash out the tartness of the rye, took their beers to an empty table, and sat down, tired but relaxed and perfectly at peace with the world.

Four cowboys at an adjoining table also idly drinking called over. "You fellers come in with them Army wagons?"

Ned looked at the cowboys but said nothing. He instead sipped beer, as dry as he had been all day, it was wonderful sitting there without a worry in the world, drinking beer.

Walt told the cattlemen they had come with the wagons. One of the range men said: "There's talk somethin' happened below the line to save your bacon . . . a herd of Mex regulars come up, drawin' off El Vengador."

Walt considered that thoughtfully for a moment before saying: "Mister, maybe El Vengador havin' to pull out like that saved our bacon, but my personal conviction is that, since we didn't lose a single damned man and he lost at least ten, if he'd stuck around we'd have saved the Mex government a heap of expense by whittlin' him down a man at a time."

One of the cowboys laughed. The others smiled a little. One of them, a tall, sun-blackened, curly-headed man in his late thirties, said: "Maybe you're right at that, friend. Maybe you're right at that. Anyway, you got away from him an' from here on you got straight sailin' right up to the gates of Camp Scott." This one signaled for a barman to fetch more beer for Ned and Walt, got up, and jerked his head at his companions. They also got up. The four of them sauntered on out into the night. For some little while Tolliver and Lee just squatted there, nursing their refilled beer glasses, watching the saloon begin to fill up with noisy men. It was good being back in civilization like this; there had been earlier reason for both of them to doubt they would ever be doing this again, which was what made it so good now.

"It's the little things in life," opined Ned Tolliver with a hint of thickness to his voice. "Walt, my boy, it's the little things in life that mean a lot, not the big ones."

Walt heard but did not particularly heed. He was staring darkly at his half empty glass of beer.

"A man lives, a man dies," mumbled Ned. "Nothing's changed much by it. Everything pretty much goes on as before. It's not even important that a big man like President Lincoln died. Life is made up for each man of a lot of little things . . . they're important, Walt. The big things . . . hell . . . they happen anyway, and they don't make no great changes any more'n the little things do."

Walt suddenly pushed his glass resolutely away and got up. "Come on," he growled. "You're headin' for bed." He took Tolliver's arm and led him out of the crowded saloon into the pleasant, purple night with its town sounds all around and its cow-town scents. As they paced southward toward the hotel Ned drew his arm away, looked down at Walter Lee with his head thrown far back, and loftily said: "You think I'm drunk, don't you?"

Lee's answer was cryptic. "I think you're givin' a real convincin' imitation, Ned."

"Well, I'm not. An' I also know something else."

Walt stopped, resigned. "All right . . . get it off your chest," he said. "Then you're goin' to bed down."

"I know that those four fellers back there in the saloon said we had clear sailin' from Acton to Camp Scott, and that's been botherin' you ever since they said it because it was supposedly four outlaws who killed O'Casey and Slattery, and also because . . . how'd they even know we were goin' to Camp Scott?"

Tolliver made a very slow, raffish smile, and winked with one eye.

Walt Lee stood gazing at him a moment. "You gave a fair imitation," he conceded. "In fact, you even fooled me. Well . . . ?"

"Well, hell!" exclaimed Tolliver, turning to look down at the jailhouse where lamplight glowed. "Let's go hunt up Cap'n Ben. If we're wrong, no one'll be hurt. If we're right, it'll prove El Vengador is a long shot from givin' up his hope to get hold of our rifles."

"It'll also prove," muttered Walt as they started off, "that he didn't lead all his renegades down to the battle below the line. I'll make you a bet, Ned . . . these four are the same four that got Slattery and O'Casey."

"Lord preserve 'em," breathed Sergeant Tolliver in a menacing tone, "if they are."

Sheriff Mittan was in the office with several unfamiliar townsmen when Tolliver and Walt Lee barged in, but Captain Southern was not there and neither was Colonel Hardin. Mittan thought Hardin might be over at the hotel, but he said he had seen Captain Southern walking up the plank walk with Miss Alice about an hour back.

Outside again, Tolliver and Lee conferred. Second thoughts inclined them to discard hunting down the captain to explain their suspicions about those four range riders.

"The mornin' will be soon enough," said Lee. "Besides, if they really are El Vengador's men after the guns, they'll let us know it soon enough."

Tolliver stroked his chin and dropped down in deep thought until Lieutenant Johnson came striding along, his fierce moustache freshly combed and stiffened, then Tolliver said— "Lieutenant."—and when the junior officer came up, Tolliver put a careful glance upon him. "Lieutenant, Private Lee and me was just discussin' . . . were you or were you not too much of a bluebelly to drink with enlisted men at the saloon over yonder and up the road."

Lieutenant Johnson raised a hand to twist his moustache wickedly. He eyed the saloon and he eyed Tolliver and Lee.

"Who has the money?" he inquired.

Tolliver jingled a pocket. Lee also jingled a pocket.

Lieutenant Johnson hooked them by the arm and turned them forcibly across the road, his course undeviatingly set for the saloon.

XV

Ben Southern washed and shaved, changed his clothing by purchasing fresh things, and met Alice Clark at the hotel dining room for supper. She had agreed to order for them both and even when Colonel Hardin strolled through, his young-old eyes glinting jealously at the junior officer, the pleasure of this moment was not dimmed.

"You could invite him to eat with us," she said, and Ben gently shook his head in reply.

She had on a gray dress held at the lacy throat with a cameo brooch. The dress fitted tightly above the waist and fell away gracefully below. Before, when he had seen her at the ranch or astride a horse, she had worn loose blouses and riding skirts; she had of course been female then, but now, tonight in the golden lamp glow of the hotel dining room in that gray dress, she was something straight out of his pre-war memories, something he hadn't seen, or even dreamed of seeing again, since arriving on the frontier.

"The whole town is talking of your battle down on the desert," she told him. "I'm very glad it ended as it did."

He glanced around the dining room. It was nearly full. There were several uniforms evident besides the colonel's, but mostly the people were cattlemen and their families or local merchants and their families. It was an agreeable world to him, particularly so since everything was clean and orderly—no sun, no sweat, no stench of gunpowder or raw curses.

He brought his gaze back to her. "I'm glad it ended that way, too," he said, "but something else troubles me, Miss Alice."

She understood. She said quietly: "It shouldn't, Captain. It stopped bothering me a long time ago."

"I don't believe it!" he exclaimed.

She raised her smoky gaze to his face. "Maybe I should have said it differently, Captain. It bothers me, yes, but a long time ago I stopped feeling the pain. As long as I thought there was any hope for him, or that he might change, might give it up and come home, I tried. But not any more, Captain . . . he's a perfect stranger to me."

They ate, and afterward he ordered them more coffee that they sipped. Later, with the benign night all around and its pleasant pale light to show the way, they strolled through Acton. Colonel Hardin's Fort Brown troopers were much in evidence, passing from bar to bar or from dance hall to card parlor. Even the colonel himself was to be seen for a short while where he leaned in cool darkness out front of the hotel, chewing a stogie and exchanging grave nods with the townsmen who saw him there and nodded as they went strolling past.

It was a hot, bland night, excellent for strolling as Ben Southern and the tall, handsome girl from the south desert were doing. "I like this town," she told him as they left the main thoroughfare and paced slowly eastward through the residential area. "My father used to own the freighting company here." He raised his eyebrows. She said: "You're surprised? You thought we only ranched? No . . . in fact when my father first came to the territory, he came as a freighter. He bought the ranch only after he got married."

She was quiet for a long while after that, walking beside him with her smooth, graceful movements. He did not desire to break the spell of this wonderful time so he, too, was quiet. When they eventually ran out of plank walk and had to turn back, she spoke again, her voice richly musical in the hush of this part of town. "My mother was Mexican, Captain. But by now you've figured that out," she said.

He did not reply. He hadn't figured it out, but it certainly explained something that had troubled his thoughts after that first close glimpse of El Vengador, her brother.

"She was Mexican . . . and was as wonderful as any girl's mother ever was, Captain."

"And your father?"

"A tall, very fair man . . . I have his coloring. My brother is darker."

"Yes," he murmured, "I know."

"He was . . . I don't know how to explain it. Sheriff Mittan calls my brother some kind of a throwback. I can't say what he is. I only know he was bad right from childhood. My parents worried about him. I've often been thankful they died before they ever saw what he'd really become."

"How did they die, Alice?"

"You'd imagine," she said, pacing slowly at his side, "they'd have died by violence. By Apache or Mexican guns. But in fact, Captain Ben, they both died of an epidemic that came and depopulated most of the desert country many years back."

He said no more. There were other questions he was curious about, but the two important ones had been answered. Moreover, she turned and gazed at him, asking questions of her own.

"Why is a man like you stationed out here, Captain?"

He raised his eyebrows. "A man like me, Alice?" He shrugged that off and said: "After the war, mustang Army officers were a nickel a dozen . . . they could resign . . . which the government hoped they'd do . . . or they could take a reduction in rank and serve on the frontier, which the state officers figured would force the most stubborn to resign anyway."

"And you," she asked, "you are going to resign?"

He smiled at her. "No, as a matter of fact I like the border country. Even now, in midsummer, I'm at home here."

They halted near a little cleared acre of land where tree logs had been carefully hauled in and arranged as benches. She, seeing his interest in this place, said: "This is where they have the plays when Mexican *troupes* pass through."

He took her hand, led her down to a particular log bench, and sat down with her there. He chose that especial bench because it had a backrest. He leaned far back, pushed out his legs and lifted his face to the high skies.

"Alice," he murmured, "marry me."

She sat perfectly still for a long time, shocked, then she laughed. He joined in, turning to watch. There were echoes to that merry sound that traveled back where two dark shapes had been hiking along. The dark shapes halted out beyond the farthest logs to look down into the small theater area.

"I wanted to see if you remembered how to laugh," he said. "I really hadn't hoped for more than a smile."

She sobered, her blue eyes made large and liquid and black in the night. "And suppose I'd accepted, Captain," she said. "Then who would've laughed. Supposed I'd accepted with a straight face?"

He was still gently smiling up into her dark eyes when she said that. "I'd have been surprised," he conceded to her. "But to be candid, Alice, it wouldn't have upset me very much. I could do a whole lot worse."

That time she didn't laugh at him; she sat there, gazing at his face, saying nothing. Neither of them had as yet seen those two silhouettes out beyond the little park, who now seemed locked in a fiercely whispered argument of some kind.

"A man without a woman is like life with spirit, Alice. Or air without oxygen. Or the desert without heat. It is a forest without leaves or an ocean without salt. I don't believe anything is very good without its leavening . . . take people, Alice . . . a girl suffers and becomes a woman. A man dies a hundred times to become a man. Without any suffering at all the girl remains just always a girl. You've seen them . . . fifty years old and simpering. Or the men whose lives have been protected, and who have suddenly been confronted with crises. They are unequal to it. The same with a man who has no woman, Alice."

She would have risen but he put out a hand to detain her. He smiled. "All right, we'll talk of something else." She eased back. "You wanted to know of the fight this morning, I'll tell you."

But she stopped him. "Not now, Captain. Not really. It's such a beautiful night." He gazed at her—that had been why she had first wished to speak to him, he was certain of that. She saw his look and understood the wonderment. "In hot daylight it's different. Now . . . well . . . now it's just too pleasant and cool and. . . ." She gestured around them where silence lay in layers, where the cool night cast its endless shadows. There was a fragrance, too. Someone nearby, among the *jacales* and homes, spared water for a flower bed. In so harsh a land there was more need perhaps than there was elsewhere for each person in some small way to feed the soul.

He waited. It was a bad time for her. That laughter had helped, but laughter at best was only temporary, the dark stirrings of a person's mind lingered on. She had been in anguish for a long time, before the soldier column her brother had attacked, appeared in Acton without casualties. She had other deep stirrings. Life was struggle and the living of it complex.

She eventually turned toward him and said: "And since you like the desert country, you will perhaps stay, Captain Ben . . . and what then, for you?"

She had some answer in her own mind; he felt that. He said: "Chase Indians that no longer maraud, I reckon, Miss Alice. Patrol the southward country for Mex guerillas. Police the border country until someday the towns get larger, civil law gets stronger, then be transferred somewhere else." He saw how she watched him and said, with a slow little smile: "Doesn't sound like a wildly exciting life for a professional horse soldier, does it? Well, I've had my excitement. Four years of it, and I still sometimes find it hard to believe I survived it. I'll take the other life now."

"Of course," she said, arising. Then she turned to watch him unwind up off the log. "Alone, Captain?"

He started to reply but checked himself, grinned, and shook a finger at her. She smiled. They threaded their way back through the logs toward the dark and silent residential roadway where those two silhouettes still stood, watching them from the upper end of the little park area. The moment they began walking back toward Acton's main thoroughfare, those shadows faded down a convenient alleyway. Ben Southern and Alice Clark passed right on by without noticing. They reached the central section of town and went down as far as the hotel entrance. There she stopped, took his hand, and lightly held it.

"Thank you for the walk . . . and the laughter," she said, dropped his hand, and walked on inside.

He remained out in the warm night with the sounds coming from the yonder saloons making him conscious of an odd restlessness in himself, and, when he turned as though to cross over to the closest bar, his route was barred.

"Cap'n," said Ned Tolliver, "you lead a feller a merry chase."

Ben gazed at the pair of them, disheveled, unkempt, like a pair of drifters. "You've been shagging me?" he asked.

Walt Lee said: "Yes, sir, but we had reason." Walt then told of the four men at the saloon. When he finished speaking, the three of them exchanged a long look.

"Maybe," the officer said, "we can manage to lose a skirmish and win a battle down here, men." Ned and Walt soberly nodded, saying nothing and neither of them having the faintest idea what Ben Southern's allegory meant. "I think with some co-operation we just might be able to surprise some gunmen."

"Yes, sir," muttered Tolliver, as solemn as an owl and just as uncomprehending as before.

"Colonel Hardin will send two drivers with us to Camp Scott so he'll have someone to fetch his light wagons back to Fort Brown for him. Those may be exactly the bait we'll need."

"Yes, sir," stated Tolliver again. "You're figurin' on rollin' out for Scott in the morning?"

"At the edge of dawn, men," assented Ben Southern.

"With a posse of these here Acton civilians?"

Ben shook his head. "You wouldn't want to scare off El Vengador's supply department, would you?"

"Well, sir," began Walt Lee, "if you was to ask. . . ."

"And perhaps let the murderers of O'Casey and Slattery ride off scotfree?"

Walt Lee's jaw snapped closed. Ned Tolliver gently masticated his cud and kept a flinty eye upon the officer in front of them. Eventually he said: "No, sir, we sure wouldn't. You got maybe an ambush in mind?"

Ben said: "That's exactly what I've got in mind. Ned, you stay here in town tonight, harness up in the morning, and ride out with the wagons. Hire two livery horses, have them saddled, and tie them to the tailgate. You understand?"

"Yes, sir . . . so's them fellers'll think all three of us are along, only maybe two of us is inside the wagons."

Ben nodded. "You come with me, Walt. We've got riding to do."

XVI

Ben Southern visited Colonel Hardin in the senior officer's room at the hotel, and, between them, they considered combing

Acton for the four men Tolliver and Lee suspected of being El Vengador's particular assassins. However, as powerful as this temptation was, and despite the force of soldiers they had at their command in Acton, they decided not to do it, for if something should alert those four, they would disappear in the night and the chances of ever getting the killers of O'Casey and Slattery would grow perceptibly smaller.

Colonel Hardin, whose area ended at Acton, said he would detach an element of his force in town to go northward with Ben, but Southern opposed that. "Too many riders, too many noticeable tracks, Colonel, and too much dust later on . . . providing Tolliver's and Lee's suspicions are correct."

John Hardin chewed a cigar, thought, and scowled at Ben Southern. "You propose," he growled, "to go after those four with just one enlisted man . . . this Walt Lee?"

Ben said that was exactly what he proposed. Then he added that, if the element of surprise could be maintained, there was no earthly reason why he and Lee wouldn't be able to bring it off. "Besides," he concluded, "there will still be Ned Tolliver and your detached pair of wagons to give 'em hell if they hit the wagons."

"Not if they hit 'em from ambush," opined John Hardin. "They could pick off five men . . . ten men . . . from a good ambushing site, before anyone could unlimber on them, Captain."

"Yes, sir. But the ambushing sites between Acton and Camp Scott are my particular charge, Colonel. Remember, we just rode down here a few days back. We know where those sites are. We figure to leave tonight when no one will notice, and start riding."

"How?" demanded Colonel Hardin. "How can two men cover the ambushing spots, Captain?"

"We split up, Colonel," explained Ben. "When we come to

the first one, Walt gets into it, hides, and gets ready with his guns. I ride on to the next one. As soon as the wagons have passed, Private Lee leaves his spot, lopes on up, and we ride to the next pair of ambush sites."

"Leapfrog," said John Hardin. "Well, it might work, Captain. But the chances would be a lot better if you'd take more men."

Ben neither argued that point nor agreed with the colonel. Shortly afterward he and the colonel parted. Ben went to his own room and bedded down. He was tired. And he was also hungry again but it was too late to do much about that, so he bedded down after first making certain which room Lee had, and also after passing the night clerk some silver to awaken him at 3:00 in the morning when it was darkest and coolest.

It seemed he had scarcely given the night man those instructions than he was there again, at bedside, gently rousing Ben. The hotel was utterly still. So was the outside roadway that Ben saw beyond his roadside window. He went along to arouse Walt Lee and led off toward the livery barn. They found the night hawk fast asleep, and, rather than go to the bother of awakening him, they saddled their own animals, left some coins, and rode out. Walt asked no questions and Captain Ben made no conversation until they were well away from Acton.

There was a faint chill to the air, but it was dry. The night—or morning—was invigorating. It was also so still they could hear every abrasive sound of their own saddlery.

Finally Walt said: "Cap'n, how about them bags of firing pins . . . shouldn't you an' me've brought them along, instead of leavin' 'em in the sheriff's safe back in town?"

Ben explained about that succinctly. "No. I don't want the pins and the rifles traveling north at the same time. We'll send back later for the pins, Walt, when no one'll have any more interest in them." Ben had other thoughts along those lines. For one thing, if he came back himself to pick up the firing pins, he would be two-thirds of the way back to the Clark Ranch, and, since he had left her no note back in Acton for a very clear reason—the fewer who knew what he and Walt Lee were up to the better—she would wonder. Well, with luck he would make it back before too long.

They passed up the broken land as far as a slight rocky escarpment, and halted up there, which was what Ben had had in mind. From the rocky height they could see in all directions, but not until sunup, so they dismounted to have a smoke and wait. It wasn't much of a wait. The sun was never tardy on the desert; it might be impeded by overcasts on the plains or forest shadows in the uplands, but upon the desert nothing ever delayed it.

They smoked and talked desultorily and watched the land steadily brighten. In the brush around them small animals and birds came to life. Cactus wrens, enormous hairy spiders, lizards by the score came forth to start their eternal daylight hunting. Walt dropped his cigarette, stamped on it, and raised his head, and Ben lifted an arm rigidly to point downcountry. The wagons were infinitesimal down below, but recognizable. A lone horsemen slouched up ahead, which moved Lee to say: "You got to hand it to old Tolliver. He's been lookin' down the barrels of guns so long he's sure to figure his luck's nigh run out. But there he is, pokin' along like he's got not one single worry in the world."

Ben agreed, but he wasn't concerned with Ned Tolliver. Unless the three of them had jumped to an arbitrary conclusion, there should be four riders skulking somewhere down there. But there were not. Nowhere Ben looked could he discern movement, riders, or even dust. He, too, killed his smoke.

The wagons came on, dust rising, the harness animals phlegmatically plodding, Ned Tolliver out ahead like a scout, also plodding, and, visible now and then out back, two saddled horses also walking along. The entire scene, Ben thought, was deceptively mild and harmless. If El Vengador's American desperadoes were watching, they couldn't help but be fooled. But as near as either Ben or Walt Lee could determine, they weren't watching.

"Well," said Lee. "Sir. . . ."

Ben knew what Walt was driving at. If they were going to head on for the ambushing sites down beside the trail, they had better move out. The sun was fully up now; heat haze would come soon. No matter what ensued, they would have no better time to do what they had come out here to do. He got astride and led out down around the back of the brushy eminence keeping two hundred feet ahead of Walt, a distance the pair of them maintained until they were in among the scrub brush of the desert floor again. Then Ben halted to permit Walter to come on up.

Ben pointed. "See those paloverdes over in that big catclaw clump? You take it. Let the wagons roll well past before you leave it an' light on up north, too."

They parted. Ben let Lee get a half mile off across the desert and beyond the crooked stage road before he turned and booted out his horse. One man didn't raise much dust providing his horse was fresh, but a tired critter that dragged its feet let the whole watching world know where a man was in this hostile environment.

Walt was lost to sight almost at once. Ben, too, as he worked his way around and through stands of brush, looking at the ground for fresh shod horse sign and also at the pale sky for dust banners, passed from sight. The only moving thing in all that emptiness was Ned Tolliver on his head-hung horse coming ploddingly up the trace, and farther back, behind Ned, the pair of wagons with their dirty canvas tops.

Ben sweated and not just from the steadily increasing heat,

either. If he had guessed wrong about those four men, there was likely to be some explaining to do, because, without something concrete to present his colonel up at Camp Scott, everything he had thus far done since departing from Scott earlier made it appear that he had only partially carried out his orders. He had been gone long enough to do everything he had been ordered to, which would only make it look worse when he got back.

He stopped where the stage road made a long curve, passing from south to northeast. There were several spire-like old pockmarked pillars there, an ideal place for an ambush. He hid his horse, kept his carbine, and went up to get into the thin shade of that place. Then he saw them!

Four riders coming at a loose lope in from the distant west. It was clever strategy, he thought, approaching from a direction no one would be expecting anything, certainly no bad trouble. They were armed with carbines as well as belt guns. They were strung out so that, although they made dust, it appeared diluted because they were not riding in a bunch. He strained hard to recognize them but gave that up after a moment because it dawned upon him that those men were making straight for the place where he was concealed.

Sergeant Tolliver was out of sight southward. Walt Lee had been instructed to remain in place until he was certain no one meant to approach the wagons farther south. These things left Ben Southern alone to face El Vengador's four killers, not a pleasant prospect, but on the other hand nothing he hadn't considered possible and for which he was not now secretly prepared for. Still, the odds were long and they did not especially favor Ben Southern.

He watched those riders coming along through the brassy sunlight; if he had been dead certain of their identity, he could have opened up on them before they could get set to offer resistance, but as it was, not knowing absolutely that these were the killers he wanted, the danger of shooting innocent range riders loomed large in his thoughts. He felt sure, but it took more than that, so he leaned back in the rocks, braced his back against a worn old shoulder of stone, and rested his carbine across a lower ledge of rock in front.

The road came on from the south, made a bend to skirt around the rocks where Ben waited, and afterward, a mile or so, straightened out again heading northward. It was this same road that ambled around up through the Camp Scott country.

The horsemen out there slowed to a steady walk, then halted altogether. He watched them straighten in their saddles, looking southward where the dust from Ned Tolliver's gun wagons rose lazily. They were gauging the distance and the time. Evidently they felt they had ample time because they made no immediate move to ride closer to the rocks where Ben waited, which was their obvious destination.

He was thankful for that. They were well beyond Winchester range, but, if they wished, they could close that gap very swiftly. He tried hard to make out their faces, and failed. There was nothing otherwise familiar about them. Still, in the battle the day before he had seen Yankee renegades among the Mexicans, but, as now, the haze, the dust, the turbulent excitement had kept him from paying too much attention to any particular man or men. Now he wished he had been more discerning the day before.

His own visibility of the southward trace was very limited. He guessed that those four riders had already previously reconnoitered the rocks, had discovered just how limited the visibility was over there, and now elected to wait out on the range where they could see the wagons, before coming on over.

That was evidently the plan, too, for, shortly after Ben saw the dust banner thicken, turn mealy with gritty substance, one of the riders hauled forth his carbine and sat out there on his horse working the mechanism to check each load. The others did not do this, but two of them drew their six-guns and hefted them, returned them to their hip holsters, and raised their reins, gazing at the fourth man. He alone showed no signs of nervousness. The others were beginning to get uneasy before that fourth man finally bobbed his head up and down.

The four of them, having decided the wagons were close enough, started riding straight for the road and on across it to the ambush site. Ben raised his carbine, pushed a finger inside the loading gate, felt the reassuring coldness of a brass casing, and moved a little with his gun so there would be no chance of sunlight reflecting off steel to warn the oncoming men. He was positive those were the killers of Slattery and O'Casey. He wanted them badly enough, almost, to risk a premature shot—almost but not quite.

The rock spires were the only ones anywhere around this part of the desert that were tall and grouped together. They resembled ancient tree trunks, devoid of tops and limbs, left over from some ancient age, and they were dark, burned that lusterless color by eons of fierce desert summer suns. There was shale at their bases where particles of stone had flaked off. Each time Ben moved, those small bits of stone ground together underfoot.

The pillars were perhaps fifteen feet high with one slightly higher, perhaps twenty feet. Behind them stood a flourishing stand of chaparral, which was where Ben had secreted his horse. He prayed now the horse wouldn't smell those other animals and nicker at them.

One man in the heart of those spires would be very hard to dislodge because, aside from having the only real protection for miles in any direction, he also could move back and forth among them for shelter against flying lead.

It was, Ben thought, probably the best place for an ambush

in many miles on either side of the roadway. One other thing he was quite certain of was that the renegades also thought that or they wouldn't be riding up now.

Each man had drawn out his carbine and was coming on with a weapon balanced across his lap. Obviously they suspected nothing, but to Ben, who was squeezing back to remain inconspicuous as long as possible, the sight of those four was not especially reassuring.

He decided to bring down that fourth man, the one to whom the others looked to as their leader, with his first shot. He eased up his gun and snugged it back. The loss of their leader might not discourage the other three, but it surely would give them ample reason to hesitate.

He had the man in his sights now. Those four were almost into carbine range.

XVII

A gunshot erupted simultaneously with a man's wild shout. Lead struck stone, chips flew, and one dagger-like rock sliver cut the back of Ben Southern's hand up close to his cheek where the hand was steadying the carbine, its forefinger curled at the trigger. The shot, the deafening sound, the pure astonishment were so mixed and overwhelming that, when Ben actually did fire, his slug whistled harmlessly over the head of those oncoming four men. They broke. One of them cried out. They scattered in four different directions. Two of them got off shots into the rock where Ben was pressing back and twisting to see where that mysterious gunshot had come from.

He never located the unseen gunman. All four of the other men were now scattered through the onward underbrush, throwing lead. Ben dropped when the bullets sang close. He turned and worked his way in behind one of the stone spires where he was quite safe. The trouble with that position was simply that he could not fire back. Gradually, as the gunfire directed against his position increased, it began to dawn on Ben that there wasn't just the four renegades he had seen earlier, or that fifth gunman, wherever he was, who had seen Ben and had fired at him to alert the other four. There were more carbines coming into the fight by the minute.

Somewhere southward he heard a lone Springfield rifle open up, its throaty bellow deeper, more ominous than the sharp snap of Winchester saddle guns. Then another Army-issue weapon fired; it was a Sharps carbine, one of the toughest, most durable cavalry weapons of all time—but single-shot. Against Winchesters whoever had that Sharps was far out-gunned.

Those two fresh weapons out there somewhere on the desert disconcerted the renegades long enough for Ben to straighten up enough to risk a peek out. He saw six men, not four, strung out through the underbrush screen. If there were six of them visible, he wondered how many more there would be who were not visible. He also marveled—until that mysterious sharpshooter had laid lead into Ben's rocks, he had seen only four men. Whether it had been a deliberate trap or not, it worked very effectively as one.

He chose a target out where the outlaws were craning around to locate those guns farther back upon the desert near the road, leveled on the man, and fired. The outlaw whipped straight around and sprang. When he fell, he was draped out across a hardy chaparral bush. That was where he limply hung until several howling companions hauled him down behind the brush out of sight and took turns pouring a deadly probing fire into the rocks where Ben crouched low and waited for the shower of stone splinters to cease.

Farther back those two Army guns were suddenly joined by another weapon, a Winchester carbine, the same kind of gun the renegades were using. The same kind of weapon, as a matter of fact, nine out of every ten civilian Westerners used, had used for many years, and would continue to use for many years yet to come.

The fire was becoming too hot for the attackers of Ben Southern. They still outnumbered Ben and whoever was out there to the west helping him, but it must have been unnerving not being able to see those other gunmen back there. The outlaws turned their backs on Ben and went back westerly beyond his sight. He heard one of them let off a roar of chagrin and could only wonder at the cause for that. Later, believing himself safe, he slipped carefully around the northernmost pillar where he commanded a good wide view. At once a gunman drove him back again with two rapid near misses. He concentrated now upon finding that gunman. It took some time, for the battle otherwise was disconcerting—one moment it seemed to favor Ben's attackers, the next moment it favored those unseen strangers out there.

He was satisfied those Army weapons were being used by the pair of Fort Brown wagoners Colonel Hardin had sent north with the gun wagons, but as time went on and it appeared there had to be more men than just two detached dragoons and Ned back there, with conceivably Walt Lee who would have heard the firing and perhaps rushed up, he puzzled over who the others might be.

Ed Mittan had been ordered by Colonel Hardin not to interfere unless asked to do so by Captain Southern, and Ben hadn't even seen the sheriff since late last evening, let alone talked with him.

It could perhaps be local range riders drawn to the scene by the gunshots, but, if that were so, how would they know which side to take? He stopped trying to puzzle things out when his opposite number drove another slug against his shielding rock. That time he spotted the puff of soiled smoke and fired back.

At once, probably because his adversary had been surprised and angered, three more savage shots raked along the stone front searchingly. Ben checked his carbine, made certain the magazine was chock-full, then sluiced one shot to the left, one to the right, levered up, and fired off two low ones and one high one. Then he dropped back to reload, and wait.

No shot came back from out yonder. He plugged in the last Winchester slug from his belt, levered one into the chamber, and got belly down to peer out. Still nothing happened. He exposed a leg, an arm, finally he got up onto one knee with his carbine ready. Nothing happened. Off to his left, farther out through the underbrush, the other fight was still furiously raging. He stood up, stepped boldly forth from behind his rocks, and, when no one shot at him, he started trotting ahead on a back-and-forth course. The only gunfire was farther out over the desert but he saw movement just before he had crossed the road, whirled to fire, and dropped. It was a loose saddle horse eyeing him with cool interest. He ran on.

The man who had been trading shots with him was lying just behind the first chaparral fringe west of the road with two bullet holes in him, one from the right shoulder downward, one from the left shoulder slantingly toward the man's heart.

He paused to gaze at that sweat-red, oily face. The man was a stranger to him, and yet he thought the man must have had some particular grudge against him to stay back and concentrate on trying to kill him so hard. Probably, he thought, one of the raiders who had been at the Clark Ranch, where some other raiders had been killed. If so, this one perhaps lost a friend down there and wanted blood vengeance.

He left the man and hastened forward. It was clear now that the renegades were pushing their attackers off. The firing still came from the west, but it kept retreating even as Captain Ben whipped in and out of the underbrush, seeking to get close enough to determine just what was going on.

Of course he had to be extremely careful. He was not only alone, without any nearby support, but he also was on foot behind his enemies; if they saw him and turned, he wouldn't stand a chance.

But as it turned out the renegades out there were too near triumph over their attackers and evidently too confident that Captain Ben Southern was pinned down east of the road in the rocks to be worried, because he actually saw two of them, and placed the other four or five with no difficulty by their angry gunfire, before they had any idea at all he was behind them.

He waited until one of the renegades was exposed, then shot the man. At first there was no general alarm over this even though the others saw their companion go down. But when he fired at the second exposed renegade, and missed, and that man spun around, low and fast, yelling he was under attack from the rear, things happened.

For a moment the other renegades stopped firing. Out over the westerly desert that Sharps carbine kept up its booming cough, along with the other weapons around it. Ben dropped, rolled up under a big catclaw clump, poked out his carbine, and waited for a target. None came but several probing shots aimed in his general direction scuffed dirt and dust. He tried once firing back, but, right after that with the outlaws pinpointing his position in the catclaw, he had to roll farther off, this time to fetch up under a nopal clump growing beside a wiry young chaparral bush. This time, too, he conserved his fire.

The outlaws were yelling back and forth. One of them had evidently seen him on the move because he called to the others that it was only one man. The others wanted to know how he had gotten behind them. Another man swore with feeling and said he didn't in the least care how Ben had gotten behind them, but to concentrate on killing him because, as long as he was back there, they dared not push the fight around front.

Now the gunmen off to the west started stalking their renegade opponents, perhaps encouraged by the lessened gunfire and all the back-and-forth shouting. Ben was gratified because it took some of the pressure off him. He saw a man stalking him, though, and sucked back to flatten down and wait.

Elsewhere the gunfire brisked up again to the west, but every now and then an outlaw would whirl to throw a reckless shot backward, evidently in the belief that this might prevent Ben from doing any accurate stalking and shooting of his own. It could not have been a very comfortable position for the renegades whether they outnumbered their adversaries or not.

Ben's stalker came down from the north on the balls of his feet like an Indian, low and shadowy and capable of gliding from place to place, from bush to bush, without casting a shadow. Ben alternated between watching him from the corner of an eye, and in also trying to divert the others again. He fired and rolled and fired again. The renegades, harassed like this, shot forward twice and backward once. It was one of those wild backward shots that did Ben Southern a great service. His silently stalking adversary was less than a hundred yards off when suddenly several of his companions turned and threw lead back in Ben's direction without aiming. The stalking man flung up both arms, pitched his carbine ten feet away, and staggered forward into the thorny heart of a big bush. One of his killers saw and wailed. The others turned. At first it did not seem to occur to them they had killed their friend; they slackened off again and turned to rake the rearward desert with sluicing ground fire probing for Ben Southern who they thought responsible. To the west a booming big voice roared out. Ben recognized that voice at once. It belonged to Ned Tolliver.

Suddenly the renegades broke. Several of them cried out and began dashing back toward the road where they had evidently left their horses. Men streamed past Ben. He fired at two of them, missed one and saw the other one wince, then he was content simply to lie there because, to his astonishment, he saw not four or six men dart past, he saw nine of them. To his knowledge there had been two killed. Certainly, with Tolliver and Walt Lee and those Fort Brown troopers out there also firing into them, there had been two or three more either downed with lead in them alive, or down with lead in them dead. He let the last one rush by and sat up, beat off dust, levered his carbine, found it empty, stood up gingerly, and used the useless Winchester to push aside limbs so he could peer around.

Where had the others come from, unless they had already been hiding out upon the desert waiting? The more he thought of that, the more plausible it appeared.

"Hey, Cap'n Ben!" someone throatily called. "Where'n hell are you?"

"Here," answered Southern, placing that voice. "Straight ahead from where you called, Ned. And be careful. They've all run toward the road, but I wouldn't bet they can't come back once they're mounted up."

Walt Lee came angling down from the northward desert and appeared first. Then the two sweaty troopers from Fort Brown appeared. The last man to show up was Ned Tolliver. Ned had picked up some lead across the shin bone. It was, as he eloquently told the others, not serious.

"No other injuries?" Ben asked, amazed. The others looked around and shook their heads. "You mean just the four of us ran off twelve or fifteen renegades?"

"Two dead ones over in front of Walt and me," said Ned. "You get any, Cap'n?"

"Two, Ned."

"Well, that was evenin' up the odds well enough. Anyway, those danged renegades fight in packs like wolves. If a feller

248

begins thinnin' 'em out, they skedaddle."

One of the Fort Brown troopers said: "Captain, sir . . . what about the wagons . . . maybe they done pulled back on purpose?"

Ben stared at that man, then whirled and called upon the others. They raced back toward the roadway, all but Ned Tolliver, who took off in the direction of the wagons.

Ben got to the road. The soldier who had made that suggestion swung southward without a word and ran along looking left and right. It was still cool but the morning sun was fast rising toward its heated heights.

Southward there was the call of a man encouraging other men to get astride and be fast about it. Suddenly the Fort Brown soldier dropped to one knee and lifted his Sharps carbine. But that horseman who suddenly arose above the nearest brush, exposed as he mounted, saw the soldier and did not stop. He swung right on over his saddle and down off the other side to land in a heap. Someone out there swore fiercely. The Fort Brown soldier, disgusted at losing his excellent target, shifted a little and fired in the direction of that angry swearing. The profanity broke off in a loud squawk and someone down through the brush began screaming he was under attack.

The renegades had run for their horses exactly as Ben had anticipated. Their purpose, obviously, had been to hit the gun wagons on the run, drive them southward in a headlong rush, and in that manner get clear of their relentless attackers, secure the guns for El Vengador, and at the same time set their attackers afoot. It was good thinking; it just didn't work, was all.

Ben shouted orders. His three seasoned soldiers fanned out in skirmish order and started forward. The firing brisked up again. The battle was being renewed, but there was something else to worry about now. The Fort Brown soldiers told Ben the renegades were retreating right into the wagons, which were southward down the roadway.

XVIII

Unexpectedly there was a terrific gun duel southward. Ben zigzagged with one clenched fist for his men to hold off a moment, to get down flat in the event some of that angry lead sailed up their way.

As before, it struck Ben Southern there had to be more men than there were. Walt Lee crept over where Ben was waiting out that fierce fight and said: "Rush 'em, Cap'n, that's why Ned went an' hit 'em like that down by the wagons."

Ben frowned. "You mean that's Tolliver behind them at the wagons doing all the firing?"

"Yes, sir. With a six-gun in each hand an' doin' like he done before . . . makin' them think there's another five or six fellers against them."

Ben stood up. It was insane; he only had four men counting himself—and Ned, now at the wagons and out of sight—with which to oppose a strong, armed force of desperate renegades. He called to the Fort Brown men and gestured them forward. He turned and made the same motion toward Walt Lee. Then he, too, began advancing, and firing as he went.

The earlier fight had at times seemed wildly fierce and deafening but it had never reached the proportions the battle now assumed down near the wagons. But as suddenly as it began, it suddenly stopped when two of the desperadoes began calling for quarter.

Very gradually all the guns ceased firing. The way they did this convinced Ben Southern that not all the renegades were anxious to surrender, so, when he bawled out for his own forces to cease firing, he gave that order as though he were commanding a company of men, instead of a squad of them. It was his hope that Ned Tolliver's inordinately rapid gunfire of a moment before would aid him in projecting this illusion. Evidently he succeeded, at least as far as inspiring the other outlaws to stop firing, even though there was no rush among them to walk out, arms overhead.

"Come ahead!" he sang out to the pair of renegades who had asked for quarter. "Leave your guns back there in the brush and walk out here with your hands above your heads!"

Walt Lee used this time to reload. So did the pair of yellow-legs from Fort Brown. Ben needed also to reload but he did not attempt it while he crouched in the chaparral, waiting.

"We're coming!" a man called out grumpily. "Hold your fire."

They came, about a hundred feet apart, one from the edge of the roadway, one from more westward off in the desert. Their shirts were limp with sweat and one of them limped from a rudely bandaged injury in his upper right leg.

Walt Lee eased up behind the one farthest off and herded the man out to the road. As he did this, Ben Southern tried talking to the others.

"Hey, the rest of you . . . come on out. It's all over."

A scratchy voice full of bitterness said right back: "It's all over, all right, soljer boy, but I got no hankerin' to swing from the end of a rope in some damned Army compound with them drummers beating their muffled instruments. You take what you got an' go on away. We'll let you do that."

Ben guessed wherever, and whoever, that one was, he was without fear. He tried working on that one particularly. "Listen, mister, it's not that simple. An attempt has been made on the lives and the property of. . . ."

"Save it, soljer boy," broke in the invisible renegade out in the desert brush. "Just do like I said. You got your damned guns in them wagons, and you did your killin', so get them rigs headed right and head for home."

Ned Tolliver came walking up. He jerked a thumb over his

shoulder. "The wagons are exactly as we left 'em, Cap'n. I think maybe we'd best do like he says. They still outnumber us."

Ben turned that suggestion over in his mind as he gazed at Ned. "That was one hell of a shooting exposition you put up down by those wagons," he said to the older man. "It convinced 'em we were a lot stronger than we are, Ned."

Tolliver didn't seem to care for the platitude. His solemn expression was unchanged. "It's the same tactic we used when we first come up, hearin' you was under attack by them tall rocks, Cap'n . . . all four of us fired as fast as we could lever up an' tug off. But these here renegades are still stronger, and directly they're goin' to find out just how damned weak we really are. Then. . . ."

"I don't think so," said Ben Southern. "I think that one meant it when he said it's all over."

Ned screwed up his face. It didn't make sense to him, a squad of soldiers backing down nearly three times as many gunfighters.

Ben called out once more to that spokesman out in the underbrush where the midday heat was casting its smoky haze. "Cowboy, if you want to walk down here, we'll talk about you men riding off unmolested. If not, we'll resume the fight."

Evidently during the interim when Ned and Captain Ben had been talking, the outlaws had also come together out there beyond sight, because, after only a moment of hesitancy, the bitter-voiced man answered back, saying: "You tryin' to pull somethin' cute, soljer boy, like maybe havin' the rest of us surrounded an' cut off while I'm up there talkin' to you?"

"Nothing like that at all," replied Ben. "You have my word."

Again there was a brief palaver, then the harsh-voiced man said: "I'm comin', soljer boy, but I'm armed and I figure to stay that way, so if any of your men think they want to earn another notch, let 'em try. Otherwise, we'll see just how good your word is."

Ben instantly signaled for the others to come up close. He told them to scatter left and right at the edge of the road and keep close watch, but under no circumstances to fire unless he fired first. Ned Tolliver was nearest Ben on the right. Walt Lee was closest on his left. Those two leaned upon their guns, following the progress of the renegade spokesman as he came with a thrust through the brush making no point of being quiet about it any longer.

When he stepped into sight, he was whisker-stubbled, sweaty, and rumpled. He was a lanky, black-eyed man with tight curly black hair to match his eyes, and a thin slash of a lipless mouth. He was a thoroughly venomous-looking man. He carried no carbine, but his six-gun rode light and easy in its tied-down hip holster. "The name," he said very dryly to Ben Southern as he quietly eyed Ben, Ned Tolliver, and Walt Lee, "is Will Smith." Unexpectedly those grave black eyes twinkled faintly. "You've heard of me, soljer boy. Why, hell . . . half the crimes in the country get blamed on Will Smith. The other half gets blamed on my old friend, Will Jones."

Will Smith turned to look elsewhere past the three visible armed men who were watching him. He shrugged as though satisfied the balance of Ben's command was hidden from his view. He looked up and down the road, too.

Ben said: "Why didn't you fellers ride south to help El Vengador?"

Smith rolled his black gaze over at Ben. "Soljer boy," he said dryly, "that stuff south o' the line wasn't none of our concern. If Johnny Clark wanted to play Mex general, that's all right with us *Americanos* from Arizona, but only until he run out of money . . . and now, out of luck as well . . . count us out. We're not greasers, so we got no interest in which side wins down there. We're not heroes, so when they turn a whole damned Mex route army loose on him over the line . . . we decided to come after the guns like he told us to. But even if he hadn't sent us, we'd have come anyway. It was gettin' much too hot below the line."

"Wait a minute," Ben said, breaking in upon the flow of words from this talkative renegade. "What do you mean . . . Clark ran out of luck? Did he get defeated in the fight below the line?"

For a moment the renegade hung fire over his reply, then he simply raised his shoulders and dropped them, turned, and beckoned. "Soljer boy, come with me. I'll show you why we decided to quit this fight. Come on . . . it's no trap."

The outlaw started walking northwesterly back away from the roadway. Ned and Walt instantly moved out the minute Ben Southern started to follow his guide through the gunshot-shattered underbrush. They went nearly a hundred and fifty yards, or out where Ned and Walt and the Fort Brown men had attacked the renegades from the rear, before they halted.

For a moment the renegade stepped back and forth, in and out, until he located what he sought, then he raised a hand to flag Ben up.

It was El Vengador, the chieftain of the Mexican insurgents and the *Yanqui* renegades. He was lying flat on his back with a bullet hole slightly above and between his dry eyes.

At first, Ben and Ned and Walt were too dumbfounded to speak, but, after their guide explained, they recovered.

The renegade gazed dispassionately at his fallen leader. "He had to run for it," the man explained. "He come hellin' it up this way, knowin' me an' the others was up here after them guns. Several of the boys came with him."

"You mean," asked Ben, "the Mexican route army sent against him triumphed down there?"

"It sure did, soljer boy," retorted the renegade wryly. "The fellers who came up here with him told us about that. It was a massacre. An' we always thought he was such a good general an' all."

"No," said Ned Tolliver, gazing at the dead man's swarthy, cruel face. "I could've told you that . . . he was a damned poor tactical officer, feller, an' I'd know 'cause I've served under more good and bad officers than most fellers. This here feller was a fool. He could've crushed the wagons yesterday . . . he had the power and the numbers. But he lacked the confidence."

"Maybe," said the renegade. "I wouldn't be no authority. All I can say for a fact is that the Mex regulars cut him to pieces an' he had to flee. So he come up here . . . an' busted right into the middle of our private little battle . . . and stopped one between the eyes. That's why we decided to call it off, boys . . . he's finished. We don't want no damned Army guns for ourselves and we're not about to go down into Mexico right now and try peddlin' 'em, either . . . not with a route army down there just waitin' for us to come back."

Ben looked at Walt and Ned. He looked back again at the renegade with the black eyes and black hair. He said: "I want the four men who killed a pair of soldiers in a box cañon east of Acton about a. . . ."

"No dice," muttered the renegade before Southern had finished speaking. "I knew them four real well. They made a bad mistake, them four. Two of 'em rode southward last night to get in on the plunderin' south o' the line . . . they're both dead. We got word of their passin' from the survivors who came north with Clark. The other two, you yourself, mister, picked off when you left them stone pillars and come in from the east, an' so help me that's gospel truth. Go ask the others."

Ned and Ben exchanged a look. Walt Lee lifted his six-gun and cocked it in the outlaw's face. "Where are your horses?" he asked.

The outlaw slumped. "All right," he growled. "That's another reason. The horse holders moved 'em westerly. They're hidin' out there, an', if we don't come along directly now, they'll pull out without us. Soljers, believe me, everything I've just told you is the truth . . . the whole blessed gospel truth." He lowered a hand. "There's the proof . . . El Vengador dead."

Ben said nothing. He stepped back, motioned for the outlaw to hike back toward the wagons again, and told Walt to keep the man covered, and, if he made one false start, for Walt to drop him in his tracks.

That was how they appeared back where the pair of Fort Brown troopers were standing in the roadway fully exposed in violation of Ben Southern's orders, straining southward where a steadily approaching dust column was rising up.

"Call your friends forward," Captain Ben ordered the man who chose to call himself Will Smith.

The outlaw looked around, his expression pained. "Why?" he said. "You was to let us go."

"Your terms," stated Ben. "Not mine. Call them out."

Smith hesitated, trading hard looks with Ben Southern.

One of the Fort Brown soldiers turned, elated. "Captain," he crowed, "yonder comes the colonel and the rest of the escort from Fort Brown, plus what looks to be one hell of a big posse of civilian riders."

The renegade raised both hands, cupped them around his lips, and called to his hiding companions to step forth and surrender because the Army was coming up in force, along with a passel of armed civilians. He had no sooner ceased calling out than his friends from far back in the underbrush started walking out. Evidently they, too, had sighted that big banner of dust.

The outlaw leader turned toward Ben. "We didn't break no laws," he said, " 'ceptin' maybe shootin' at you boys a little."

The column came up. It was Colonel Hardin and Sheriff

Mittan, exactly as they had anticipated after seeing the dust. The colonel took over their prisoners and promised to see they were jailed in Acton and later tried there. He also suggested Ben and Ned and Walt Lee get out of their outlandish civilian range rider clothing and back into the proper military attire. When Ben took both Hardin and Sheriff Mittan out to show them the body of El Vengador, they recognized the outlaw and were as amazed at his being there—dead—as Ben had also been.

The orders were passed for El Vengador to be taken back and tied over a horse for the return trip. Colonel Hardin said he thought it might help the dead outlaw chieftain's sister if Ben went back, too, but Captain Ben declined. He felt, without ever saying it, that Alice should be allowed to recover by herself. He had valid reasons, too, that the others did not know of.

Besides, he had a perfect alibi for returning to Acton several weeks hence, when Alice would be recovered, and also when the rifles would be safely stored up at Camp Scott—those firing pins in Ed Mittan's safe back in town.

He took his final leave, he and Ned Tolliver and Walt Lee, of Colonel Hardin, the troopers from Fort Brown, and of Sheriff Ed Mittan and his posse men, set their onward course straight for Camp Scott, and this time, because Hardin had allowed it, there were two uniformed men to each gun wagon.

They drove slowly. The heat was murderous. When Ned and Walt could no longer remain awake, they tied their animals to one of the wagons, climbed inside, rolled up the canvas, and sacked out. Captain Ben withstood this same temptation until he was positive they were well beyond the zones of any kind of renewed peril to their cargo, then he climbed inside to make himself as comfortable as a man could who proposed napping atop gun crates, and, instead of dropping off, fell to thinking of a beautiful, willowy girl back down on the desert who he felt very warm toward. Thinking like that, he, too, finally dozed off.

ABOUT THE AUTHOR

Lauran Paine who, under his own name and various pseudonyms has written over a thousand books, was born in Duluth, Minnesota. His family moved to California when he was at a young age and his apprenticeship as a Western writer came about through the years he spent in the livestock trade, rodeos, and even motion pictures where he served as an extra because of his expert horsemanship in several films starring movie cowboy Johnny Mack Brown. In the late 1930s, Paine trapped wild horses in northern Arizona and even, for a time, worked as a professional farrier. Paine came to know the Old West through the eyes of many who had been born in the previous century, and he learned that Western life had been very different from the way it was portrayed on the screen. "I knew men who had killed other men," he later recalled. "But they were the exceptions. Prior to and during the Depression, people were just too busy eking out an existence to indulge in Saturday-night brawls." He served in the U.S. Navy in the Second World War and began writing for Western pulp magazines following his discharge. It is interesting to note that all of his earliest novels (written under his own name and the pseudonym Mark Carrel) were published in the British market and he soon had as strong a following in that country as in the United States. Paine's Western fiction is characterized by strong plots, authenticity, an apparently effortless ability to construct situation and character, and a preference for building his stories upon a solid foundation of historical fact. *Adobe Empire* (1956), one of his best novels, is a fictionalized account of the last twenty years in the life of trader William Bent and, in an off-trail way, has a melancholy, bittersweet texture that is not easily forgotten. In later novels like *Cache Cañon* (Five Star Westerns, 1998) and *Halfmoon Ranch* (Five Star Westerns, 2007), he showed that the special magic and power of his stories and characters had only matured along with his basic themes of changing times, changing attitudes, learning from experience, respecting Nature, and the yearning for a simpler, more moderate way of life. His next Five Star Western will be *Iron Marshal*.